Upstream

Poison River Series
Book 2

Jennifer M. Lane

DEDICATION

For every small town that's named after a direction.
And for all the people who leave that small town and face the
same question time and again.

Yes, it's direction. And a location. It's also the town's name.
Thankyouverymuch.

CHAPTER ONE

JULY 9, 1901

The ten o'clock train rumbles on the track and hisses as I pass, an impatient visitor letting off steam. It shudders, eager to leave, like it's late for something and denied what it came for. That makes two of us.

It's been a year since that train brought me here, and I still haven't proven Pritchard and his coal town have been poisoning the water, killing people, and covering it up. I wave steam from my face, cursing the train under my breath for reminding me, plowing through its plume with my head down and my notebook in my grip. Harrison is about to speak at the brickyard. I promised Weylan I'd write this story for the next issue of the newspaper, and I'm already late.

I finally make it through the crowd and stand on tiptoes so I can see Harrison on the dais. It's really just a small, wood platform about three feet high that Weylan's father uses here at the brickyard to see his property and his workers—and to hunt deer and turkeys sometimes—but it's the perfect place for Harrison to make his case for the mayorship. He's crouched down, shaking hands with workers and families. Maybe a hundred people or so have come from this end of town to hear that man who, God willing, will put an end to the lies and schemes, and the intimidation and violence of Whitaker's administration.

Harrison peers out over the crowd with his hands on his jacket lapels. He seems more confident lately. People around me note it too, how much taller he seems. How he smiles more easily. I make a note of it in case I forget by the time I sit down to write.

He's grown more charismatic since people started listening to him and applauding when he speaks, almost as if he needed a vote of confidence before he found his voice. It's made him more relatable, at least to me. But he's an academic man, the kind whose head is always somewhere else, his eyes not really seeing what's in front of him. That just makes him better for the role, in my opinion. But I'm not here to form an opinion. The election is only nine days away, and I'm here to report on what he has to say, so I cut through the mass of people and slink up to the edge of the crowd, keeping to the back fringes where I can also see people's reactions, and where the sun won't be in my eyes.

I want to hear him talk about the poison in the waters. I want him to finally say that he won't take bribes from men with deep pockets, that he won't be a safe harbor for the upstream sins of a corrupt coal boss. He needs to say that he'll sink their ships in his own words, so I can print them in the newspaper, because printing my words instead of his would be an opinion, not fact, and it would put The Record at risk.

Someone shouts my name from across the way, and a hand

shoots into the air, waving frantically. I hop up on a brittle log and stand on my tip-toes to find my brother, Emmett, and his friends, Vernon and Max. I wave them over, but Harrison straightens, his long, lean form stretching to the sky. He looks the way I picture a young Abraham Lincoln, tall but not lanky. A little stooped, as if he feels unworthy of his height and with a gentleness that will form deep lines as the strain of the years settles in. He licks his lips—a sign of his nerves—as he grips his lapels, and I pull out my pocket notebook and pencil to make note of his demeanor. Unassuming. Earnest.

Bea pops up out of nowhere and bumps my shoulder. I nearly lose my notepad.

"Did you speak to Weylan yet?" She gives me the same critical look she gives me every time she asks, because she knows I haven't.

"Of course not," I whisper. I promised I would, and I need to do it, it's just never the right time. "I will. I swear."

"Charlie, you could break the tension in the print office with a sledgehammer. You need to talk to your fiancé." She presses her straw hat to her head and blinks against the blast of hot summer wind, and I'm glad she turns her head so she doesn't see me roll my eyes.

"We're not engaged."

"You might as well be," she says. "He asked."

"And I answered." Somewhat. What I actually said was *yes, but not yet*, which is a terrible thing to say to a man who asked you to start a life with him, but it's what I said, and I'd meant it. "I'm not ready yet, Bea. As soon as we get married, I'll have to give it all up."

"Give what up? You'd still be able to write for the newspaper, wouldn't you?"

"Hardly," I huff. "First, we'd find a home and have to settle into it. There'd be all that cooking and cleaning, doing laundry for two. Mending his clothes. He wouldn't demand it of me, but I'd want to do it, and before long there'd be no time at all to keep up this fight. I'd remember my parents with nothing but regret for having given up on finding justice for them, and I'm not ready. Not yet."

Bea's pursed lips loosen, and she chews the bottom one. "I understand that. I do. It's just that maybe Weylan doesn't, and it's making things difficult for all of us. And it's been a year of it."

A year that's seemed to creep and fly by at the same time. Ever since Pritchard showed up at the Water Festival and I turned down his offer of my childhood home in exchange for giving up my fight, I've been trying to trace the bribes and coercion he uses to hide how he poisons and kills people. Progress might be so small it's imperceptible, but it's on the horizon. I can feel it.

"I'll talk to Weylan," I say. "I know things are uncomfortable."

"Good, because he seems miserable." Bea's eyes drift across the crowd. She returns Emmett's wave. "Look! The boys are here. I'll be back."

A scattering of applause ripples across the crowd, and of course, I've missed what Harrison said to elicit it.

He raises a hand to ask for silence. "And I will not accept bribes and look the other way as our town is poisoned and crippled."

That's more like it.

The crowd offers another, louder, round of applause, and I put my notebook in the crook of my elbow to join in.

The crowd behind me has swelled since I arrived, and I scribble down a note of it. Growing crowds mean more people want to hear what he has to say. Behind them, though, back by the station, one man catches my eye. There's nothing odd about him at first. Just another man walking close to listen, but there's a sense of hesitancy in his steps. It's as if he doesn't belong, as if he's creeping up on something he doesn't understand, and when I lock eyes on him, I realize it's me. He's watching me.

The man has dark, wavy hair that's a little too long, pinned up and out of his face. His eyes are piercing, somewhere between blue and gray. They match the swath of fabric tied about his neck, just beneath his high collar. His jacket is perfectly tailored. He has a strong jaw, a thin nose, and a steep dip to his thin upper lip that would give him a handsome appearance if I didn't know him to be a scoundrel already. He's close enough for me to see the whites of his eyes and the narrowing of his gaze, and he's strikingly familiar in a way that makes my blood run cold. I know him, but I'm not sure why. Then the corner of his mouth lifts a little with a smile that's naturally sinister, and I know exactly why I recognize him. I pinch my pencil so tight the wood splinters.

Silas.

He was a fixture in Stoke. Pritchard's manager. He oversaw the workforce. Of course, *manager* was a term Father had used both loosely and strictly. Silas had a southern charm that could wither the sun, a face made for moving pictures, and a twinkle in his eye that would make any woman swoon. But he used it to wield the Coal and Iron Police like a weapon, and he'd grin while he starved you.

I'd only seen him a handful of times before. Once at the company store and a few times at the church.

He walks closer and stops some twenty paces away, hands in his pockets. It gives his shoulders a slouch that he probably hopes is unassuming, but his spine is straight and his eyes are on me.

Harrison's voice breaks through my fog, talking about how the election is only nine days away, and how one of his first acts will be a new carriage for the constables. Though I have a spine-jarring memory of how desperately they need a new carriage, and I ought to write it down, I take a step in Silas's direction. If he thinks he can come here and implement the kind of strong-arm intimidation tactics he uses to flatten Stoke, he has another thing coming.

Silas turns and walks away. I glance at Bea. She's listening in rapt attention.

If Silas gets on that train and leaves, I might not find out why he came until it's too late. Did he meet with Mayor Whitaker? Did he give him a bribe? I turn to race after him and run straight into Weylan's father. I grab his shoulder to stop myself from falling, and he grasps my hand.

"Charlotte. You are well, I see. How is Weylan?" He has kind eyes. Not like Weylan's, though. Weylan has his mother's gentle eyes. But his father's eyes are dark and soft at the corners, and he always seems to be smiling through the grief I know he lives with after losing his wife and his oldest son. I don't know him as well as I should, though, because he works endlessly and shuts himself away from the world. He barely knows his own son, and they live together. Grief is his steady companion.

"Sir. It's lovely to see you." My cheeks resist the smile. I broke his son's heart. Things have been tense between Weylan and me since I said I wouldn't marry him yet, and I'm sure his father knows the reason. "Can you excuse me? I was just following a man, who—"

I crane my neck to see around Weylan's father. There's no sign of Silas, but he can't have gone far.

"Go." Weylan's father pats me on the shoulder. "You have

important work…"

I thank him and promise to come right back, not wanting to seem impolite to my possible future father-in-law, the man who gifted Weylan the newspaper that feeds us all. I rush toward the train, but there's no sign of Silas. I can't even find his footsteps in the hard-packed dirt, there are so many. I heave open the train station door. Three women stand at the ticket counter. A child kicks his feet against the back of the bench in front of him. A man mutters to himself while looking at the departures board. But no Silas.

"Charlotte!" Vernon's father leans out the window and waves an envelope at me. "Letter for the newspaper here. Man just dropped it off."

"Of course." My stomach sinks to my shoes. "Did you see which way he went?"

He nods to the far door. "Left here on a horse in a hurry."

"Drat."

He passes me the envelope and turns to the wall of nooks where he sorts the mail. "Do you want to take the rest of the mail while you're here?"

"Certainly. Save the postman the trip." I accept the stack of envelopes. "Did he say anything, the man who left the letter?"

Lifting his hat, he scratches a spot behind his ear. "Nay. Not a word. It was stamped, though. I suspect he was passing through."

I plop on the bench far from the boy kicking the seat and away from the door. I peel open the flap and shake out the letter.

Cease and desist?

Fanning myself with the limp envelope, I skim down the page. It's addressed to the newspaper, but it's all about me. *A woman in your employ makes enemies with her printed lies… has family in*

Stoke… monitoring their well-being as she undertakes this endeavor to slander…

"Oh, for heaven's sake." I know Pritchard's reach extends far past Stoke, rare for a coal boss. And if he's sending his manager all the way here to leave threatening notes for me, they must truly be afraid of us.

I flatten the page on my knee.

We will seek damages against the newspaper owner, and against Charlotte and Emmett Morris…

What does Emmett have to do with this?

…and seize assets of The Record unless our demands are met. You will publish a retraction of the slanderous, libelous accusations in the article printed on the 3rd of June alleging collaboration between us and your mayor, who by all reports has brought prosperity to the town.

"Prosperity? That's a twist on things."

They want us to print a retraction by the twenty-sixth, which is only in three weeks, which is hardly enough time to generate and rehearse that kind of theater, even if I were the kind of person who might entertain it.

I fold the letter, shove it back into the envelope.

Three months have passed since Weylan presented me with the gold wedding band that once belonged to his mother. Three months have passed since I closed his hand around it and said, "Yes, but not yet." For three long months both our hearts have been broken, and we've avoided each other like molten hot iron because I fear—and perhaps we both know—that when we do talk, it will all be over.

But now I really need to talk to Weylan.

CHAPTER TWO

JULY 9, 1901

I can't deliver this news to Weylan without a plan or at least thinking through what I have to say, and the deadline for our next issue is bearing down on me. If I show up with this letter and no article, I'll only have myself to blame for disappointing him on all possible counts, so I head for the apartment instead. Hopefully I absorbed enough of what Harrison had to say to craft a story worth the ink.

The door slams shut behind me. The windows are all open, and the curtains flutter over the table where we eat, rustling a stack of signs for Harrison's campaign. Ruthie's doing. They're in various states of being painted, stacked underneath and on the table, draped over chairs, and tacked to the wall. There's so many of them we can barely see her handiwork anymore. Peeking from under all the campaign signs that paper the wall are delicate little scraps of paper painted with little birds on twisted branches. Flowers and starry skies. Sketches and water colors of storefronts and bottles on windowsills with the sun glistening through. She has the kind of talent that you hope the world never dims, that polishes itself the way a rock spheres under rolling waters, and if the girls' parents hadn't agreed to let us all live here together, I never would have seen it happen one day at a time. I can't wait for the campaign to end so I can see her work again.

It was a leap for their parents, letting us all move in together. It started with Bea's. Leta and Mitchell never made me feel unwelcome, and they insisted I stay as long as I'd liked, but with my pay from the newspaper, I was eager to not make myself unwelcome. Bea pleaded the case to move out with me and said she didn't want me to be lonely, but I knew then that she was even more eager to enjoy some freedom of her own. We're right down the street from Leta and Mitchell, after all, and we're in their store all the time. Ruthie followed, then Hazel, and before we all knew it, the four of us were cramming ourselves into a hatbox apartment. Bea's father was slow to warm to the idea of us all living here together on the grounds that young women just don't do this sort of thing. He spent a lot of time scowling at our stove, wondering aloud how we'd ever get on. But it's amazing what a bunch of women can do when we're left alone to get on with it.

It's small, only four little rooms. One bedroom on each side of an eat-in kitchen with windows that look out to the neighbor's houses. Bea and I share the smallest of the two. A little bathroom is tucked on the other side of the wall from our feet. It makes our room so tight you can barely turn around, but it isn't an outhouse, so it feels like a luxury. The kitchen makes up the bulk of the space we share above the candy store, and most of that is the stove. It's old, with a crooked door, and it doesn't always heat the water tank like it should, but we all have the hang of it now. And we've gotten pretty good at repairing it when we need to.

There's no place to sit at the table, so I clean off a spot for myself and try to recall what Harrison had said, but even after sitting with a blank piece of paper for ten minutes, I still can't think of anything but that cease and desist letter.

Weylan always takes stress in stride, but there's been so much of it lately. The newspaper took off in a way we couldn't have predicted, and the press couldn't keep up with subscriptions. We needed more advertisers to pay for equipment and help. The further he stepped in that role, the more he said things like "it's just one more little thing," and "we can handle this," but there was rarely a 'we' about it. Weylan rubbed at his eyebrow and always dove in, and he got quieter and more distant. And then he proposed, and it all got worse. I unfold the letter and smooth it out on the table, inspecting it as if there's some clause or relief to be found in the space between the lines.

Ruthie spills in from outside, sweat-drenched and fanning herself. I pull a towel over the letter.

"This blasted heat." She sifts through the piles of signs I moved to the chairs. "Have you seen my brownie camera?"

I shove my pencil behind my ear and lean back. "I set it on your bed."

"Thanks." She dives into her room and is back again in a flash. "Are you helping finish these signs tonight?"

"I'd love to, if—"

The door creaks open as if it's straining against thick molasses summer air, and Bea fills the doorway, fanning her face with a newspaper. She nudges the tin can full of rocks that we use as a doorstop to prop the door open. "Muggy in here," she says.

Hazel repeats her question for Bea who swears she has no other objective tonight than to clean up the kitchen before all this paper combusts in the heat and sets us all on fire.

"I swear I'll help if I can get this story written," I vow. "Do you remember a thing Harrison said?"

"I was only half paying attention." Bea falls into the chair across from me and unearths handfuls of small peaches from her shopping bags. She holds one to her chest as if she's pined for it forever. "I've been waiting for these for months."

She bites into one and wipes her chin with the heel of her hand. She offers one to me, but I decline. Hazel takes one and heads to her room, poking at her hair in the mirror.

"I thought you were having dinner with your mother tonight," I say.

She swallows another bite. "Change of plans. Mother's meeting with Sarah to put together all those stories they compiled into one organized list."

"Like a book?" Hazel asks.

"Somewhat," Bea says.

I lean back. "They're finished already?" If so, that's one less thing to worry about. Leta and the suffragists have spent the last year visiting women in towns along the river, promoting their cause for votes for women and asking about illnesses and deaths that could be linked to the poison Pritchard spewed into the water. Half of the women were afraid to talk lest someone with more power than compassion came looking for a fight, but the other half wouldn't stop talking. It seemed an awful lot of people thought they were crazy for linking sickness and death to exposure to the river, and once someone was ready to listen, they told them everything they wanted to know. Leta rarely said much more than that. I suspected she wanted to protect their stories until the time came to make use of them. But with Pritchard demanding we cease and desist, I wondered what would become of their stories.

"Right, Charlie?" Hazel leaned out of her bedroom door, eyes wide and chin tucked in, waiting for me to agree with her about something that clearly brought her joy. Having missed everything they said, I merely nodded.

Maybe it wasn't a waste of time. If Leta is organizing all those witness statements, our case will be even stronger, but we still lack proof to back up the claims and there's no one to present it to. If only we'd been able to find that scientist in Baltimore who Weylan overheard at the train station two years ago.

"I need to finish this article." I tap my pencil on the blank page. "Then I'll help with these posters. I promise. Maybe there's something in my old notes I can use. I can work on my bed so you can have the table."

The bedroom door clicks to a close behind me. I really should do what I said I would. What I know I should. This article needs to be written so I can focus on this letter, but I feel like there's a knife lodged in my chest. I need to be closer to ending this thing with Pritchard, not further, so I can get on with my life.

If I could think of a direction, a way to use the stories Leta compiled, I might be able to convince Weylan to oppose this cease and desist. But I wouldn't dare hope for as much if I approached him without an article about Harrison. Perhaps there's something inspiring in the old notes shoved in my wardrobe that will spark some memory. It's packed to the gills with my things and Bea's. My old sewing projects I wish I'd finished and the scraps of my old favorite skirt are balled up in the bottom corner. We each took half of the top shelf, but Bea only had a hat to put there, so all my notes and letters and research on Pritchard and Whitaker are piled up in heaps, and God forbid I ever need them. It would take forever to find anything.

I drag everything to my bed in armfuls and start to sort it. The ripped sleeve from an old blouse. Lengths of ribbon. Balls of thread. As for all the paper, I have one pile about Pritchard and another about Whitaker, but a woeful lack of overlap.

Bea pokes her head around the corner. "You need a desk. Or a new obsession."

I ignore the barb. "There isn't room for a desk." The wardrobe is so close to the ends of our beds that the doors don't open all the way. "I thought I'd be doing all this at the newspaper office but work and home are the same thing anymore. A desk would cramp things, wouldn't it?"

"We could fit one in between, under the window." Bea frowns at her peach pit, lobs it out the open window, and wipes her hand on her skirt.

"Things are really disorganized around here, aren't they?" It would be funny if it weren't so challenging. I sit on the bed, and papers spill off their stacks and crinkle around me. "I'm sorry I'm so hard to live with lately."

"You're not any harder to live with than the rest of us." Bea tilts her words at the end, and I know she's not truly mad at me for the mess or the distance between us. Even so, I still feel like I have a lot to make up for.

"I've been distant, Bea."

She tilts her head. "Preoccupied, I'd say. It's understandable."

"Obsessed seems fair. You were right earlier. I do need to fix things with Weylan. I will. I swear to it. Thank you for putting up with me, because without you and the girls, this place wouldn't feel like home at all."

"You mean without us and Weylan."

"Of course," I say, a bit ashamed of the omission. "A desk? Are you sure?"

"It would help both of us. I could use a place to sit and write sometimes, too. Something that isn't the kitchen table. Hey!" She jumps. "I almost forgot. I saw Sidney. I'm sure you'll say no because you have a million other things to do, but he asked if you could sew something for him, and I promised I'd pass it on to you."

I look up at the ceiling as if it holds clarity, but the only thing there is an old water stain. "I don't have time to sew for myself." Ages have passed since I last sat down to sew anything.

The disappointment must show, because Bea drops a hand to my shoulder and purses her lips in sympathy. "This will calm down soon and you can get back to things you love."

"I sure hope so."

Bea returns to the kitchen, and I dive back into the stacks of notes, sorting Harrison's campaign from Whitaker's crimes and hoping something Harrison said today would jump out at me.

"I have an idea," I call out to Bea. "Maybe I can just write about how enthusiastic the crowd was today."

"I'm sure that would be sufficient," she says.

"There's not that much free column space anyway," Hazel says, her voice muffled as she fixes her hair.

I could easily send Harrison a few questions and run a follow-up article in the next edition. Besides, the longer I wait to tell Weylan about Silas and that letter, the more I'll make up tragic scenarios.

Weylan might shutter the paper rather than deal with the backlash. Or worse, he could cower and print the retraction. If we give up now, Pritchard will win. And if we don't, he could ruin Weylan.

Everything we'd printed had been the truth. Pritchard had bribed Whitaker, participated in planting explosives here, framing me and Emmett and making it look like we'd schemed to detonate it at the town festival. All of it was proven in front of a judge when Mannix sued him on Emmett's behalf. Whitaker even admitted to it, though he said he was a pawn in Pritchard's scheme. Printing a retraction would offend every one of my sensibilities.

But what I fear most is Weylan doing nothing at all and having his dream taken away from him before he truly gets to live it. Just that thought alone makes me jittery and my stomach sour because I already watched him crumble once. He hid it well when I said I wouldn't marry him. Someday, yes, but not yet. And then there's all the sediment that's formed while we avoid stirring up the murky waters between us. I dread that more than anything else. Even more than what Mannix will say when he finds out we've stumbled into yet another legal tangle.

And why I hadn't thought of taking this letter to Mannix was beyond me. I should have stopped there on my way home. I checked the time and folded the letter, shoving it deep in my pocket, and I headed for the door.

CHAPTER THREE

JULY 9, 1901

I'm out of breath by the time I reach Widow Wilkins' picket fence, but I push myself to keep going so I don't interrupt Mannix's dinner or risk him not being home. We're lucky he thinks so fondly of us, considering he's the only lawyer in town, and he's the only person I can think of who can help me coat this cease and desist letter with some sugar to make it more palatable to Weylan.

I cross the bridge over the creek, round the building, and tap on his back window. It's not a fool-proof way to be sure no one sees us talking, but it's the plan we came up with in the early days after Emmett sued Whitaker for framing us.

I worried about being seen going into Mannix's office at first, concerned that if people knew we were in regular communication, Whitaker's men might conspire to put me behind bars again. Whitaker, himself, was only locked up for two short months after framing Emmett and me. He planted that blasting powder by the flat rock where I like to sit along the creek. Then he tried to make it look like we did it with an intent to disrupt the Water Festival, and though he's been rather quiet and stayed home since, that doesn't mean he isn't scheming behind closed doors. So I throw the least amount of kerosene on the fire that I can when I need to see Mannix to talk about laws and breaking them. Besides, knocking on his back door always makes me feel like I have a smart uncle who can solve all my problems and is always happy to see me.

"Charlie." Mannix wiggles the window open. "Leta is here. She was just about to leave, and I planned to close up for the day. What brings you around?"

I pass the letter through the gap, and he waves me in the back door.

The heat and humidity make the door stick in the jamb, so I shove it open with my hip. The window rattles in the frame when I close it. The narrow hall with its yellow striped wallpaper leads all the way to the front door and an open space that serves as his sitting room, but I step into the first door on the right and plop myself in the armed windsor chair across the desk from him. Next to Leta. She smiles at me the way a mother would—like she knows I'm up to some sort of trouble, and I'm a grown woman now, and she's afraid to ask.

Mannix's office is a small square room made even smaller by the built-in shelves crammed with leather-bound books. In the summer, it smells like I imagine a university does. Hot leather, ink, thick air, and damp paper. His desk is rarely clean, messy in a way I can relate to. Stacks of paper turned this way and that, scraps peeking out with scrawled notes. Weylan would shudder looking at it and itch to line up all the corners. It looks like chaos, but it makes sense to people like Mannix and me.

The letter curls out from his fingertips, and he peers at it over his glasses, his chin tucked in. He's almost at the end.

"I'll do none of this," I say. Using as few words as possible, I tell Leta about the letter's contents.

He lowers it to his desk and laces his fingers over his belly. "This is very frustrating, Charlotte. I told you this was a bad idea."

I look down at my hands. "At the time, we were trying to flush out more stories. People in other towns were subscribing to the newspaper, so we thought if we printed stories about the poison, they'd be more inclined to talk to Leta. And we very much wanted to find that scientist. Perhaps if he saw it—"

Mannix's chair groans when he sits forward. "What is the newspaper doing now? More of this?"

"No." I shake my head. "Nothing. I promise. We sent a few letters to banks that do business with Pritchard. Like the one he used to offer my old house to me. We asked if they would talk to us, but no one responded. We were following the money, like you suggested, same as any other newspaper would do, and I did my due diligence like any good journalist. Bea's been following the money around here, which you know. She's working from the bottom up. Weylan and I worked Pritchard's angle, but that was weeks ago. I refuse to print a retraction."

I could feel it coming as a splotchy redness crept up his collar and onto his jowls. He was about to demand it of me, and he might have if Leta hadn't cut him off. He untangles his glasses from his ears and lays them on the table as he sighs.

"They must be worried about what you'll uncover," she says. "Sending you a letter like that? They want to silence you."

"You are not the Baltimore Sun." Mannix jabs his finger into his desk so hard I expect it to pucker. "You are not the Washington Post. You don't have the resources to defend yourselves. You'll bite off more than you can chew if you don't comply with this." He pushes the letter across his desk. "I cannot help with this."

"I'm not asking for help." My voice is small. Smaller than I want it to be. I suppose a small part of me did hope that he would clutch the letter and swear to make it all go away, but I didn't truly believe he would do it. "I thought you might have some advice. Some magical wording you could suggest that might find its way into a loophole and—"

"I must protect myself." His voice is flat. Stern enough that Leta stiffens beside me. "I am dedicated to helping the suffragists with their cause. If I embroil myself in the affairs of a coal boss, any good I could do will be severely diminished. Harrison's election is only nine days away, and I must stay focused on assisting him or Whitaker will make my life very difficult, indeed."

"I know. Quite sorry, I didn't mean—"

"Oh, come now, Mannix," Leta croons. "Surely you can give them some advice. The newspaper is an important asset."

Leta's words of support straighten my spine. "Is there anything we can do other than print a retraction? Nothing we printed was illegal. We did our due diligence. I swear to it."

He huffs. "I know that. I'm your due diligence, remember? I'm the one who told you it's not illegal. But I also told you it was all a terrible idea."

"That isn't what you said, though. You said you thought it wasn't the best idea."

He purses his lips and gives me that *you know what I meant* look.

"Anyway, every disaster is an opportunity, right?" I ask. "Every action is a chance for equal and opposite action. So what can I do instead of a retraction?"

"They can sue you, Charlotte." His voice hitches with an anger I've never heard from him before. "And the paper. They may or may not win, but the financial strain will ruin you and Weylan and the newspaper. And what about Emmett? This was the most irresponsible—"

"Emmett doesn't work for the newspaper." My words trail off and my voice gets small because my bravado is only a very thin sheen on top of my eternal fear that life is fragile and Pritchard almost took my brother once with his poison.

My deep breath isn't cleansing, and Mannix keeps looking at me with a mix of exasperation and *why are you like this.*

"It's a newspaper!" Leta doesn't match Mannix's fury, but she's as angered as I've ever seen her. "Drawing attention to the biggest news to affect the town is certainly in their purview. It had the desired effect. Some people who spoke to us were swayed by the knowledge that the matter was being taken seriously, which is more than they'd gotten from members of their own family who wanted to sweep the whole thing under the rug and forget it happened! Move on in their grieving."

Mannix clenches his jaw. Some time goes by before he mumbles, "That's fine, do as you wish. But don't get me involved in it."

I take the paper from the desk without disturbing anything else, and I fold it along its crease.

"Sorry to bother you. It won't happen again." My voice is so small I can barely hear myself, and it drips with a shame I resent.

Nothing we did is worthy of regret, but I admire Mannix. I can handle this on my own, though. The response will be easy enough to write once I figure out what to say, and with a little time, I'll come up with a way to tell Weylan that won't give him a heart attack. What I need is a plan. A proposal. Pritchard and his men in Stoke want something from me, right? Why can't I use the information I have about them and leverage their demand to learn even more?

I slip out the back door and take two steps when the door opens again and Leta reaches my side.

"Of course, you're disappointed," she says. "Take heart. Mannix is merely busy. Worried. If Harrison doesn't win, Whitaker will come for all of us." The clouds of hair coiled and piled on Leta's head wiggle as she talks and fiddles with the handbag draped over her arm. "He's holed up in that town office meeting with every scoundrel who will support him, making all sorts of promises to keep them out of trouble if they help him get the votes he needs."

"I understand. I'm sorry that Mannix is so disappointed in me, but I can fix this myself. I'll just use the information I have about them and leverage their demand to learn more, if I can."

"How? Do you think they'll hand you a key to the town because you refuse to submit to their demand? Put you on their police force?"

"Don't get my hopes up, Leta. No, there has to be a way to pry more information from them. Maybe I can agree to write their little retraction if…"

If what? There is no government agency that cares about what Stoke does, and that's the whole problem, so there's no one to send to inspect the place.

Or is there?

I snap my fingers. "We haven't been able to find that scientist, but what if there was someone like him? What if someone pretended to be from the government and wanted to inspect the air or the water?" I whisper because the trees here have ears. "Or maybe we could hire a scientist of our own."

"Then what? Write back and agree to write the retraction if they let someone in to study the place and write up a report?"

"Exactly!" I exclaim. It's an idea to present to Weylan at least. Pritchard sent Silas here. It's my turn to send someone there. "Can I ask you two questions?"

Leta nods and leans forward, as if she has all the time in the world for me. I hate to take up much of it, or take her for granted in the slightest, because ever since she took me under her wing, she's always opened her door for me and my brother. I've already infuriated Mannix. I don't want to lose Leta too.

"Do you think I can put off telling Weylan and Emmett until tomorrow?" I ask.

The corner of her mouth puckers. "Might as well. Nothing they can do about it tonight."

"Great. My last question… Did you hear Harrison speak earlier today? I'd love to know what he said, because I somehow missed everything."

CHAPTER FOUR

JULY 10, 1901

"Good morning, night owl." Bea hunches over a paper at her desk, unmoving except for her eyes, which follow me as I plop a small basket of tomatoes in front of her.

Ruthie is focused on her writing, chewing on her pencil. Hazel types away on the typewriter that's new to her but was old to her father. The tapping and clacking echoes off the concrete walls.

"Sorry I'm late." I toss the folded pages with my article about Harrison on my desk. "Hope I didn't keep anyone up last night."

Luckily, Leta had remembered what Harrison had said at the rally so I was able to finish the article, but the relief wasn't enough to grant me any sleep. My mind bounced between Mannix's frustration with me to what Weylan would say when I handed him Pritchard's letter then to my endless worry over whether I was holding up my end of the cleaning arrangement with my roommates. It seems like I'm either not enough to please the people around me or too much to handle these days, and as soon as I focus on one, I manage to neglect the rest.

"You didn't keep me up at all," says Ruthie. "It was too hot to sleep."

Bea agrees. "I was up, but it was no fault of yours. I tossed and turned all night."

Hazel's tapping stops. "Where'd you get those?" She eyes up the ripe red tomatoes.

"Mrs. Weaver. She gave them to me on my way past her house. She grew them in her greenhouse. They're for everyone."

"You should be late more often." Ruthie is hot on Hazel's heels.

Chairs scraped the floor. Ruthie swaps her pencil for a juicy, ripe tomato. I bite into one myself and catch the juice and seeds as they trail down my hand. Then the door opens and we all turn to see Leta, her arms full of papers she hugs to her chest. She bends as she lowers the bundle to the counter like it's a small baby she's putting down for a nap.

We know it's the stories they collected from women upstream, and gape at the volume of it in silence for a moment.

"Golly, Miss Leta. That's a lot." Hazel marvels.

"Is this from the women's recollections?" Ruthie asks.

"Heavens no. This isn't even half. You can do as you wish with these." Leta separates the stack into two piles and declares the smaller stack to be accounts of suffragists who faced opposition for their dedication to the cause. Some papers she stores with Mannix, others she stores here, like a squirrel burying nuts for future consumption. "Keep them safe, and trust no one," she says.

Ruthie jumps and returns to her desk, extracting a rolled tube of posters held together with twine. She holds them out for Leta. "For you."

"Perfect. We'll get these plastered all over town straightaway. You girls have outdone yourselves. We expected half as many."

As Leta runs her nail along the pages and counts down all the stores eager to show their support for Harrison, I shrink back to my own desk, hoping Leta doesn't mention that we saw each other last night. I haven't told the girls about the letter from Pritchard yet, and I'd rather tell Weylan first. Luckily, Leta seems to be in quite a hurry. She thanks us for the posters and turns to leave.

Pausing at the door, she glances back at me. "I do hope when the time comes you'll use all those stories responsibly. No names in print."

"Of course." I give her our assurances that we'd take great care with the stories entrusted to us.

We each take a few pages and sit at our desks as the sun stretches across the floor. Every once in a while, one of them gasps at the atrocity of it all, at the way illness took people's teeth and made their gums bleed, how their bodies failed from the inside out. I give up trying to concentrate and focus on my Harrison article instead. There's no harsher editor than daylight after a sleepless night. I don't change much, but before mid-day arrives, the back door opens and closes, and Weylan's footsteps echo down the hall. He comes to a stop in his office. Ready to get it over with, I collect the letter and Leta's stack of pages, bumping into Bea's desk on my way by.

"Is everything okay?" she asks. "You look…"

"Pale." Ruthie draws out the word like she's not sure it's the right one, but as clammy as I feel, I bet it is.

Bea looks between me and the hall, and it must dawn on her that I'm about to talk to Weylan finally, because she lets out a long *ooooh* and smiles in a way I'm sure is meant to be reassuring but doesn't hide her pity. I have a feeling Marie Antoinette saw that same look from gawkers while on her way to the gallows.

Weylan's door at the end of the hall is shut. I can tell because the usual ribbon of morning sun isn't stretching across the floor. He's either busy or irritated this morning, and either way I have to break in and give him the awful truth.

I knock twice.

He clears his throat. "Come in."

I slip inside, holding my breath, and close the door behind me. With my back against the door, I hold out a tomato like the wicked queen tempting Snow White. But he eyes me like I'm the snake tempting Eve.

He walks to me slowly, head down, blushing. "You do know this is a dream of mine?"

I hold it out, dangling it before him, and I let it fall into his outstretched hand. As much as I wish I could hold in the smile, I can't. He still makes me giddy when he looks at me like that. I feel like the only woman in the room, and when I am the only woman in the room, I can't resist his pull.

He steps back and plops the ripe, red beauty on his desk. I plop the papers on the table where he works.

"Leta brought the victim statements," I say.

"I'll go through it all this afternoon."

"I have something else to say, and I need to get it out before I lose my nerve."

He puts up a hand to stop me. "Me first." In an instant, he extracts an envelope from the mess of his desk and puts it in my hand. My stomach tightens into a knot. I'm getting really sick of letters.

"What is it? You're making me nervous." As if I'm not already.

"Do you remember that scientist who tested the water here?"

"The elusive, mysterious man we can't find? Yes." How could I forget?

"Well, a few weeks ago, one of the women Leta talked to about the water wrote to me. Their conversation sparked her memory of that scientist, but she couldn't recall the details at the time. She finally remembered his name and thought I'd want to know."

I sit hard in a chair at his little table. "Really?"

"Really. I looked up his name in the city directory and wrote him a letter but didn't hear back."

"That's disappointing," I say. It seems both of us have been keeping secrets. Mine are a bit worse, though. "You never said—"

"I didn't want to get anyone's hopes up. Anyway, I then wrote to the Baltimore Sun hoping they might know something about him. Thinking maybe they'd do a little digging on behalf of a fellow newspaperman. And they did."

I stand again, pressing the letter to my heart. "Did they find him?"

"They did. But he's dead. Natural causes."

I skim Weylan's letter and the obituary clipping, but it's just as he said. Nothing new. I'd been hoping to send him to Stoke. My heart sinks toward my shoes, but not all the way. It's just one door closed, that's all.

"That's terrible," I say. "But it's not the end. If he could study the water, then surely someone else can, too. We'll just have to find someone and start over. And we'll have to do it soon because I have bad news too."

Wrestling Pritchard's letter from my pocket, I put it in his hand, and I stand back against the door again waiting for something. Not a scream, he never does that. Not an outburst. He wouldn't lash out at a fly. A warning, maybe. An admonition. I never should have pushed for us to publish an opinion piece. If ever there was a good time or reason for him to break things off with me in a big explosive way, this is it. I brace for it, but all I get is a sigh.

"Say something," I implore.

He sits on the edge of his desk. "I knew what I was signing up for."

"With me? Or the paper?" I take a chance on levity.

"Both." The corner of his mouth lifts. "We'll fight it."

I lean next to him. "I took it to Mannix first. He was on my way, and I thought he might have an idea or two, but he was very frustrated with me for having written the opinion piece at all. I think I should write them back and agree to write a retraction if they'll let someone in to inspect their operation and prove that I'm wrong about the poisoning. It would have been perfectly timed if the scientist were still alive, but we can find someone else. Once they agree, I'll write something, but it won't be the retraction they're expecting."

He nods. "Something tongue-in-cheek that fits the bill but doesn't let them off the hook."

"Right. I just don't know who I could send there or where to find them." The first little thrilling spark of conspiracy ignites between us. I forgot how good this felt.

He chews the inside of his cheek. "What about your family in Stoke? Emmett? The veil over this threat is pretty thin. If you push Pritchard too far, someone could get hurt."

"If Pritchard harmed them over this, he'd lose the only leverage he has over me. I'm calling his bluff."

"Alright, then who do we send?" he asks. We both drum our

fingers on the edge of the desk. After a few moments, Weylan goes to the shelf and pulls a newspaper off a stack, rolling it up and slapping his thigh. He gives me an *I have an idea* look that edges on mischief.

"The Baltimore Sun?" I ask. "You want to swat them with rolled up copies of the Baltimore Sun?"

"Not quite." He taps the paper against his head now. "I don't know why I didn't think of this before."

"Think of what?"

He chews his bottom lip. "We have all the victim statements Leta and the suffragists collected. It's time to think bigger."

"They're two different issues," I say. "We need to respond to the cease and desist now. We can't wait until we've read all those pages before we come up with our next step."

"That's true, but I think we can kill two birds with one stone. The Sun has been writing about a similar case out west."

"I know, but we aren't a government entity, Weylan. We can't sue Stoke. That's the problem. They haven't committed a crime because there's no law against what they're doing, but we can't make a law against what they're doing because we can't prove it. We need proof, first, and—"

He places a hand on my shoulder, and the stiffness melts out of me. "Let me send a telegram. I have an idea. Just give me until tomorrow morning."

"Fine. Whatever you're thinking can't hurt."

The corner of his mouth lifts, taking his eye with it, and it's like we're a team again, the way we were before I told him *yes, but not yet*. Some of the knots inside me have untied, and I don't know if it's the ease between us, the thrill of conspiring with him, or the relief that it all happened without a big conversation about who we are together and what we mean to each other. Part of me wants to wrap my arms around him, but I'm afraid to break the spell, so I walk to the door instead.

"I ought to tell Emmett," I say. "He eats his lunch by the creek. At least I think he still does. If I head out now, I can probably meet up with him there."

"Did you tell the girls yet?" he asks.

"No. I didn't want to worry them with a threat against the paper."

"I'll tell them while you talk to Em?"

"That sounds like a good idea."

He takes a step closer. The old wanting is back in his gaze, a burning in his eyes that sears my insides. "Was there anything else you wanted to talk about?"

Yes, but not yet. The words echo in my head, turning him down without turning him away, and if I knew things would get better between us and not more awkward, that it wouldn't result in an ultimatum that would send us in opposite directions, perhaps my mouth wouldn't be so dry and my tongue wouldn't be glued to the roof of my mouth. My spine turns to ice.

I don't want to lose him and I don't want to hurt him. I just want us to be a team so nothing falls apart. Us. The newspaper. The mission.

I swear I could drown in his dark eyes. He has a poet's eyes that seem to memorize every word I say and study every expression I make while his mind is elsewhere, thinking grand thoughts. He has a way of raking his hand through his hair when he's lost in some reverie. And he always smells like paper and ink, like all the best books, but he's so much more than any fantasy or epic legendary tale, and he terrifies me. The thought of losing him terrifies me just as much as the idea of marrying him. I wish I weren't such an idiot.

"No. I don't need anything else. Just this." I back up to the door.

He nods with half a smile, and I wonder if he heard the same echo. *Yes, but not yet.*

The girls have scattered back to their desks, so I grab two tomatoes for Emmett and find him just where I thought I would, across town, sitting on a log, eating cold meat and bread, and staring at the water.

"Tomato for your thoughts?" I get a little pleasure out of startling him.

"You know, I can't eat those things. So much stuff comes out of me, I turn the privy into a general store."

"Lovely, Em." I wrinkle my nose. "Will you ever grow up?"

"Not if I can help it. What do you want anyway?"

I plop down beside him, pluck bark from the tree, and tell him about Silas's letter. "You can't tell a soul. I don't want Whitaker getting a whiff of fear and saying anything to Pritchard."

"Fine by me," he says. "Do you think it's the best idea to be using Weylan's newspaper to poke bears like Whitaker and Pritchard?"

I reel back. "Um, yes. A newspaper is the appropriate entity to ask questions like this. And Weylan wouldn't do it if he didn't want to."

He puts both hands up. "I'm just saying you could print stories about what's for sale at the stores and cats up trees and live a quiet life."

"I'm not getting into this with you." He knows this is as important to Weylan as it is to me. "No, I am. The newspaper isn't an arm of my search for justice, Em. It's not a weapon to me. These facts belong to the people, and the newspaper is how they can get them.

Should we not print this stuff because it matters to us?"

He lolls his head back and looks at the tree canopy. "How many times are you going to hurt Weylan before you're done playing with him, Charlie?"

"Don't kick me when I'm down, Em. I already feel bad enough." I throw a hunk of bark in the creek and relish the plunk. "How did people at the brickyard feel about Harrison's talk?"

"Sure. Change the topic." He lifts a shoulder. "A few people are mad at Whitaker, but most are numb. They don't think anything will ever change. The dummies I work with just want life to go back to the way it used to be a long time ago. Like you can snap your fingers and clean up the water. The smart ones know it won't be that easy. They want new industry. Opportunity. They figure Harrison might not make that happen, but he can't be any worse. I would like to do something other than make bricks all day."

"I told you to come work at the paper. You could help operate the press."

He feigns choking on his sandwich. "Forgive me for not wanting to work with you."

"Fine. You think they'll vote for Harrison?" I ask. "They're not afraid of Whitaker finding out who they voted for?"

"Nah. People don't stand around and talk about it, but most of them are going with Harrison."

"That's good to hear." I stand and brush shards of brittle tree bark and moss from my skirt. "I have to get back to work. I just wanted you to know about Pritchard."

Halfway up the hill, I stop. I didn't tell Em everything. Silas had been here, staring me down, letting me know he knows how to find us. Emmett needs to hear it from me, because I'll regret it forever if anything happens, but telling him will only make him angry. We're already estranged enough, growing apart. Living our lives. He thinks I've let Weylan down. If I tell him Silas was here, he'll have more reasons to doubt me. Besides, Silas was merely here to drop off a letter, and the situation is under control. Weylan and I are working on a plan. And if Silas wanted to hurt us, he had a chance. And like I told Weylan, if they hurt Emmett, they have no leverage over me anymore.

"What's wrong?" Em asks. He hurls a peach pit across the creek, and it rustles some old leaves when it lands.

I turn to face him. More than a year has passed since we first came here, when he stood on the bridge I'm about to cross and dabbed at his bleeding gums with his sleeve and asked me to tell him it would all be alright. He was a boy then. Now he's chiseled with a strong arm and a stiff upper lip. Maybe he's wrong about my relationship with Weylan, but he's plenty old enough to handle himself. It's funny how time changes things. There was a time I couldn't imagine not looking out for him. Now I don't even know the man he's becoming.

He squints at me. "What's that look?"

"I'm proud of you, that's all. I might not agree with you, but you've come a long way. Father would be proud too."

"How could you possibly write a retraction of that opinion article." Ruthie leans against the kitchen cupboard, winding the dish rag around her hand, waiting on Hazel to hand her a clean plate to dry. With her eyebrows pinched, she has a look that sits somewhere between aghast and exasperated. "What could you say that would appease those people?"

Bea pushes the Ladies Home Journal across the table at me and pokes at an ad for a tan leather pump shoe that costs three dollars.

"Don't know yet. Weylan and I are thinking about it." I wrinkle my nose at the shoe. Bows on shoes turn my stomach. "In the meantime, Weylan's looking for someone we can send to Stoke who might be able to inspect the water or something."

"Pritchard will throw them a state dinner." There's a sparkle in Hazel's eye. "I love a good controversy. But we won't lose our jobs, will we?"

"I don't think so."

I start to hopscotch through my conversation with Weylan when three quick knuckle raps on the door cause all our heads to swivel.

"I'll get it." Bea flips the page of her Ladies' Home Journal back, feigning injury. "Look at these bodices. Who's shaped like that? Her waist is pushed so far forward, her rear nearly reaches her shoulders."

"I'll bet a week's wages it's Weylan," Ruthie says.

"No takers on that bet," says Bea, her hand on the knob.

"He needs his own key," Hazel says.

"That is a horrible bodice." I hold up the page so Hazel can see. She wrinkles her nose. "Who buys these things?"

Bea smooths her hair and flings open the door with a dramatic flourish. "You're lucky we're all decent, boss man. We could be in our night clothes at this hour. Are you here to woo our Charlotte?"

"Ladies." He steps in, hat in his hands. "I'm sorry for disturbing your night." If he were two inches taller he'd have to duck in the short doorway. I don't know if it's the way his hair falls in his eyes when he dips his head or if it's his height. Despite the worries around the newspaper and my fears of a life-changing confrontation if he tries to define what we are, he still makes my skin tingle. "It's about work, unfortunately. I need Charlotte."

"I bet you do." Ruthie nudges Hazel's elbow. "By work, you mean a long walk in the moonlight?"

Bea glares at Hazel when she snorts. She nudges me with her hip, inching me toward the door.

"I knew I should have dressed for the weather before I came," he says, "but my suit of armor is still hanging out to dry."

Ruthie snorts when she laughs and I make a quick exit before they make him any more uncomfortable than he already is.

Neither of us says a word as we set off in the direction of the park. No words are needed as we follow the creek. We aren't far, and we both know the way with our eyes closed. I also used to know the landscape of his heart with my eyes closed, but now there's a chasm between us, and I can't see across it. It should feel comforting or at least comfortable walking beside him, but my mind races with a thousand things other than work that he may want to say, and all of them fill me with guilt and the outer ripples of a heartache on my horizon.

The sky melts, glazing lavender, as we turn down the street that leads to the sliver of land by the water and the gazebo where we sometimes sit. I don't want things to end between us here. So many great memories are tangled up in this place. Emmett's words come flooding back to me, raising the level of my guilt.

"It's been a while," he says.

"It has. Weylan, you would tell me if anything I wrote was risking the newspaper, wouldn't you? It's your dream."

"I would, but you haven't. It's kind of you to think of it, but it's not just my newspaper. We're a team, Charlie. At least I hope we are. And putting a stop to that poison is as important to me as it is to you."

"I know." Maybe the night is sharpening my senses, but unease seems to swirl around Weylan. Much more than usual. I try to bite down on some thought, one thing I can say that will set his worries aside and put him at ease, but all I can come up with is, "Of course we're a team." Though it's not enough.

He folds his arms. "I'm glad to hear it. I asked you out here for a reason."

Oh, no. I wiggle my fingers into the crook of his arm, craving the old closeness as we move to the open lawn, and a breeze sweeps across the water and pushes around us.

He places his hand on mine. "I found the article I remembered in the Baltimore Sun. It's about a case before the Supreme Court. I stopped everything and took it straight to Mannix, but he doesn't seem interested in helping with this—"

"I noticed," I say. "I thought it was me."

"I think he's upset with both of us. He did let me use his telephone to call the newspaper and ask to speak to the man who wrote the article. I wanted to know who the lawyers were in the case."

My heart does a little leap. "Is the case similar enough to ours?"

"A little different. Missouri has sued Chicago and the State of Illinois for contaminating the Mississippi River."

"That's brilliant." I stop. Weylan stops. "Our case is as good as won, then. Once the Supreme Court says that you can't poison water, they'll make Pritchard stop. Weylan, this is wonderful news."

He spins to face me. "It's sewage, not coal."

"Okay, more disgusting than wonderful. You're saying that case isn't enough like ours?"

He shakes his head. "It's not. But the case is about the right to clean water."

"And if the court says that people have a right to clean water…" The words come out of me slowly, as the thought forms. "Then perhaps we can go up against a private industry with deep pockets like Pritchard's after all. Did you get the name of the lawyers?"

"I did." He's trying not to smile, but it isn't working.

I stamp my foot and try to force my own smile to submit. "Stop toying with me. Out with it."

"I rang their number right away. They said they'd meet with us tomorrow."

"Tomorrow?" But that's so soon. "We do need to move quickly with that cease and desist looming over us, but do we have to meet in person? Can't they just tell us everything over the phone?"

Weylan grabs both my hands. "We can get more information out of them in person, Charlie. It's so hard to hear on those things. And you need to be there, because you've interviewed people, and I haven't."

"But the train ride. It's so long." My mouth is dry. Talking is like forcing my words through raw cotton.

He bends down to catch my eyes and force me to look at him. His hair flops in his eyes, and I'm inclined to give him anything he asks, but this feels like too much.

"What are you afraid of?" he asks.

"Honestly? Lawyers." I'll never forget how upsetting it was sitting in Mannix's office for the first time, telling him everything I remembered about Stoke and my parents being sick and how it was all Pritchard's fault. He had to ask all those difficult questions, trying to find the holes in the tale, but it made me feel guilty. Like it was my fault somehow. Lawyers are smart and sly, and it's like they speak a whole different language.

"This isn't like you," Weylan says. "What's going on?"

I let my hands go limp in his. This is Weylan. I should be able to talk to him about anything. "Convincing people in a small town to fight for their rights is one thing. Convincing argumentative lawyers to listen to us is something else entirely. I'm not the right kind of person—"

"You're exactly the right kind of person. You're more prepared to talk to them than anyone. We're not backing down because you're intimidated by a lawyer and a long train ride, Charlie. Pritchard brought the fight to you with that letter. You have to meet it or give up. Which one will it be?"

I've chewed the inside of my cheek raw. "Fine."

"Yeah?" He lets go of my hands and reaches into his vest, pulling out two slips of paper I know to be train tickets. They land in my right hand like hot slabs of molten metal.

"Good," he says. "Tomorrow. We leave at eight."

"In the morning?" My voice is high and a little wild. "So soon? And there are only two tickets."

"Who else would go? The clock is ticking on that letter, and Monday is too late. We have to do this tomorrow."

I swat his arm with the tickets. "It's terribly presumptuous of you to think we should be alone together on a train."

"We won't be alone. There will be a hundred other people on the same train."

Emmett could have come with us, I'm sure. Or Bea. I search his eyes for a way out, for a clause, for a loophole I can slip through and escape. But all I see there is a bit of pride that he found those lawyers and a hint of confusion at my hesitancy. What about the train is making me so nervous? Being alone with him, trapped in a train car? It shouldn't. Most people think we should be married by now. It's me who's made things awkward between us, and I'm the only one who can fix it.

"It will be fun." I study the ticket. Washington, D.C. "To see the landscape and the Capital."

He takes my hand and gives it a squeeze, sealing the date, and we start to walk back. I smile up at him, but it feels unnatural, and judging by the twinge of hurt in his eyes, I know he knows I'm forcing it.

"I'm sorry we never found the scientist you overheard that day," I say. "It could have solved everything."

"There will be other avenues. Other paths to pursue. We have the full weight of the newspaper behind us now. Pritchard will be held to account for what he's done. I promise you that."

"How can you be sure?" I ask.

"Because it's the only way I'll stop feeling guilty. It haunts me."

I know it does, and I can feel it grip him in the way he clasps my hand. That guilt grips me too. If I could unwind the clock and go back in time, what tiny action could I take that would have changed it all? Would have moved us away from the air and the water, stopped the poison from eating my parents from the inside out? Tiny actions won't change anything anymore. Weylan and I both know that.

He has a way of smiling when he brushes things aside, with a raise of his right shoulder as if he's trying to convince himself that it doesn't matter. That it doesn't hurt or it won't for long, and I hate that he uses it to mask his regrets. I've seen that look from him a lot lately, and I know it's my fault.

"We should walk together more," I say. "I miss that we used to do this."

He shrugs. "It was a long winter, then a wet spring."

I wish precipitation was all that stood between us. I meant it when I said *Yes, but not yet.* Somehow, I have to close this gap between us. I lean into him, hoping he knows my heart is still here, even if it's wrapped up in all temporary apprehensions.

He inches his hand around my waist and rests it on my ribs, and a little thrill runs down my spine and coils in my middle. He still gives me butterflies, even if they feel sickly and on death's door.

CHAPTER SIX

JULY 11, 1901

I wish I'd never asked Hazel, consummate consumer of the Ladies'
Home Journal, for help with an outfit. I've never regretted a dress
more in my life. Sitting next to Weylan in a stiff borrowed bodice, I
can't take a full breath. I'm not sure what's to blame, my nerves, his
countenance, or the clothing, but I do know my blouse is starched,
the collar scratchy, and I'm saddled with a purple purse made of
beads that makes too much noise and is far too small to contain
anything of value. It won't even hold the old netting needle I used to
carry around out of habit. It does, however, match my skirt and the
rather smart blazer, the cut of which I'd love if only it had pockets.

The whole affair makes me even more self-conscious than I'd
have been if I'd rolled out of bed and hopped on the train in my
dressing gown, especially since the train's natural to-and-froing
keeps tossing my leg into Weylan's. Of course, he seems to be
enjoying the adventure, smiling as our hands brush when he turns
his newspaper page, resting his knee against mine, and nudging my

shoulder with his. How can he be so at ease, and why am I always such a bumbling, stiff, uncomfortable mess? By the time the train crosses the bridge that joins the two banks of the Susquehanna River, I'm short of breath, and I feel like an entire flock of crows have taken off within me and immediately began fighting to their death. Clinging to the window's edge, half of me prays the train will stay on the tracks, and the other half begs the universe to launch me into the abyss. Surely there could have been a way to communicate with these lawyers that didn't involve so much emotional turmoil and touching.

"You seem tense." Weylan shuffles to his right, making the tiniest bit of space between us.

"Yes. It's the dress. It's all Hazel's doing. I thought I needed to look a bit more polished, so I put my fate in Hazel's hands." I raise my left shoulder as high as I can, releasing tension from my ribs.

"You do look nice, if it's any consolation."

"Thank you. Hazel chose a pretty dress, I think." Albeit stiff and scratchy.

"I can't give Hazel the credit for the prettiest part." He winks at me when he says it, then returns to his paper.

I blink at the passing landscape, at the little purple and yellow flowers among the lush greenery next to the tracks.

"Do you want to move to another seat? Perhaps if you had more room?"

"No," I said and placed a hand on his knee. "Not at all."

"Mister. Missus." The conductor nods as he passes, checking our tickets.

Smiling politely, I take my ticket back and secure it in Hazel's dainty purse. Meanwhile, Weylan pulls his monstrosity of a briefcase onto his lap. It's a giant leather thing with hooks and clasps and four different handles. He unfastens the strap and pulls out type-written papers and newspaper pages, tidying them in a neat stack.

"You look very business-like," I say. "As if you're off to make a deal."

I love and admire that about him, how easily he slipped into the role of being the man he had to be in order to achieve the dream he wanted.

"I am a businessman," he says. "I bet you could use a diversion. How's this?"

He shuffles the papers and puts a yellowed article on my lap.

"Oh, perfect. How did you know that I've been longing for homework? Also, how is it possible that you know just what I want to read and have it there in your handy briefcase?"

"You're an open book, Charlotte Morris." One corner of his mouth lifts, one eyebrow arches. He leans until our shoulders touch. "There's no test. It's just hope. This man, Henry Adams, claims that steam is the future. I thought you might like to read it."

I can't pretend to have an attention span any more than I can bring myself to have one. I skim the page, though, and accept another while my mind volleys between Emmett's pointed observation that I'm damaging Weylan's livelihood, Bea's concern that things are getting too tense, the story I must write in praise of the murderous coal criminals, the electric jolt I get from Weylan every time we touch, whatever is happening to my ribs, and the fact that I have absolutely no idea what to say to the lawyer we're hurtling down the tracks to see.

I stare at page after page, my eyes following the lines, absorbing none of it. And I'm grateful that there is no test at the end, because if Weylan wanted to discuss any of it, I'd be at a complete loss.

Hours pass before the train pulls into the station, and despite Weylan's assurances that he knows where we're going, we take a turn around the block like we're assessing a dance floor before we find the law office.

The building is made of gleaming white stone, and its corner is angled like the newspaper's door, as if someone sliced it off with a knife. But this is nothing like the newspaper office. There are giant brass doors with thick glass windows, and inside, the floor is made of marble and, behind an elevated counter crafted from more wood than my apartment, is a man who gawks at us as if we don't belong. And, oh, how right he is.

Weylan makes our introduction and enquires about the lawyer, but the man we've come to meet isn't here.

"He's had an emergency across town," he says. His glasses sit on the end of his nose. "He asked if you wouldn't mind waiting an hour."

"We'll run a few errands and be back." Weylan checks the time on a pocket watch that dangles from a chain attached to a button on his vest. I hadn't noticed it when we were sitting on the train. He truly does look like a businessman. Keeping track of appointments. Keeping track of time.

The sun is high and blaring hot, and if my dress would allow me to sink when we step out the door I would. Instead, I stand ramrod-straight on the sidewalk, gaping at the horses and carriages and smelly, noisy automobiles that share the road while Weylan looks both ways.

"It's like another world," I say. "Have you ever done something like this before?"

"No," he says. Then how does he seem so comfortable and confident while I feel like I've fallen through a hole in the earth and been spit out, upside down, on the other side?

"Let's sit." He nods to the little park that sits on the adjacent corner.

The lawn is sparse and wide, home to a few large pin oaks and a scattering of young trees, tall and narrow, jutting like pencils stuck in the ground. Bare paths crisscross the trimmed grass like they're lacing up nature. Benches sit here and there, facing nothing in particular, and Weylan aims for one, startling a squirrel who shoots across the park and clings upside down to a tree, chattering his dissenting opinion.

All the trees start to close in on me. The clouds press down. The buildings loom higher, their walls growing closer. I can't catch my breath. Why can't I breathe?

"Are you alright? You're whiter than that marble floor."

He takes my elbow. When did I stop walking?

"Sit. Breath in. Slow." He inflates slowly, waving a hand to demonstrate what breathing should be like, and I try to mimic him, but I can't. It seems I've forgotten how to breathe.

"What are we doing here, Weylan?"

"Don't get cold feet. He'll be back. We'll meet with him."

"It isn't that." My breath ratchets. Tight little bursts in. Small puffs out. "They're brushing us off. We're a waste of their time."

"That's not true," he says. "They wouldn't have offered if they didn't want to."

"I can't do this."

"You can." He sits beside me with his briefcase at his feet while I compose myself.

"This is frustrating," I say. "It's daft, and these coal people are going to win because money always does. I can't afford to pay big lawyers in a place like this. Those doors cost more than my entire life."

"They're just people." He looks at me softly, and I appreciate that he isn't exasperated at having to deal with me and my lack of composure. "They do good work, which is how they can afford all that fanciness. We need their knowledge and wisdom right now."

"But this is going to take a whole day, and we don't have a whole day to lose. What's the best that could happen here? Even if they do take on our case, I have to live in a tiny apartment with two other women. I can't pay these people."

"It's just advice. Direction. An avenue. They've been down this road, and they might know who could study the air and the water. Isn't that the thing we want more than anything right now?"

I fiddle with this tiny stupid purse Hazel made me bring while Weylan runs his hands over his knees. Maybe I wouldn't feel so much like an imposter if I didn't look like one. If the Weylan beside me were still the same Weylan he always was instead of a man with a briefcase and a pocket watch on a shiny chain.

"What if it's all lies?" I ask. "Maybe they don't want to meet with us. What if we lose control of it all to a bunch of lawyers, and in the end they give up because they don't care as much as we do? More excuses and lies from men in suits."

"Charlie, it's just a conversation." His voice is low and quiet. He's trying to calm me, and it isn't working.

The purple purse keeps sliding off my lap so I fling it into the space between us where it clatters on the bench. "This is stupid.

Skirts are stupid. I want to wear pants. With pockets."

I don't even have to look at him to know he's trying not to laugh at me. "I love that idea. You'd be gorgeous in pants. Or in a potato sack. I'll help you get out of that dress and change when we get home."

"I know you're just trying to make me laugh, but talk like that will ruin everything."

His smile fades, and he swallows hard. "I doubt anything could ruin what we have."

"I shouldn't have said that." He probably thinks there's nothing left to ruin, and I can't blame him. "I don't want—" To talk about this here. Or at all. I pull the purse onto my lap and run my finger along the beads while he sighs and sinks back on the bench.

"What is it that you do want, Charlie?"

I huff, though I wish I hadn't, and I look the other way, to the corner where two men step from a carriage and enter a coffee house. What *do* I want?

"I want calm and peace. A solution to all of this. I want to beat Pritchard and make him stop. My life is on hold because of all of that, and I want it to go away, so I can move on and put an end to this feeling that the clock has stopped ticking on my life. Or hasn't started yet, as the case may be."

"Alright." He probes a tooth with his tongue and nods, his eyes fixed on some distant roofline. "What are you willing to do to get it? How much discomfort are you willing to endure? Because all you have to do is go in that door and talk to a lawyer."

"I'm willing to do anything. All of it," I say. "But that doesn't mean it won't hurt or be hard."

And I realize now that all my fear of not reaching justice just keeps me from trusting people, not for the first time, and it's impacting Weylan more than anyone. I disrupted his whole life, and I'm lucky he has the patience to wait for me, because I don't know how I'd do all this without him. God, I'm so stupid. I will take a train all the way to Washington D.C. to meet with a lawyer in hopes of taking one step toward solving a problem, but I won't have one conversation with the man I love in hopes of bridging our divide. What is wrong with me?

I turn to face him as best I can considering my torso won't twist, and I look him in the eye for the first time in a while.

"I've been really unfair to you," I say. "I'm lost, and sometimes I don't know what this thing between us looks and feels like anymore. It's uncomfortable, and I keep avoiding it hoping it will get better, because I feel like you're…" My deep breath strains my bodice. "You have something to say. To me. About us. And I'm not running away from you this time. If you want to say it, this is a good time. No one will walk in on us or tease us. We have all the time in the world. Or until that man comes back from his appointment, whichever comes first."

I want to hear it, even if it makes for a long, heart-broken train ride home.

"I do want to talk about it. Desperately. But you don't want to do this here." When Weylan stands and paces, a corner of my heart chips off and falls away.

"I do. I can handle it. Things are tense all the time, and I've handled that just fine. I caused it. But I don't want it to be like this anymore. Uncertain and wobbly."

If it's going to end, it might as well be now.

He leans against the tree next to me. "I'm not strong in the ways you are, Charlie. I want to be with you and make you happy. We went from perfection to *not yet, but yes.* What should I do? What should I feel in this *not yet* time? I just can't turn that off like you can, like it's a phonograph and the music just stops for a while until you put it back on."

"I said *Yes, but not yet.* The *but* came after the yes. And I didn't turn off my feelings. I will never stop loving you, Weylan." I close my eyes and try to make sense of the tornado of feelings before they suck me in and spit me out in pieces. "I don't know either. I feel all the same things for you that I've always felt, but there's this guilt and fear in the way, and I'm so afraid that if we start this conversation it will end with us apart."

He kicks off the tree and stands in front of me, eclipsing the sun. "I fear you'll find someone else. I don't know how I'll cope."

"Someone else? That's not possible. Weylan, I still want us to be together. I just don't want to be married yet."

He sits beside me, small and sheepish. "Are you sure?"

"Of course, I'm sure. I'm entirely certain about you. You're the only future I see. But if I start building a home and a life with you now, it will only be half of a life because the other half of me will be in this fight. And if I stop fighting Pritchard my parents will never rest peacefully. Either way is a path to regret. But I will never regret you."

Weylan places his hand on mine, which is a greater act of affection than I deserve after causing him so much pain. Even so, I feel as if the weight of one of these tall buildings has been lifted off my chest.

"I do love you, you know," I say. "I missed you. And us."

"As did I. I love you too." He squeezes my hand back. "With that settled, would you allow me to take you on a date to that little shop over there? A cup of coffee, perhaps, or tea?"

"I'd be delighted." I push to my feet and take Hazel's purse in one hand and loop the other through Weylan's arm. We walk to the coffee shop in a silence far more comfortable than the one on the train, and though we enjoy a little table by the window, sipping coffee and enjoying flaky pastries, my mind and my fears are across the street. Speaking my mind to a lawyer isn't half as easy as giving my heart to Weylan.

Stitching together the months of distance between us is like returning home. My heart has always known the shape of his smile and the lilt in his voice when he talks about Ruthie's sketches. The knots in my stomach loosen. My bodice seems to loosen too, giving me room to breathe, and by the time Weylan looks at his watch and declares it time to cross the street, the worry has been replaced with a bit of resolve. When we return to the cold, marble lobby, I face the man at the counter as if he owes me and the bill is past due.

CHAPTER SEVEN

JULY 11, 1901

Simon Dietrich, Esquire, has a lush office on the third floor with soft upholstered furniture on both sides of a broad wooden desk. Gas lights with green domes dangle from the ceiling. The walls seem made of books, matching spines lining the shelves with little volume numbers. It's like Mannix's office but amplified a thousand times. No wonder lawyers always look so tired. It must take a whole day to find anything in here.

"This is about coal, you said? And this is impacting a town?" The man frees himself of his wire-rimmed glasses and lays them by an open book, peering over his laced fingers as if he's waiting to be entertained.

"It's destroying towns along the water south of the coal plant." I grip the purse in my lap as he reaches up and flips on a gas lamp. Light flares on a stack of law books. Those books have to be a better trail to justice than the violence in Stoke that seems inevitable. I may not understand them, but I need to trust them.

"Thank you for meeting with us," I say. "It's kind of you to give us your time. You have a very nice office."

"It's frippery. Makes people think we're capable."

Weylan settles next to me in a giant wood chair with carved arms. He looks at home there. It suits him. Like if he sat there long enough, he would spontaneously create grand pieces of literary art.

I sit up straighter, trying to look the part, but it only makes me feel more out of place, like a child trying to sit still in a parlor full of adults. But I refuse to allow my lack of confidence to betray my resolve.

"To get to the point, sir, the coal plant in Stoke is poisoning the air. It causes an illness that leads to death. The owner denies the cause. We also suspect they're poisoning the water downstream, where fish kills have happened and people have been sickened. A scientist once studied it and arrived at that conclusion. He was overheard telling the mayor, but there's no paper record of it, and he has since passed away. We have collected witness statements from several towns. We also run a newspaper and publish articles and editorials about the poisonings, and the coal plant has demanded a retraction."

"Not just that." Weylan cleared his throat. "They've threatened her family with unspecified physical harm if we don't comply."

The lawyer scowls and shakes his head, nudging a notepad on his desk. "This letter you received. Who sent it? A lawyer?"

Weylan unlatches his briefcase, whips out the letter, and passes it across the desk with enviable grace.

"No. The coal boss," I say. "On coal company letterhead."

"His name?" the lawyer asks, inspecting the letter.

Pritchard's name gets caught in my throat. Once it crosses my lips, this talk is no longer hypothetical. We won't be discussing a situation, a snarl that we're in. We'll be talking about people and real dangers. Men with power protect each other, and I can't put the stopper back on this bottle once I spill the contents, so I splay my fingers in my lap.

Weylan clears his throat. "Nels Pritchard."

"Pritchard must be worried." Dietrich strokes his trim beard. "Whether you're onto facts or swaying opinion, you've ruffled feathers. If they thought they stood a chance at defending themselves, they would have filed a suit. If they thought they had a case, it would have come from a law office."

Weylan sighs. "They're more than willing to skirt the law."

"What have you done so far?" Dietrich asks, handing the letter back to Weylan and glancing back and forth between us.

"I've contacted people from Stoke who might talk." I rub my sticky palm on my knee.

"We wrote to a bank they use. They didn't respond." Weylan finishes my thought. "And we know Pritchard is fond of bribery. We're hoping new mayors who aren't under Pritchard's thumb will be willing to speak."

"Don't be surprised if your candidate inherits an office that's been cleansed of its paper trail."

I agree. It's a thought we've considered. "Two questions then: Are there any existing or past court cases that can help us here — like the one about water rights — and how can we steer our case to the courts?"

The man stands and browses his books, and if there is an answer, I hope it's among the spines. "Others have gone down similar paths with coal companies. Steel and iron, too. If you win, you'll be destroyed in the process. If you lose, you're destroyed in the end."

"That's what I hear. Is it hopeless then?" I purse my lips. I refuse to accept defeat before we've begun. All this talk and coming so far, this can't be the end of our peaceful options.

"Not necessarily." He slides open a drawer and pulls out a small card. "Take the cheapest path first. Find out if other towns have suffered in similar ways."

I sit up straight. "We've done that. We have quite the collection of statements, but no evidence to back it up."

His head bounces as he nods. "You're on the right path. Leave no stone unturned."

Weylan reaches across the desk to accept the card Deitrich extends.

"But we've reached the end of our path," I say. "How do we find proof? The scientist who studied the water before has died. It's a dead end, isn't it?"

He extends his arm and twists his wrist, wobbling his hand as if to say the waters are rough. "It's so hard to topple these big companies. Evidence doesn't sit on the surface, but you don't always need it to move forward. If you have enough victims, like you say, you can often find a lawyer who believes in the case enough to fund an investigation himself."

"They'd all have to sign onto the idea." Weylan and I exchange glances. He's reading my mind. The case will be stronger if they do, but most of them asked to remain anonymous, and convincing them will be harder than herding clouds.

"I can see your concern," Dietrich says. "Cases like this get messy. Victims have different concerns and expectations. My suggestion is to make a lot of noise. Let people know you're moving forward. The braver you appear, the more people will follow you. And the more eyes that are on you as your party grows, the safer you will all be."

His metered way of speaking ratchets my breath, and the doom implied by his words makes me break out in a sweat. I exchange glances with Weylan. Making noise is my strong suit. Leta knows a lot of suffragists. Men might not be willing to discuss what they know, but their wives might be.

"We can build alliances with the most powerful people in each town," I say.

Weylan agrees. "Like the Missouri case."

"Good. Tell no one you've spoken with me. Gather as much information as you can, then send me a letter or telegram. The more people impacted, the stronger the case will be. You need people all along that waterway who will allow testing on their property. And you need towns willing to support a law that will stand up to that coal boss. In the meantime, I will ask my contacts for someone who might be able to test the waters."

"What happens then?" I grip the arm of the chair. "And what if it doesn't work? What if Pritchard manages to bribe every politician he comes across? Everyone has a price."

Weylan places his hand on mine. "It's possible no evidence will ever be uncovered to prove he knew he was hurting people but covered it up to make a profit. What can we do if there's no evidence?"

Deitrick gives us a flat-lipped grin and I know I've exhausted all the questions he'll answer for free.

"That's a bridge to cross another day," he says. "For now, get people on your side. The entire state, if you can. Everyone up and down stream."

A quick glance at Weylan, and I know we're thinking the same thing. It's a relief to have a plan. We have steps to take, a path to follow. With Leta's connections to suffragists, we should have no trouble finding support.

Dietrich places his glasses back on his nose, walks to the door and holds it open for us. "When you know more send me a note or telephone me."

The whole way back to the train station, I grip the purse with the business card in it, little sequins digging into my fingertips. Weylan and I speak little, though we're both light on our feet, and when we reach the tracks, the train is waiting. We're among the last to board and we find two seats together where we huddle and make notes about what Deitrick said. Then we pull out his map and list out all the towns that trail down the waterways like breadcrumbs.

"What would your father make of this, I wonder?" Weylan muses.

The world passes outside the window as I try to decide. "I don't know. I don't think justice seemed possible to him. It belonged to rich people in cities, not coal workers owned by their boss. And certainly not with the Coal and Iron Police around."

Weylan's knee rested against mine, warm and intentional. "Maybe he'd be glad you found it so fast."

"Maybe now. But I also wonder if he'd say I was daft for trying. It seemed so impossible just a few days ago. I sure do wish I could tell him."

"He knows, Charlie."

I lean my head back and watch the world pass by the window, lulled by the rocking of the train and the long day.

Hope can be an expensive thing, especially when you have

nothing left to lose. It's the kind of thing you spend wisely after watching fools part with their hope too easily. But I'm willing to spend some now. I know Leta and the suffragists have done their best to find good candidates who will support votes for women and uphold stronger values. With luck, they uncover evidence along the way, a money trail that will lead right to Pritchard.

I clear my throat. "As soon as we get off the train—"

"Straight to Leta's." He's reading my mind again. "One at a time, we'll win over those towns."

It all seems so possible and simple that by the time we cross the Gunpowder River, I'm relieved enough to finally sleep with my head on Weylan's shoulder. And when I wake as we cross the Susquehanna, he brushes the hair from my temple, and it feels like the puzzle pieces have finally formed a shape. We have a plan. Things with Weylan are back on track. There's a new type of hope. But more than that, I have a renewed sense of purpose and a reason to get out of bed in the morning.

The train pulls into the North East station and I find I'm sad to see the trip end.

"Can I walk with you to Leta's?" he asks

"Isn't it out of your way?"

"Not at all," he says. "I want to stop by the newspaper office, so it's only a small detour. I want to check to see if we have mail first, if you don't mind."

We enter the station and dodge a small crowd at the ticket window to find Vernon's father. There are only a few letters for the newspaper and something for me.

"It's from Sophie." I clutch it to my chest. "What a treat."

The first few months I lived here, the mayor and his men stole all my mail, and even once I started receiving it again, I worried it was being read by Pritchard. A letter from Sophie still fills me with joy, especially if it's still sealed shut.

Weylan holds the door while I tear open the gummed envelope and unfold her single-page letter. Her writing is always so tidy and neat and goes on for miles, but it's hastily scrawled, and I stop in the shade.

It can't be. I stop dead in my tracks.

"What is it?" Weylan asks.

"My two young cousins." I lack the breath to say it out loud. It doesn't seem real. "They've been killed. In a mine collapse."

His hand lands on my shoulder. "You should sit. I'll get you some water."

"No," I say. "I haven't time. I must tell Emmett. We have to go to Stoke."

CHAPTER EIGHT

JULY 15, 1901

A few days later, I pay Vernon's father for two tickets on the northbound train and wait inside the station for Emmett until the stifling heat sends me out for fresh air. My need to be early often clashes with his need to test my patience.

The conductor walks down the track some twenty yards away, and I start off in his direction to ask how much longer the train will be here because I don't want to choose between waiting for my brother or heading off alone but Leta leaps upon me from out of nowhere. She pulls me into a hug, brushes at my hair, and coos her sympathies.

"Your dear cousins. I can't imagine what your aunt is going through," she says.

"I'm still in shock, I think." That, and I'm too tired after a sleepless night to put my feelings into words.

"At first, I thought it was that terrible poison, but Bea said it was a mine collapse? How horrid." She heeds the call of a shopper at her market cart and turns to make change for a basket of beans. I linger awkwardly, watching the street for Emmett's arrival.

"Bea says you and Emmett are going up north for a night."

"Yes, ma'am. To pay our respects and help where we can. We don't want to stay too long and be a burden."

"Or risk your neck, I'd imagine," she says. "This is your first time going back, isn't it?"

"It is. I've been trying not to think about it." I won't see the town beyond my aunt and uncle's door, and I have no intention of seeing what's become of our old home. My heart couldn't bear it. Some other family lives there now, I'm sure, and if I think about it too long, I might crack this hard shell I've been building up. Leta has a way of nudging me to talk about things, and I'd rather not, so I change the topic.

"Did Weylan come to see you?" I ask. "He said he would talk to you about a meeting we had with a lawyer."

He'd walked me to Emmett's door and sat with me while I broke the news. Then he walked me home and helped me pack. He'd sat at our dinner table and told the girls everything the lawyer had said, but he left just before dinner and headed to Leta's to repeat it all and ask for her help. I don't know what I would have done without him last night.

"Weylan did visit." Leta's shoulders tighten a little. She glances about to be sure no one can hear. "I'm happy to call upon the people we spoke to, to gain their support for a legal case, but many of them were reluctant to be named. Progress moves slower than words, I'm afraid. If you knew your husband had been bribed, would you tell anyone? If *you* had accepted a bribe…"

Her voice trails off as she glances about the platform. It's mothers and children and men in suits, none of them paying us any mind, but she clamps her mouth shut and purses her lips.

I hadn't considered the likelihood or willingness of people to speak out. The mountain of their losses, the utter tragedy of so many women and men dying and seeing it all in stacks of paper had shocked me, both because it happened and because they were willing to speak about it. But talking to a sympathetic woman about those losses was a different animal than speaking about it in court. And I hadn't given it thought because Leta had those connections. Finding those people was out of my hands. And any thought of their hesitancy seemed to flit out of my mind as we all read the accounts. I suppose I got carried away thinking the threat of the poison and the pain it caused were motivation enough to prompt people to join together for a legal remedy. Now it sounds like people won't speak.

"Do you think it's an impossible task?" I ask.

"Impossible, no. Long and arduous, yes. Women want safety. They want better, but sometimes the fight for that progress makes things worse first."

She doesn't have to tell me about things getting worse before they get better, but I'd really like to know when better might be, because I've already lost almost everything I can stand to lose. Working with that lawyer was our best hope. It can't take years. It just can't.

I nod, trying not to look as disappointed as I feel. "Like how a long walk gives you blisters."

"Except these blisters can hurt your sons and daughters too," Leta says.

My cheeks hurt with my agreeable smile, and it doesn't reach my eyes, I know, but it's better than saying what I truly feel. There may be things I don't understand yet, but there's an awful lot they should have understood by now, and I'm tired of being too young, too much, and not enough to fix the broken things.

Leta looks at me as if she's afraid I'll break if she says one more thing, and I ought to say something to thank her for her trouble in trying, but I feel like an empty eggshell with sharp edges. Patience isn't my dominant strength, I'm afraid.

"I didn't expect it all to be resolved within a week," I say.

Whatever reassurance Leta is preparing to give is overshadowed by Emmett appearing through the train's steam cloud with his suitcase in hand. I hug Leta and give her my thanks, and Emmett and I board the train. Not three minutes later, it pulls out of the station, heading north. Once we reach speed, I take Hazel's typed article for the next issue from my bag, hoping to read it on the way, but I can't concentrate.

"You still think it's a coincidence?" Emmett asks out of the blue.

"What's a coincidence?"

"First, That letter from Pritchard. Then our cousins are dead?"

I keep telling myself that Pritchard wouldn't collapse a mine and kill valuable workers just to murder two of our cousins in retribution for some articles I published. Even if his deadline to print a retraction had passed—which it hasn't—I'm still not certain he would actually do it. Workers are assets, and they mean more to Pritchard if they're productive and afraid than they do if they're dead. But it would be easy for paranoia to overtake reason if I gave it enough air, so I refuse to.

"It's such an unsafe place to work, Em. The chances he killed twenty of his own workers just to annoy us is pretty slim."

He grunts. "What did Leta want?"

"Well, there's news." I tell him all about Baltimore and the lawyer, about the suffragists' progress.

"They've spoken to the wives and daughters of mayors, to women in towns between Stoke and North East, and so many of the stories are the same. Illness. Bribes. Death."

"Things we already know," he says.

"True, but it's all in one place now."

"Then why don't you seem excited about it? It might take a few decades for women to get the vote, but you'll have your court case against Pritchard a lot sooner than that."

"Maybe we will, but we need evidence to back up the claims, and I don't count chickens before they hatch."

I'm also preoccupied with this cease and desist, because we were going to tell Pritchard we would comply if he would let someone study the water, but we still don't know who that would be, and I need to send a response in four days. There's a very good chance we won't be seen at our aunt and uncle's house but there's still a risk in being there. The real terror will begin the moment Pritchard learns we're going to hold him accountable in court.

* * *

The rest of the ride takes eight long and dusty hours, and we pull into a Stoke that's much changed since the last time we were here. No young children play in the street. No women lean over fences, trading foods from their gardens and gossiping about the neighbors. The *click* and *clomp* of horses' hooves echo off the houses, and birds titter between the trees and shrubs, but all else is quiet. The silence seems to rise out of the ground like a fog, steaming up from the hard-packed street and wrapping around the buildings to suffocate the town.

My backside aches as we pull up in front of our aunt and uncle's home, but it's nothing like the sharp stab to the heart when I take my bag off the back of the carriage and face the house.

Aunt Edith and Uncle Harvey's is a two-story brick of a house with its short side facing the street. The last time I was here, I'd dropped off a set of plates. They were chipped and cracked, and no one would buy them, but they were perfectly good, and Auntie had said she would take them if no one else wanted them. Emmett and I moved to Maryland two days later.

Red paint peels from the wood siding, flecked with black coal dust. The awning above the door is gone now, finally having collapsed after years of hanging on by a thread. In some ways it's like time stood still, yet in others, it feels like a shrunken version of what lives in my memory.

I pay the driver the last of our fare, and as he unstraps our bags from the back of the carriage, the front door flies open and Sophie soars out, all skirt and arms. I find myself in a bear hug before he's even returned to his seat.

"I wish we were better prepared," she says into my shoulder. "I just got your letter yesterday."

"There's nothing to prepare for. We'll squeeze in. We're here to help you, not the other way around. I can't believe the letter got there so soon."

"How is everyone?" Emmett asks, his bag dangling from his left hand.

Sophie gives him half a hug. "About as good as can be expected, I suppose. Mother tries to keep her hands busy, so she starts sewing or cooking, then the misery sets in, and she takes to her bed. She's reading her Bible by the window now, but I don't think she sees the words. Father is quiet. Angry. Who could blame him? He had to go back into the mines the next day. They all did."

"No time to mourn?" Sarcasm drips from Emmett's voice. Of course Pritchard wouldn't give them a moment of ease.

"No," Sophie says. "He comes in from work and sits at the table until he's tired or drunk enough to go to bed. He just got in."

I could hardly blame him. "And how are you?"

"Busy keeping things together, thankfully," Sophie says. "Alice Walsh is sick. You remember her?"

I nod. "Pritchard's laundress."

Her nostrils flare with her sigh. "Pritchard didn't lift a finger to help her. Terminated her as soon as she was unable to work. He abandoned her to her son's care."

"That callous man." But I'd expect no less of him.

"Come," Sophie says. "Let's get you dusted off."

"I'd like some water to drink if I can visit your well," says Emmett.

She takes a step toward the house, and Emmett follows, but my feet won't budge. I need a moment before I face more death. Once I step into the aura of grief, the loss will be real. I know it's awfully childish of me, especially after wearing that same stained misery for so long, but I wish like hell I could climb back in that carriage, make that horse walk backwards the way we came, and erase the whole thing. All of it. To bring them back. To put the light back in Sophie's eyes and ease my aunt and uncle's pain.

Emmett looks back at me. "Charlie?"

How dare he rip these lives away with poison and bloodshed, destroying these families with such careless abandon and expecting them to continue on as if it didn't happen. If he truly cared about his profits, he would care a little more about the survival of his workers.

Suddenly, it dawns on me. "Pritchard didn't do this on purpose."

Sophie huffs. "Don't let my mother hear you say that. How can you, of all people, defend him? He knew that mine wasn't safe, and he sent those boys down there anyway."

She looks at me as if I've lost my mind, but she's mistaken. I'm clearer headed than I've ever been.

"No doubt it's his fault, and it wouldn't have happened if he weren't such a vile, selfish man, but I mean that he—"

"It's like you said." Emmett grabs my elbow. "It's just a coincidence."

He's right. It isn't revenge against the workers, and that's worse somehow. Pritchard is more heartless than ever and twice as reckless. When Father worked down in those mines, this was what they fought to avoid.

"Father always said Pritchard was intentionally negligent," I say.

This was the eventuality that became an inevitability, and now it's happened, and I don't know what to say or do.

Emmett nods in the direction of the house and duty pulls me in like quicksand.

The silence from outside seems thicker indoors. It's funereal, as if the family buried their words and sighs because they had no bodies to bury instead. There's no ending to this type of grief. Just imagining what those boys went through over and over, how dark it must have been. How much fear they must have felt in those last minutes as the roof fell in. And my family, robbed of the ritual to say goodbye, to gather and reflect on a life well-lived and witness that return to the earth, ushering in a new phase of living our lives without them. This grief is an unnatural one.

Aunt Edith sits by the window with the Bible open on her lap, tracing the lines with her thumbnail.

The smallest nephew scrambles to his feet from the rug by the fireplace where he'd been pulling apart a pinecone. He rushes at us, all knees and flopping feet, clad in a straight, calf-length tube of a shirt. He slams into my leg, pinning my skirt to me.

"Charry," he calls me, and I scoop him up. He weighs two sacks of potatoes more than he did a year ago. I'm surprised he remembers me, but children can be wise that way.

"Hello, George. You're very tall now. How did you do that?"

"Uncle Em." He wrinkles his freckled nose. "Tom and Dabid aren't coming back."

It's a matter-of-fact declaration from a child. He's not musing or trying to understand. It isn't a question, it's a statement.

"I know," Em says. "I'm very sorry."

"They're dead," he says, and my heart breaks all the more. A child this age shouldn't understand death.

He squirms, and I let him down to the floor. He's gone in an instant, plodding back to the rug and his pinecone.

"The others are in the mines." Aunt rises and walks to us on unsteady knees. She's always been rail-thin but she's almost twig-like now, and I'm afraid I'll break her as I offer her a hug.

"We came to work," I said. "To help out where we can. We can only stay a day."

"So far to come for one day," she says. But Emmett has to work, and I promised Weylan I wouldn't linger and draw suspicion. "Even so, there's nothing to be done. Dinner's on the stove. Everything is…"

Sophie fills in where my aunt trails off, giving me a look that says things are far from under control.

Aunt Edith isn't strong enough to stand much longer. She dips and she feels behind her for the chair, and Em guides her to it before she falls. She waves us on, and Em promises to bring her a drink.

We trail Sophie past Uncle Harvey, who sips his beer and tips his bottle in greeting at Em like they're two old friends who happened to collide at the tavern. He's soot-drenched, which hides his expression, and his eyes seem to glow through the grime. I expect Sophie to stop, for Uncle to say something, for a pause to say hello, but Sophie pulls us through into the kitchen. He's in no shape for talking, I presume.

The kitchen is immaculate. Not a single dirty dish sits in the sink. No speck of coal dust clings to the table. I know this scene, this deceiving setting that's born out of a misery that won't let you settle. A pot simmers on the stove, and Sophie plunges a spoon into it.

"Been refreshing this for two days now," she says.

"It smells delicious," I say.

"Pork stew," Em says, peering into the pot. He glances at the dying fire. "You need coal? I can get it."

"We're almost out of house coal. Saving it for nights if we need it. We've been using the wood out back."

"I'll go chop more and fill up your water pail at the pump." He takes the bucket and slips out the back door. There's a pointedness to his look when he passes, and I know he'll slip money into Sophie's hand to help them with the coal.

"Let me do this. Sit." I wrestle the spoon from my cousin and whisper. "I brought you some money. It's not much, but I wanted to help. Your parents won't take it, will they?"

When Sophie shakes her head, I vow to leave it with her to spend as she sees fit.

We reminisce while Emmett chops wood, until Auntie joins us in the kitchen for tea. When the boys finish their workday, it takes some time for them to calm down and clean themselves up to varying degrees. They settle outside on the bench to eat, to spare us the effort cleaning the kitchen again. Aunt and Uncle, Sophie, Em, and I sit at the table to eat together in a kind of foggy haze.

"I wish you'd come away with us. Join us in Maryland." I break off a piece of my bread and dunk it in the deliciously thick and starchy soup.

"Not a chance," Uncle Harvey says. "Got debts to pay, and they follow you no matter where you go. Besides, this is home."

"You saw what happened to Father." Emmett leans back in his seat, smoothing his shirt, saving it from spills. "It's a long, slow death."

"That don't happen to men who work underground," Uncle says. I look to Aunt Edith, because clearly it does, but her eyes are fixed on her bowl. "We owe Pritchard, and he'll come looking for his debts to be paid no matter how far away we run with them. We live here. There's pride in that work down there."

Pride in the work.

The coal boss has fed that line to these workers as long as I've been aware of my surroundings. He uses freedom and pride as the bait but debt is the hook, and it sinks deep into every man who nibbles at the line. There's a lot to be proud of here, doing the hard work that makes industry happen and keeps people warm and fed, but the boss uses the Coal and Iron Police to press down on them hard. If they try to rise up and ask for good enough—let alone better—they get beat back. Bad. A good number of them use pride like a shield, like a buffer between their spirit and the coal boss's weights. But I long for the day they can have their pride and their pay, their soul and their safety.

Father and friends tried to reclaim all that. I know how hard they tried, because I polished their words. And it hurts my heart a thousand times over to see Uncle fall into that abyss, not because he lets me down or doesn't live up to some imaginary standard, but because it means he's given up.

But Emmett hasn't. "You could have so much better," he says. I'm sure he regrets his words as soon as they fumble out of his mouth, because he purses his lip and chews on his jaw while he shreds a hunk of celery with his spoon.

"I know you children mean well," Uncle says with a clearing of his throat. "But don't come here and say this isn't good enough."

Aunt Edith looks up. "It would be good if it got cleaned up. Like it used to be. It's a good town with good folks."

"I know that," I say. "That's why I'm working so hard."

"At what?" Aunt Edith asks. "At your newspaper?"

"No. Well, yes, and I'm trying to find someone to investigate, so we can make laws that will force it to be better. Of course there's pride in mining. Everyone thinks so. The work should be safer. The town shouldn't be full of poison. They shouldn't be spreading it, bribing people to keep it quiet while people suffer and die. And I'm going to make him stop."

Uncle waves his spoon. "That sounds downright dreamy, but I strongly advise against that. Some girl isn't going to stop Pritchard—"

"Father, Charlie isn't just some girl." Sophie looks between us, her eyes resting on neither of us but for an instant. "You know what she heard in her father's house. And her newspaper has done great work."

"Fine and good. But they'll take it out on the workers here. You sit down there and make those demands, but you don't have to live with the consequences."

His words fall like a hammer on a ringing rock and the eerie feeling of him being right grates my bones and echoes through me. But it's more complicated than that, and I've been through this so many times, the matter is already settled in my mind. The only alternative to doing something is doing nothing, and Emmett and I wouldn't be here grieving the deaths of two little cousins if everything were fine. The consequences of doing nothing are the worst option, because those consequences come with a guilt that burns so bad it mars your soul forever.

We eat the rest of our dinner in silence. Em and I clean up afterwards, talking with Sophie and the boys about the town and the people we know in common. Their names wash over me from a distance that seems greater than the fourteen months we've been gone.

Cousin Elgar, who looks all of nine years old despite being thirteen, swears he'd come with us and do any job but mining but there's no chance his father would agree to that. Emmett tells him to keep learning and when he's of age, maybe he can escape this hell. I think my brother finally sees how lucky he was to get out when he did.

Later, as we get ready for bed, we brush our teeth back by the well pump. Then we all settle into the bedroom like sardines. I sleep on the floor next to Sophie's bed, and Em sleeps on top of three blankets at my feet.

"Everything seems worse than when we left," he says as he shuffles around to get comfortable. "I hope Pritchard doesn't find out we're here."

"That makes two of us," I say.

I roll away because I don't want to talk about it. Worries always seem to get bigger when you say them out loud, so I pretend to sleep as Elgar blows out the candle. Sleep doesn't find me, though. I can't stop thinking about how Uncle and Emmett might both be right. When you live in something this awful, it's possible you get used to the worsening of it. You distract yourself with sewing or chopping wood, scrubbing the counters and clawing the laundry across a washboard. You live with bad things all of the time and seeing them get incrementally worse isn't nearly as bad as the explosive consequences of kicking up a fuss. You only look up when a few people, like my father, start pushing back, and things start getting ugly. That's what makes it so easy for Pritchard to undermine benevolent societies and worker calls for reform. And maybe the chance of making people suffer in unforeseeable ways isn't worth it. What's the point if you can't guarantee you'll succeed? Had that kept Father up at night? I bet it had.

My mind spirals, thoughts bouncing off my fears. I can't stop thinking about what Leta said about needing to be patient, and how there's no time to waste on patience anymore. I wish I were home instead of here. Home, where I could be walking to the park with Weylan or sitting in the newspaper office, reading drafts of articles.

Unable to sleep with such a loud head and a full bladder, I tiptoe over my family, slink down the stairs and out into the night. The outhouse smells like hot death, and I curse Pritchard yet again for his lack of indoor plumbing.

As I step back out into the moonlight, I hear footsteps in the woods behind the privy. There are bears in these parts, big black ones that dig through your garden and pick through the scrap piles. There's a good chance he'll want nothing to do with me, but I take gentle steps backwards praying I don't disturb the ground, eyes wide as I can make them, trying to pick up any movement.

"Don't scream, Charlotte," a man's voice says from the darkness.

CHAPTER NINE

JULY 16, 1901

I take a deep breath to do what the man says and keep quiet, but he lunges at me, one hand over my mouth, and I realize it's Silas. I stomp on his foot, and he lets go of me, stifling a yelp. I fumble in my pocket for the netting needle, but it's not there. It's in Maryland.

"I'm not trying to hurt you, Charlotte," he whisper-yells. "We need to talk. Please, be quiet."

He knows my name. Who I am.

"I will not talk to you." I kick him hard in the shin.

He grasps his leg and hops on one foot. The yelp he holds in dissolves into a whimper. "It isn't what you think. I need your help."

"Do not sneak up on a woman as she exits an outhouse. What do you want, and how did you know I'm here?"

I have a thousand more questions, stacking up one after another, but I'm too angry to choose which one to hurl next.

"Did you think you'd get here without anyone knowing?" he hisses, testing his weight and rubbing his shin. It's satisfying to watch him wince. "It's my job to know everything that happens here."

"It's not your job to know about me. I don't live here, and I'm not your subject. Don't come one step closer, or I'll scream and aim higher when I kick next time."

Silas takes a step back with both hands up, his weight still on his other leg. I actually hurt him. I'm a little proud of myself.

"I've been sitting back there for at least two hours. Figured you'd have to come out sometime. Do you know how big the spiders are in these woods?"

I do know. He shudders in a way that seems too sincere to huff at.

"What do you want from me, Silas?" I ask.

His hands are up, and he's not holding a weapon. His pant legs are smooth, his pockets likely empty. His vest is tight. Unless he plans to choke me with a watch chain or has a knife in his boot, he's come unarmed.

He probes a tooth with his tongue, and studies me like I'm the one who can't be trusted here. "I want to work together."

A bark of laughter escapes me, and I clamp a hand over my mouth. "You can't possibly think I'm that stupid."

He doesn't miss a beat, hands out, palms down, like he's reasoning with a tiger. I'm glad if he thinks he is. "I saw you in Maryland when I dropped off the letter. I wasn't sure it was you at first, and I was as shocked as you probably were."

"Why didn't you talk to me then?" It would have been far more convenient than whatever this ambush happens to be.

"I didn't have a plan yet. I was only there because I had family business in the county, and I stopped to deliver the letter on the way.

I was curious about all the commotion, so I went to look while my horse was drinking, and there you were. You being here now saves me the trouble of a trip later. We need to work together."

With the last flush of terror cooling my skin, now I'm just amused. Silas wants to work together? The notion is absurd. I fold my arms. "Let's talk, then. I have plenty to say."

He inches back toward the trees. "I want you to stay and finish the work your father started."

"That…" Isn't going to happen. Doesn't make sense. And is clearly a trap. Knowing I need to put space between us, I take a step back on shaky knees.

"Isn't what you expected," Silas says. "I know."

My heart thunders in my ears. I could be surrounded. He could have Pritchard's henchmen all over these woods.

"What are you playing at?" I ask.

"I know your newspaper has been probing around at our bank, and asking questions. If you want answers, I can take you to them." His hands are out, palms facing up. He pushes at the air at the start of every sentence like he can press his point into me. "Half his correspondence, the proof about his debts, and information about all people he pays is in files in the administrative building. I can find work for you there. The other half is in another building, but I can find a way to move it."

"Then deliver it to me in Maryland. We'll read it." I fold my arms to keep my hands from shaking.

"That won't work. I can't transfer all our files to another state. They'll notice."

"You think I can just walk in there?" My voice shoots up an octave.

He jerks his head to the side. "Of course not. I can set you up as an employee."

"Why would you do this? If you want to kill me, you could do it now. You don't need to lure me here with the promise of evidence."

He laughs. It's more like a snicker. "Why would I kill you when we're on the same side?"

It's my turn to laugh. "We are not on the same side."

"More than you think. You lost parents. I lost a wife and daughter. I want Pritchard brought to his knees as much as you do."

He flinches when he mentions his family. It's nearly imperceptible, but his eyes cloud over for an instant, and his claim is, at least, believable.

"How did you know about me?" I ask.

"It's my job, like I said. I manage the people. I was your father's boss's boss. The fact that you wrote for your father became common knowledge here. People who never set eyes on you know your name. Pritchard believes you have more information than you let on. Frank Morris is considered a martyr, and if you'd stayed quiet in that Maryland town, he'd have left you alone, but you didn't. You have that newspaper behind you, and he's afraid of what you'll find out."

That much I know is true. It's why Pritchard sent that cease and desist letter.

"Stay." The world rolls on his breath, a delicious enticement. I can only imagine what I'd uncover if I had access to Pritchard's secrets. "Collect what you need. I can help."

"Why do I have to be here?" I ask. "If you want to give me facts, just give them to me."

"It's not that easy. I want to clean this place. Scrub it of Pritchard's dirty dealing. But if I hand you the proof, he'll find out it came from me, and I won't be able to take over when he's gone."

"Oh. Right." Of course. Silas wants to slip into the power vacuum.

"Pritchard will take me down first, and he could harm what's left of my family. But if you walk in there as an employee and walk out with what we both want, my hands stay clean."

The first wave of potential hits me and knocks me back a step, filling my chest with warmth.

"How would it work?" I ask. "Hypothetically."

He folds his arms and plants his feet. "Rhodri runs the company store. Lost a son in the blast. He's not handling it well. I'll give him time off to deal with the loss. You can fill in for him until I can make room for you in the administration building."

I shake my head before he even finishes. "No. Pritchard knows what I look like."

"He never goes inside the company store."

"I know that to be true." Pritchard doesn't recognize most of his workers, and he never mixes with them.

"He never goes into the administrative building either. He works from his study, in a back room in his house." He leans forward. "I can move you around undetected. House number four is empty, and I can have it ready for you. We'll make up a story. Say you're my niece, traveling to a teaching job out west. Staying for a while because your job was delayed. I do have a niece moving west, and it won't be unexpected."

The offer was tempting. I could play a role like that to get what I wanted. It wouldn't be that hard. I'd just have to keep my head down, stay quiet, and be friendly. It would require a massive leap of faith in Silas, but it would give me an even larger leap in the fight against Pritchard.

"I've never worked in a store before," I say. "What would I have to do? For how long? Days? Weeks? How will you protect me?"

"A few days at the store to start. The work is easy. If you fumble, no one will think twice about it. You'd be a teacher, not a shopgirl. Then a week or so in the offices. I have to arrange a need for your help there, so it isn't suspicious. You'll be isolated down that street in house four, and there's no need to talk to anyone because you're only here for a short time."

"Then what?" I ask. "I just walk into a train with the evidence?"

"Exactly. Then we both have what we want. You expose Pritchard, put his reign to an end, and I take over a profitable business and fix it."

"No more poisoning the water. I won't do this unless you promise. No more mine collapses."

He steps closer. "Ms. Morris, I didn't want to lose my wife and daughter any more than you wanted to lose your parents and your home."

The beat of silence between us is anything but quiet. Crickets call out at a rapid pace. My heart thunders in my ears. And so many thoughts rattle through my head, but I can't look away from his eyes. They go dark when he focuses on his resolve. His Adam's apple bobs with a sharp swallow, and his jaw clenches as he grinds his teeth. If he's lying, he's far better at it than any other man I know.

His eyes widen and he glances behind me. "Candlelight," he says. Someone's awake. I glance back and confirm his assumption. "I need your answer. Now."

"I'm supposed to leave in the morning."

"You'll regret it if you lose this chance."

"I need to talk this over with Emmett."

His chin puckers as he chews his thoughts, eyes fixed on the house. "If you decide to stay, say goodbye to your family as if you're going to the train, then meet me in the backyard of the house at number four. It's on the empty side of town, and the back is wild and overgrown. You can't miss it."

"I know where it is."

He melds into the shadows, into the trees and the woods. I walk backwards until my heel hits the doorstep, then I find the knob and let myself in.

"You couldn't sleep?" Sophie's voice rings out in the dark. She's taken the seat Auntie occupied all day. "You startled me. I didn't know you were out there."

"No. Sorry to frighten you."

She turns back to the window, gazing out to the street. The moon only picks up a few puddles from yesterday's rain. Everything else is so dark or coated in soot that the moon reflects nothing at all of this place.

"I can't sleep either," she says. "I keep thinking about how scary it must have been down in that mine. And what happened to them. Is that morbid? Maybe I'm losing my mind."

"No. I don't think that's morbid," I say, remembering the days after my own losses when my straying thoughts were equally morose and erratic. I sit across from her in Uncle's chair and look out at the street, though there's nothing to see.

"Tell me what you're up to." She kicks out her ankles and tugs her nightgown up to her knees. It's hot, and hair is sticking to my forehead.

I can't tell if she means tonight or in general, so I take the easy route. "Pritchard wrote the newspaper an angry letter."

"About that article you wrote, accusing him of bribing that man in Maryland?"

"You know about that? How?"

"It was in your newspaper. It found its way here, somehow." Sophie raises a shoulder. "The whole town knows. Father sounds dismal about fixing this place, but he's just afraid. Most people are happy about what you've done. Sometimes I run into one of your father's old friends at the store, or I hear people talking after church."

"What do they say? Tell me everything."

"I don't hear as much as you ever did, but I know they're still trying. No one's giving speeches in front of the company store anymore. Not since it got violent. It's more subtle." She picks up a fan from the table. It has a picture of birds and flowers on it, and it flaps as she fans herself. "There's a bit of impatience, though. Some people wanted a bigger movement. Fewer people know what's happening, it seems. But there's a rumbling."

"I suppose they had no choice but to be more quiet about their efforts."

"Some men got a pay raise, though. First time in many years. But only to buy their silence, it seems. The store is still as expensive as ever. I heard that a man who stole soap was beaten nearly to death by the Coal and Iron Police outside the recreation hall. They talked about shutting it down. No more dances or bowling. Happened in front of everyone."

"That's awful. Over soap?" This is the life and death situation Silas better be willing to talk about when we meet, because if I'm giving him ten minutes of my time, I'm using half of it.

Sophie reaches across and takes my hand. "You cannot stop.

Whatever you are doing, you must keep going. You're the only person outside of this town who understands what is happening. Your newspaper was everywhere here. It was on every table. It gave people hope."

"Not Uncle."

The house settles. The stairs pop. Sophie glances over her shoulder. "Don't listen to him."

"I wish I could stay longer, but I have to get home. Pritchard gave us an ultimatum, and I promised Weylan I wouldn't be gone long."

"I more than understand." She stands and wiggles her nightgown straight. "The privy calls, and you should get some sleep."

Tiptoeing back up the stairs and praying I wake no one, I step over Emmett and snuggle onto the pile of blankets.

My stomach is full of butterflies, but not the angry kind. The idea of staying here and getting under Pritchard's skin is too exciting to lay still with. I could find the proof myself instead of waiting for Leta to convince other women to drag it out of their men one week at a time for God knows how long.

Maybe it's the lingering rush from being startled or the whirlwind of curiosity, but I don't have an ominous feeling about working with Silas. He's no angel, but we want the same thing. He's a far better resource in this fight than the Pope would be. I feel a peace I haven't felt in a long time. I have to see what Emmett thinks about this, of course. Staring at the ceiling all night is going to take some patience. Not my strong suit. But who needs patience when solutions jump out of the woods?

My mind wanders until the wee early hours, and I'm up with the sun and a horde of cousins. I help with some sewing before breakfast, to lighten Aunt Edith's load. While my hands are busy,

Silas occupies so much of my mind that I'm clumsy. The needle finds my thumb more than the little pants they ought to sew. After we dine on griddle cakes and coffee, I help Sophie hang laundry while Emmett cleans the kitchen. I can't wait to get him alone, to tell him he's leaving without me, and I chew the conversation over in my mind. He'll hate it, no matter what I say.

"Charlie?" Sophie holds out one hand, the other pinching the corner of a bedsheet to the laundry line.

"Sorry." I pass her a pin, and she wiggles it over the fabric.

Emmett leans out the kitchen doorway, gripping the frame. Morning dew still shines on the window. "It's nearly eight. We need to get going."

"Can you get our bags?" I ask.

"They're already by the door," he says.

Sophie throws one of the boy's shirts over the line and wipes her hands on her hips. "Time went by too fast."

"It always does, unless you need it to."

We hug and make our promises along with our goodbyes. Sophie promises to visit one day, though I know how hard that would be. Then Emmett and I step out the front door. Halfway down the gentle hill, I glance back and return her wave. It's odd parting in such earnestness when I'm merely going across town. The deception makes warmth creep up my neck.

I pause at the bottom of the gentle hill, where I'll need to turn right to get to house number four.

"Em? I'm not going with you."

He leans his head back when he sighs, and he looks just like our mother when we'd exasperated her. "Yes, you are."

"No." I grab his elbow and pull him close so I can whisper. "I talked to Silas last night." I explain all the details as quickly as I can, because I don't want Emmett to miss his train. "I need you to tell Weylan where I am."

"What about the lawyer and all those women Leta talked to?" His shoulders are high, and his voice is higher but the edge in his voice sounds like father's. His bag dangles like a broken branch in a storm. "You'll miss the election. It's in two days."

"Ruthie can cover the election. This is more important. I can get what I need faster than waiting for Leta to convince people who don't want to speak out. This is actual proof. Better than anything we'd get from any other source."

His nostrils flare.

"Em, this could fix it. Finally."

"How can you trust him?" Disdain stains his question.

I shrug. "I can't. But I know he's not going to kill me because he knows you know everything. That's why you need to go home without me."

He lifts his arms and lowers them again and spins around. "You know… fine. I can't tell you no. You'll do what you want to do anyway. I have a job I have to get back to."

"Ask Bea to pack up some of my things. She'll know what I need. Send them on the next train out."

"H— But." He stammers. "How?"

"You'll be home at mid-day. She can send some clothes on the three o'clock train, and they'll be here at nine tonight. Send them addressed to Sophie, and I'll figure out how to get them. I'm staying at house number four." I nod down the hill to the vacant end of our cross-shaped patch town. "Don't tell anyone where I am except for Weylan, okay? Especially not Mannix."

CHAPTER TEN

JULY 16, 1901

"You are being monumentally stupid," Emmett says. He's probably right, considering how entangled bravery and stupidity can be, but I can't let on how uncertain and terrifying it is to stay here. Alone.

"I'll be fine," I say. "I can just get on a train and come home if I want. Silas won't hurt me. He's using me to get what he wants." This much I know is true.

"You can't stay here." Desperation lifts his voice.

I meet it with wide-eyed defiance. "You can't tell me what to do."

"The only people who say that are children and people who need to be told what to do."

"I thought you were in favor of this."

He glances over his shoulder at the steam rising above the trees from the waiting train. "I'm in favor of fighting Pritchard. Not you staying in Stoke to dig around in his paperwork."

Emmett digs his hand in his pocket and gives me the last of his money. He sputters demands at me. To come to my senses. Get on the damn train. He must realize that he's only talking to himself, because he trails off and storms down the hill, and I turn to the south. The street isn't long—a dozen houses, seven on one side, five on the other, none of them inhabited except the one on the corner. At this time of day, everyone's in the mine or tending to their work.

On this side of town, the houses are older, spread further apart than the newer ones that stretch to the west. Tall grasses and untended mountain laurels separate the vacant homes. There's no sign of life here but for the deer grazing when I reach the end of the road.

Number four could fall out of the sky and land on me, and I wouldn't feel more winded. Two stories high with a small front porch, the house is painted deep red and flecked with coal dust. It's the kind of housing offered to middle managers and married couples. There are times at our little apartment in Maryland when all four of us are home and stacked on top of each other that I yearn for this much room all to myself. So many times I wished to be back here, close to the home I'd lost. But Stoke seems so desperately lonely now, and this house feels so isolating. It isn't a bad house, though. At first glance, it's clearly older than most houses in Stoke, but in better condition than many. I had no reason to think Silas would give me any comforts, but at least there's a chance the windows will work. With luck, it will have a well that isn't dry and a stove that functions.

The grass is flattened where Silas must have walked around the back. Hot breeze rolls down the gravel street, picking up dust and blowing into my eyes. I rub and shield them as I follow his steps.

The back garden is surrounded by a wood fence that's too low and weak to deter anything. In the far corner, the leaning bones of a deserted outhouse cast shade on a knot of plants. Silas hadn't undersold the wild tangles that lean and stretch into the rocky paths. I move over and around them to reach the back door, and they release their tangy, earthy scent when my bag brushes against them. The door is ajar, and I nudge my way in. Silas is seated at a table across the kitchen. He stands and brushes his hands down his vest.

A ribbon of sunlight slashes across the kitchen floor but it isn't enough to light the room. A faded but comfortable rug blankets the space, rimmed by bare wood. Dust and bits of dried grass collect in the corners, but I don't see any mouse droppings. A small relief. The six slat-back chairs surrounding the table seem overkill for just me, but the table is covered with a pretty green cloth that almost matches the walls. A folding table sits in the corner with a lantern, wash bucket, and pail. I'd forgotten what one of these kitchens sounds like, the hollow doors of the wood cabinets clattering as I look inside. There are enough dishes to cook and eat with. There are a few canned goods that should get me through my first few meals, and the stove is ancient but clean. It's ice cold to the touch, though. It will take forever to crank up.

"This is the dumbest thing I've ever done," I say to myself.

"I doubt it," Silas says.

"Does the stove work?" I ask. "Is there wood? Coal?"

He nods. "I had the gas turned on for you. An older couple lived here until February. He died. She moved away. Let's get to the point." He strikes a match and lights a lantern, the kitchen filling with the sulfur plume. In the thin light, it's obvious it will take a lot of time and effort to clean it up and make it feel livable.

"You'll be working in the company store for a few days," he says. "Rhodri and his wife are burying their son and visiting family. In a few days, I can get you into the administration building, but until then, you just need to play the part of my niece. You're on your way west to a teaching position and for some reason you've stopped here."

"What if people question me?" I ask. "We look nothing alike."

"What family does? They may think you're young, but they'll also think I have every reason to trust you. Just don't get too close to anyone, answer any questions, linger in conversations too long. I don't tell those people about my personal life, but we don't want to be found out because small talk made anyone suspicious."

"That's fair."

He kicks out a chair and motions for me to sit. A ledger is open on the table between us, a big, thick book with ink-covered pages.

"This is the debt book."

I trace a column of numbers with my finger. Scrips. Imaginary money, earned by working in the mines that can only be spent at the company store, and there's nowhere else to shop, so they charge a lot more for things than they should. Three times as much as Mitchell's market back home. Basic necessities are unaffordable here, but the company is generous, so they extend credit, and when you're so deep in debt you can't get out of it, they let you pay it off by sending your kids into the mines to work it off for you.

Debt book, indeed. They don't even try to hide it.

Silas explains how the bookkeeping works, how to record debits when people buy things and credits if they make a payment on their account.

"The people in this town will try to hoodwink you. Do not extend more credit than prescribed in the books. Even to your family. They need to pay more down or have more kids."

I lean back. "Maybe you should try to create safe working conditions so you don't kill the ones they already have."

Silas glares at me. "That isn't funny."

"I didn't mean it to be."

I meet his stare, though it isn't a battle worth waging until I have enough ammunition. He straightens the book, flipping it open to a middle page.

"Every family has a credit threshold." He jabs at the yellowed paper. "It's next to the account number on the top of the page. Don't let them exceed it. Scrips go in a cash box. I pick it up at the end of every day. Be at the store at seven. I trust you know where it is."

"Of course."

He rounds the table and stops in the doorway that frames the living room. "What name will you go by?"

I hadn't thought about it. I don't know where Harriet comes from, but the name rolls off my tongue.

"Harriet, it is," he says. "I promise you won't be in this store for long. I just have to pull a few ropes and create a reason for you to handle the company records. If you need anything, take it from the store and leave a list in the back of the ledger."

"How will I find you, if I need you?"

"You won't. I'll find you."

Silas leaves me alone with the house and its creaks, with the groans of the roof in the wind.

I have all day to come to terms with this town and this house, to strip away the skin and cut at the sinew of this place, to break its bones and rip a hole in its chest, plunge my hands in and squeeze its heart until it stops beating and bludgeoning my people. And I'm suddenly so numb that *numb* is too vibrant a word to describe it.

I start at the kitchen and work my way outward, pausing at mid-day to eat a can of oysters Silas left in the cupboard. An anxious current runs through me, and I use it as fuel to scrub the floors and wipe the baseboards. By dinner, I've shoved the spiders into the yard and rid the windows of grime.

Late evening sun paints the walls a vibrant pink, and I run my damp rag over them, taking away the thin layer of coal dust that's collected there. Soon, I'll have to find a way to collect my things from Sophie's house. It won't be long before the train comes in, and a man collects all the deliveries on his wagon and hauls them through town. Sophie can be trusted, more than just about anyone else I know, but I can do without a repeat of the conversation I had with Emmett.

* * *

The sun goes down as I'm on my hands and knees, wiping down the wall beneath the window, and the unmistakable sound of footsteps on the gravel lane sends me into a panic. One set of footsteps. I duck down, crouching below the window with my back against the wall, hugging my knees. I curse myself for having the gas lamps on. Now, the house looks occupied. But I forgot it doesn't matter. I'm allowed to be here. I'm Silas's sister, Harriet, and I'm here because my lodging out west is delayed. Helping out where I can. That's all. There's no reason to hide.

It could be Sophie, after all. Perhaps Bea and Emmett sent a note with the crate telling her I'm in house number four.

I stand and inspect the wet, dirty knees of my skirt, disappointed that I'll have to launder this one. I hope Bea sent enough of my clothes, or I'll use half my time washing two skirts and two blouses.

Tap tap. Tap tap.

Feet shuffle on the porch. The hollow scrape of a case or a trunk. I inch to the window, soundless, and peel back the edge of the curtain, expecting to see Sophie, but there's a man on the porch with a case in his hand, and I know the round of his shoulder.

I fling open the door.

"Weylan!" The word chokes off at the end. I expected Sophie or an intruder or a miner to come to see why the light is on. Or Pritchard having found me out already. This is somehow worse. The train brought more than just my clothes. By the look on his face, it brought a fight.

"Are you angry?" I ask.

"That's one way to say it." He heaves his suitcase over the threshold, steps in, takes off his hat, and puts it on the mantle I cleaned an hour ago.

"I'm not going back with you," I say.

The suitcase is more like a trunk. He must notice me eyeing it because he wheels it at me. "Our clothes, Charlie. I got your things from Bea. Do you think I'm letting you stay here alone?"

He doesn't look furious. He looks tired. Of course, he's been on a train for five hours and had to pack and make excuses for where he'd be.

"Did you tell your father where you are? What did you say to the girls?"

I guide him to the kitchen and he follows. The case bumps the doorway and he leaves it in front of the empty ice box before falling into a chair where he sits and frowns, like he smells something awful, squinting in the thin light. He's never lived under coal dust and ash. Everything in his world has been washed clean by a river. Here, the dirt is in the air. You can feel it sometimes. Like now.

"My father thinks I'm on a business trip. The girls know I'm here with you."

I stomp my foot. "I told Emmett—"

"He didn't tell them; I did. I could hardly lie to them. And yes, I'm furious. This is irrational and ridiculous, and they could be drawing you in with the most obvious ploy. Why would they ask a nineteen-year-old woman to come here and do this?"

I open my mouth to explain everything, but he waves both his hands in the air while rolling his eyes, and rather than prove myself to be absurd, I clamp it shut again. It does sound like an obvious ploy when he puts it that way, and if I were a man in my thirties in charge of an entire workforce, I wouldn't trust a nineteen-year-old woman to do anything. But I didn't choose to be in this position any more than Silas did. There's no use in my saying so, though, because Weylan has already given up arguing.

He rolls tension from his neck. "I don't blame you for staying. I know it all just lined up this way, and there's a good chance this Silas man really is telling you the truth. I would have done the same thing in order to finally put this thing to rest, but it's still stupid, and I'm too tired to argue about it."

He pulls a piece of paper from his pocket and tosses it on the table as he falls into a chair. I sit across from him.

"You're staying?" I ask as I unfold it. "What's this?"

"I'm here as long as you are. That's our response to the cease and desist. I mailed it from town before I left so we don't have to worry about it anymore."

It looks the same as the draft I wrote days ago except for a few small changes that I can't focus on because Weylan is here, and there's only one bed upstairs. What are we supposed to tell people? He can't hide in this house the whole time he's here.

"I'm going by Harriet. You'll need another name."

He raises a shoulder. "I'll go by Parker."

His middle name.

"This is going to be rather awkward." I grimace at the thought of sharing a chamber pot with Weylan. "A chamber pot. An outhouse."

"I've used a chamber pot. We can figure this out."

"You look tired." I rise and take the first step toward the stairs, offering to give him a tour, but Weylan takes the lantern off the table and wanders into the living room. I join him there instead.

Seeing it through his eyes, the living room looks completely different to me. It takes up half of the first floor, with raw wood to walk on and paper peeling off the walls. The ghost of a rug squares the center of the floor. Two sitting chairs face a fireplace with a table between them, and wood-framed drawings of Bible scenes speckle the walls with a crucifix nailed by the kitchen entry.

"Catholic?" Weylan holds the lantern up to a charcoal sketch of a saint that hangs next to the fireplace.

"Yes. A lot of people here are. Italian. Irish. Don't mention it in public, though. There's an unhealthy divide between the Catholics and Protestants here, and you don't want to accidentally step into a fight unprepared."

"Good to know."

"Silas said they were older, the people who lived here." I run my thumb across the top of the picture frame. All my fingers are black, the fine lines of my fingerprints filled in with coal.

I bite my bottom lip, snagged by a memory of sitting by a window with Sophie as a heavy rain pushed rivers of black down the street, and little silty streams trickled down the window panes.

Everything in this house sets me on edge. Now that I'm not scrubbing it, now that I stand back and look at it, I'm reminded of all the things my parents were lucky to avoid by living just outside the town's limit. Traipsing in black dust, breathing it in, and wiping it from cabinets twice a day. The ghosts of my childhood are all around, playing with Sophie by the stove, sprawling out on the floor with our dolls. My aunt flailing at my uncle's clothes with a carpet beater every night before throwing them in a tub of water out in the yard. I'd always pictured living in Stoke, but couldn't ever imagine living a life here. Perhaps because my parents had taken great pains to raise us so we'd never have to hitch ourselves to the company anchor. I never realized the difference until now.

"No sense in delaying further, I suppose." Weylan grabs his bag. "I'll go up. You think they gave you new beds?"

"There's only one bed."

The color drains from his face, his eyebrows arching from incredulous and furrowing to confused. He stammers a few broken syllables about making do or getting by, and I can't bear his discomfort on top of my own. As increasingly glad as I am that Weylan is here, this is business, not pleasure. We have a mission, and we've both accepted plenty of inconvenient emotions already, so there's nothing left but to get through it.

A flight of stairs curves up the wall, leading to the second floor, and he joins me there, both of us looking up. Heat creeps down the staircase to meet us, hot and damp for being shut up so long and smelling mildly of onions. It feels ominous, like the house is warning us not to go up there, and I can't agree with it more, but there's no sense lingering in the kitchen until we're too tired to stand, and this suitcase won't unpack itself.

I sigh out as much air as I can and replace it with a last deep gasp before plunging into the heat. His large suitcase banging the stairs as we go.

The stairs open to a little hall with a washroom and a cabinet. There isn't much in it. No medicines or bandages. There are a few tatty washrags left by the last residents, though.

An open door leads to the back bedroom where a window overlooks the yard and the small, tumultuous garden. The side window offers a view of the street, empty but for a little tuxedo cat racing between buildings. From here, I can see the sunken roofs, the caved porches. A plain brown wardrobe sits along one wall, covered in dust, with its doors propped open by a pair of slat-back chairs. The bed sits along the other wall with a clean set of sheets resting on top. I can't even look at it. Its very presence unnerves me.

There's a second bedroom, though, just through the doorway that connects the rooms. It's papered prettily enough with yellow stripes and small pink roses, but it has no furnishings. If it did, we could have separate rooms, and I could sleep at night without thinking about where my hands are and where his hands are or if I've made embarrassing noises he'll never let me forget, but the room is empty.

An odd sort of hopelessness cracks open inside me, splitting all my worries into little islands.

"I'll sleep on the floor in the other room." Weylan sags to lean in the doorway, looking like a giant wedged into a dollhouse. He shrinks back a step, tilting his head back and blinking at the ceiling as if prayer might get him through this.

"Don't be silly." I sound oddly matter-of-fact for someone who's afraid to look at a bed. "You can't sleep on a floor all this time. We'll take turns. We can handle this."

"*You* can handle this," he says. "You've always been better at the distance."

"If I'd known it was a competition, I might have tried even harder." It's a terrible joke. Weylan doesn't even smile. I leave the lantern on the dresser, and pull back the curtain to stare down at little red tomatoes ripening on the vines. I could tidy the patches and let in some sun. I could even jar a few and bring them back to North East for Ruthie and Hazel and Bea. On second thought, they could be poisoned. Better not to touch them. I wonder if the well water is safe.

"You shouldn't have come." The words tumble from my tongue. "You're the smart one. You should have known better."

I don't hear him rise or cross the room, but his hand on my shoulder is all comfort. His chest warms against my back. The way his heat bleeds through his clothes and through my clothes and sears my skin is familiar the way pleasures can be, like the anticipation of ice cream's cool sweetness on my tongue.

He plants a kiss behind my ear, stilling my breath. "I wouldn't let you do this alone, Charlie."

Dear Lord, if I let my feelings get ahead of me, I would be more comfortable in this situation than any unmarried woman ought to be. The thought of it is terrifying, and the whole earth seems to tilt. Nothing makes sense. Like standing on a boat and being blinded by the light of an oncoming train. The emotions are all mixed up.

His hand grows hot on my shoulder, but it feels distant, like someone else is feeling it and telling me about it, and his breath is warm on my ear. Yet it sends chills down every inch of me. He isn't trying to do it, but he does. Some rational part of my brain, the kind that warns you of being burned or drowning, tells me to pull away, but some other animal part of me wants his company, his comfort, and touch even more.

"We should talk." He wraps his arms around my shoulders and whispers into my ear. "Before we unpack. This is uncomfortable, and it'll only get worse if we don't."

The crack widens and the islands drift, swirling around in the deep waters. It's an odd mix of a future I never pictured unfolding in a place I never wanted to be. And it crashes onto Weylan's shore.

"Let's not." I wriggle free and turn to face him, brushing dust from his jacket so my hands will have something to do. "This is just a test. Right? We can figure this out, one step at a time. It's funny, if you think about it."

"Right." Weylan twists and tugs at his jacket pocket, and he pulls out a little leather box. "It's not what you think. Or maybe it is. This was my mother's."

My heart stops beating, then it starts again at a thunderous pace. Surely Weylan understands that I can't do this.

He starts to open the box, then doesn't. He holds it out instead, and I realize, now, that he's wearing one too. It looks right on his hand, as if it belongs, and all of the worries I haven't allowed myself to entertain yet start fluttering around like drunken moths in my stomach. We'll be alone together. In a house. In situations I'm not at all prepared to think about. And he's proposing? Again?

"I don't want to make a big deal of it," he says. "It's just that we can't draw attention to ourselves, and we need a story."

"So, it's—" I can't steady my voice enough to say it, but he seems to understand, because he nods and gives me the polite kind of smile he gives to the woman behind the register at the general store.

"For show," he says. "So we don't look improper."

Before I lose my grip on the box and drop the ring, I take it out and slip it on my finger, and I feign interest in the moonlit garden because silence is awkward. Weylan is so tense he might get a back injury if he breathes too hard.

He stands next to me, takes my hand, and twirls his mother's ring around my finger. "It is a bit farcical. If this happened to Emmett, I'd think it was hilarious."

"I'd join you in that."

"I have money," he says. "Plenty enough to buy what we need. We can buy extra blankets tomorrow."

"In the meantime..." I wag a finger at him. "Stay on your side."

"I swear to it."

"And no touching in the house. Jesus and the saints are down there watching, after all," I say. "Along with the rest of the town, unfortunately. Living in their walls is making me uneasy."

"Are you changing your appearance? In case you're recognized?" he asks.

"I wasn't planning to. I don't think enough people ever saw me in person to make it necessary."

He frowns and little lines appear on his forehead. "I think it would be a mistake not to."

With the lift of a shoulder, I disagree. Wigs are itchy and hair dye stinks.

"Speaking of fears." He lets my hand go. "The railroad strike is getting closer. I read about it yesterday, and on my way here, I overheard some of the workers talking about a strike."

"If it happens, there will be food and medicine shortages here.

Why are they striking?"

"Not sure." He lifts a shoulder. "Could be unrelated to Stoke."

"No, it's entirely about Stoke, I'm certain. Pritchard is their biggest customer, and he's wanted to buy that railroad for many years. He undercuts them. He finds ways to pay less than the contract. Maybe the railroad is finally demanding he pay up?"

"Perhaps. I'm very curious. Maybe I can find out more while I'm here."

I place a hand over his heart. "Lay low and don't draw attention to us, please. It would only make this more difficult."

He places his hand over mine. "I promise." He's more cautious than I am. I don't doubt him. "I brought plenty of money to get us out of here, in case we need to leave quickly, but we need to make a plan in case we run into trouble getting a train."

I cock my head to the side. "I wanted to come back home so badly, yet I turned down Pritchard's offer to have it back. Now that I'm here against my wishes, I might be stuck here forever."

He throws open the lid to the suitcase and extracts a crisp white shirt. "Be careful what you wish for, I suppose."

CHAPTER ELEVEN

JULY 17, 1901

Coal is everywhere in Stoke. Chunks fall off the rail cars, and little lumps shine on the street after the rain. Picking up a piece of it is illegal. Pritchard sees it as theft, and he'll send his private police force after any man who walks along the rail line picking up chunks to heat his house. It's all his, after all, because he's the one who owns the land and puts forth the effort to extract it from the ground and process it. He charges an arm and a leg for it at the company store, too. So I take an odd bit of pleasure in picking up a chunk the size of a quarter as I pass two men going the other way. They aren't looking at me, though. Their heads are down, and they're racing to work. I pocket the coal, because I can.

The morning is thick and damp. My hem is dingy by the time I reach the company store. It's dark inside but the door is unlocked, and Silas leans against the counter like he owns the place. The fact that he almost does — that he will if we succeed — isn't lost on me. He's my employer now, at least in name, and I hate it so much I want to burrow a tunnel all the way back to Maryland with my bare hands, but he lays the ledger on the counter between us and hands me a key.

"Good news. Rhodri's miserable. He'll be mourning for days." No remorse curls his words. There's no glee, either. He's matter-of-fact, and that's worse, somehow. We both know the clawing ache of powerlessness against death. It's made us both cold in our own ways, but at least I still have my empathy. "It will be a day or two before I can open a window of opportunity to get you into the administration building. Until then, the store opens at seven, closes at six. If you need a break, put a sign on the door."

I slip the key in my pocket and turn to inspect the bins of flours, grains, and rice. The shelves are lined with boxes and canned foods, jars of fruit and vegetables, dried meats and cheeses, and clothes in bags labeled by size. I find a dented can of peaches, rusty around the rim.

"I know it's inconvenient for you to start here," he says. "But your visit created a unique opportunity. I need a few days to make your move to the office convincing."

The store is exactly the way I remember it, yet smaller somehow. Like the world got bigger when I left this place, and now all those experiences and all the shiny new places I've seen are pressing on Stoke so hard that all this coal should turn into diamonds. Instead, it's just crushed dreams. This is nothing like Leta and Mitchell's store.

"Some of this stuff doesn't look so good." Smells co-mingle in the back corner, like the sulfur stench of a broken egg mixed with sour, spoiled milk. The lights are off and I can't see under the shelf, but I can see well enough to know that the whole place could use a coat of paint and a good cleaning. People deserve better than this.

"I suppose Rhodri does the best he can. People track mud and dirt in here all day."

I wipe the lid of the rusted tin and sit it back on the shelf. "It would at least give the illusion you treat people with dignity."

"Dignity isn't in my job description. I manage the workforce."

What is that awful smell? I wrinkle my nose and step back, trying to see under the shelf.

"That ledger is a great responsibility. I don't give it to you lightly. Do not erase or change anyone's debts. Do you understand?"

The temptation would be great. I'm tempted to point out that the risk could be avoided if they paid people a living wage and charged a reasonable amount for the goods, but it's probably better I keep my mouth shut and stay on Silas's good side.

"Weylan is here, by the way." My face is nearly to the floor, my voice muffled by the shelf. There is something back there. I'll get it when Silas leaves. "He's going by the name Parker."

"That newspaper man of yours?" he asks with disdain. "You were supposed to keep this to yourself."

The fury in the clench of his jaw is so tightly composed that it's impressive.

"You said Emmett could stay, but he didn't. Weylan is here instead. We'll say we're married. On our way west, just like you planned."

He purses his lips and folds his arms. "No one here will believe I'd let him stay for free. He'll have to work."

Grit sticks to my palms, and I brush them off as I stand. There has to be a broom behind the counter somewhere. "He's not going in the mine."

"No. He couldn't handle it." Half his face scrunches with disgust and confusion, and I ignore the barb. "I can find him work at the tavern. They always need help, and I owe them a favor."

"Weylan working for them is hardly the same as you paying a debt." There are rolls of fabric, stacks of paper, crates of cans and God knows what else. I find the broom behind it all tucked in the corner.

"It is to me," he says. "I'll visit Weylan and work out the details. You just follow the rules and close the shop at six."

"How will I find you?"

The door clicks to a close behind him. All for the better. The uneven energy around him puts me on edge. I find the offending eggshell and the sticky egg it unleashed when it shattered, sweep it all into a pile, and usher the refuse into the trash. Then I position the stool behind the counter and I slump over the ledger, looking up names I know and coming to terms with the debt they live under that can never be repaid, watching their debt grow along with the prices while their income stays the same. It feels wrong to know this about people, like it's the kind of thing they'd want to keep private, so I slam the ledger shut before succumbing to the urge to look up my aunt and uncle, and I study the contours of my little lump of coal.

Father used to carve little animals from coal. I had a whole circus once. The lion I found on the day Em and I moved to Maryland still sits on the windowsill next to my bed. I never learned by watching him, so I don't know where to start, but I find a knife on a shelf behind the counter, probably for opening bags and cutting twine, and I carve a duck from coal. It's a crude imitation of a decoy, lacking eyes or feathers. It's only the size of my thumbprint, but it makes me smile.

The rest of the morning is quiet, with everyone in the mines. With nothing else to distract me, I walk along the shelves and line up all the items so I don't fall asleep. The entire night had been restless. Weylan and I sat at the kitchen table playing cards until we couldn't avoid sleep anymore, then we climbed into bed next to each other. I curled up inches from him where my stomach ache and nausea went from small, hard knots to giant churning coils, and I've never had so many bedfellows. We laughed about how awkward it was and faced opposite poles, but his presence alone and the effort it took not to seek out his warmth kept me awake.

The bell rings out above the door, and I leap to my feet, cracking my head into the bottom of a shelf and rattling jars of beets. I clamp my hand to my head and wince, biting back curses as miners and women trickle in. A cluster of three, then a few more. They fan out among the shelves as I slip behind the counter, rubbing at the stinging wound.

A woman plops a bar of soap on the counter. "Rhodri's visiting family?"

"Shame about his son," says her friend. "Outright tragedy."

"It's criminal, if you ask me." The words fall out of me before I can stop them. If I don't squeeze my lips shut, I'll never pass for being a relation of Silas's. Fortunately, the men are louder about it than I am.

The woman hands over a few round goldish coins with Pritchard Coal etched in an arc, and a triangle punched in the center. I haven't seen one of these in more than a year. It sits warm in my hand, currency from a past life.

"Put the extra toward my debt," the woman says.

"I don't know the accounts quite yet. Do you know your

number?"

"One thirty." The woman throws her elbow on the counter and leans, chatting with the friend behind her. None of them pay me any mind at all.

That night I carry home some canned peas and deviled ham, and I find the front door unlocked and Weylan jubilant at having coaxed the stove into working. He presents a dinner of chicken he slaughtered himself along with some vegetables he scavenged from the untamed garden. It's much grander than anything I'd planned.

"Silas was here," he says between bites. "He's a wily one. Everything he says makes sense, yet it seems like it shouldn't."

"At least he's somewhat honest about being a scoundrel."

"I went to the bar with him. I'll be cleaning tables and pouring beer. Not bad work. The place is dark and sticky, and it's loud. Smells like beer and moonshine."

"Is it awful?" I wrinkle my nose. "It sounds awful."

"Not at all, actually. The work is easy, and the people seem friendly. The couple who owns the place is hilarious. The woman has a great sense of humor." He leans across the table like he has a secret to share. "And I met a man named Carlin."

"Carlin," I repeat. "That name's familiar."

"He was burned terribly. So bad that I couldn't tell if his wounds were fresh. He must be sick of people wondering because he told me the whole story before I even said hello. Seems it happened a while ago in an accident that shouldn't have happened, if you know what I mean."

"My God." Chicken falls off my fork, and I collect it again. "Someone did that to him on purpose?"

"It sounded that way. Carlin really hates Pritchard. By the sound of it, far more than you do."

It seems I've lost my appetite. I put down my fork. "I can't blame him, if Pritchard did that to him on purpose."

"Right. He's a talker. He probably would have said more, but his friend showed up and they huddled at the end of the bar. They stopped talking whenever someone got close, but I managed to catch a few words because the more they drank, the more they trusted me. They seemed to accept me as a bumbling guy just passing through and working for his keep."

"Everybody talks around you, Weylan. You have a way—"

Weylan leans forward again, but this time it isn't a secret he's sharing. It's a point he wants me to see. And I do.

"They talk around me, Charlie." He smiles. "They're planning something. I can feel it."

* * *

Two days later, the store pops and creaks in the mid-day sun, and I've nearly unpacked a crate of canned peaches when a man in a floppy hat enters the store and goes to the back. He studies a can of tomatoes. His head is down as if he's inspecting the label, but it's taking him an awful long time, and his face is shielded. I feel his eyes on me, sizing me up like I'm cattle at an auction, but there's a gentleness to his energy that scatters my worries.

He approaches the counter with a limp, his head lowered, and when he looks up and takes off his hat, wadding it in his hands, my heart clenches at the sight of his burns and wounds. His nose is nearly gone, pale skin spider-webbing his face. His forehead bears no eyebrows, and his eyes have no lashes. I swallow hard, imagining what he's gone through, and I look away, not wanting to stare. The pain he must have endured is unimaginable. This has to be Carlin.

"Can I help you? I noticed you looking at the canned tomatoes."

His voice is thin, raspy, carried on forced air. "Are you running this store now?"

"It's temporary. Rhodri will be back." I settle on the stool in front of the ledger.

"If you're smart, you'll stay to yourself. Don't get too close to anyone. Why're you here, anyway?" His skin is tight at his temples, but even without the lilt at the corner of his eyes, I can see a glint of suspicion. He may already know the answer.

Even if he is one of Father's old friends, he can still be dangerous. He could let it slip to the wrong person. And to be recognized within my first hour working at the store? I'll never hear the end of it from Emmett if this all goes wrong.

I clear my throat and run my hand over the ledger's leather cover. "I don't know what you mean. I have family here."

"Of course you do. You're Frank Morris's girl."

I begin to object, my face contorting with the lie, and I stammer a few syllables, but the man drops his chin and looks at me with the questioning eyes of a teacher who knows a lie when he sees one and isn't to be trifled with.

I open my mouth to protest, to say he's wrong, that I'm Silas' niece. His assumption must be corrected. I need my anonymity here to remain intact, so I shake my head and start to say I have no idea what he's talking about, but he speaks before I do.

"Don't deny. I spent enough time at your kitchen table, eating your ma's cooking, to know a Morris when I see one."

I touch the end of my plaited hair, wondering if I should have dyed it or dressed differently as Weylan had urged me to, but it doesn't matter now. The man recognizes me, as only a very small handful of men could. And if he knew my father half as well as he seems to, he could be someone I should trust.

He blinks and brushes dampness from his pink eyes, not tears but damage from the burns, and he leans forward, placing his fists on the counter like he's about to make a point. Like he's clutching invisible silverware, eager for dinner to arrive. The gesture throws me backwards by years, to men around our kitchen table, whispering over lantern light. He'd looked different then, not scarred by fire, but his eyes were the same. His hands. I remember him now.

"Carlin."

"You look just like your mother, lucky for you. Frank was a revolting bastard," he says with a laugh. "I met that man of yours. Parker? He never worked in a tavern before, and he certainly don't belong around here. Followed him back to that house you're staying in and caught a sight of you. That your newspaper man?"

"It is," I say. "Please don't tell anyone I'm here."

"I won't. Secret's safe with me."

He glances at the door. Someone across the street is sweeping the night from their porch, the gentle *swish, swish* of the broom the only sound. "We're still working here. Organizing. Trying to fix things. It got quiet for a while and went underground, but we're up and running."

I take in a sharp breath, throwing my elbow on the counter, the stool wobbling on its one short leg. "Tell me."

"We read that article about Pritchard paying people off to keep 'em quiet. And your newspaper from that place downriver. The one you printed with all those stories last year. You could do that here too."

Parts of Stoke that have been frozen in time thaw and reanimate. The sound of father stoking the fire downstairs while I was supposed to be asleep. Men's footsteps as they hit the creaking board just inside the door. The low rumble of their voices as they plotted and planned. Mother's rocking chair creaked when it rocked back, rhythmic wood on wood. It would stop sometimes, and she would hush them, saying Emmett and I were asleep upstairs, but I heard more than she ever knew.

My eyes sting, and I blink back warm tears. I miss them, my parents. I never wanted to grow up this fast or this hard. It's like a giant wall went up in the middle of my life one night, and every part of it that I left here in Stoke is still here but I can't reach it.

I don't have the heart to ask about our house or who lives there now, but I want to know everything else all at once.

The man's eyes dart around the room, along the shelves behind me, out the window to the street. He seems possessed by a permanent sense of fear and paranoia. He's probably right. Someone could walk in at any moment. Our time is too short for many questions.

"What happened to you?" I can barely get the words out. "When?"

"About a year before your father died. He kept a lot from you. The story's too long for a visit this short."

My father knew about this. Suddenly all the times I wondered about their scheming came rushing back to me. Maybe Father had been involved in something bigger than I knew. And if he was, I might be stumbling around the edges of it too.

"What do people think of Silas? Can I trust him?"

He chews his lip. "Trust him to put himself first."

I glance at the door. "Visit us tonight. Maybe we can help. And I need to know what my father was up to. Can you come without anyone seeing you?"

"I'll be there at eight."

CHAPTER TWELVE

JULY 19, 1901

Weylan took down the painting of Jesus while I was at the store. He said it didn't feel right being in the house with it, and I agree, but the absence of it makes me think of other things I'd tidy up before company comes, except Carlin will be here any minute, and there isn't time for all that. Carlin won't judge us anyway. It's not like I need to impress him. It just feels strange cooking a meal for company, even if it is just reheated Irish Coddle pork sausage soup that smells like earthy potatoes, onions, and thyme from the garden.

Weylan wipes the table down. Ever since he got home, it's been too quiet. He washed up and changed his clothes while I started dinner reheating, and I washed up while he cleaned the house, and the lack of conversation distraction made a void into which my mind wandered. Now I'm nervous and anxious, and I don't know why.

"I should have made a list of things I want to know." The kitchen fills with steam when I take the lid off the pot.

"You still can. He's not here yet."

"The problem is that I don't even know what I need to ask. I want to know everything he knows about the railroad, and what Pritchard did to him, and what my father was involved in, but I'm afraid to know the answers."

A knock at the door relieves me of the impending uncoiling of my nerves. Since Carlin walked out of the store earlier in the day, I've been standing on this cliff's edge as it crumbles beneath my feet. I've always known my father was involved in something more than giving speeches inside the social club building. There had to be more to their effort than that, considering how much Pritchard hated him. But I refused to believe that he'd done anything violent. That wasn't the kind of man my father had been.

Weylan purses his lips and nods a little before he answers the door. He knows better than anyone—except for Emmett—how much it would destroy me to hear that my father and his friends pushed Pritchard too far and earned the reputation he tried to pin on them.

Carlin strides into the kitchen in clean boots with his tan shirt tucked into his brown pants. There's no trace of his day in the mines left on him.

"It's nice of you to have me," he says, pressing his hat to his head as he dips his chin.

Weylan slaps him on the shoulder and shows him to a chair. "We've got beer in the ice box. Can I offer you some?"

Carlin accepts, and we muddle through the awkwardness of finding seats and filling plates, and promising Carlin that the house is safe, that no one knows we're here. Yes, he'd been able to find us, but only because he followed Weylan, and no one else has reason to suspect we're anything other than Silas's relations.

"How many people here know as much as you do?" I ask.

"A few. Not many. More did, but they died," Carlin says with his head down, eyes pinned on the sausage he saws at with a dull knife.

Weylan peppers him with questions about illnesses and how people suffered, asking if their bodies failed the same way his mother's did. The pain he felt watching her fall apart lines his face in ways he rarely shows.

Carlin wags his fork at me. "Pritchard could have helped your pa, you know."

"I always thought so. The doctor even said as much. He had the medicine. It was just meant for more important people."

"Nobody was more important than your father around here." Carlin sets his fork down. "He was doing more than just talking."

Our eyes meet, and I try to read his but he gives nothing away. It isn't until Weylan asks if I really want to know that I have the words to say I do, no matter how hard it is to hear.

"Go ahead." My potato takes the brunt of my anxiousness as it smashes under my fork. I don't want my memories to be stained or unraveled, but I'd rather hear the truth while I can. "Tell me everything."

"He was trying to form a group of men from every part of Pritchard's operations. Collect information and take him down from the inside. I don't know how far he got, but it all fell apart after he died. Pritchard found out later. Your father weren't violent like they made him out to be, but if the poison hadn't taken him, Pritchard would have."

The false accusation is a knife in the back of my father's reputation, and it pierces me. "He wasn't an aggressive man." He carved circus animals out of pilfered coal and brought his favorite chickens into the house when it snowed. The sausages and potatoes swim behind a veil of tears, and I blink them back while I shove a bite in my mouth.

"Ms. Morris?" Carlin waits until I meet his gaze before he continues. "It might be true that the doctor could have eased your father's pain. But Pritchard ordered him not to. And even if he had some medicine that would have fixed him, Pritchard would have made him a martyr for our cause in the end."

It's like Pritchard killed my father twice. My mouth is too dry to swallow. Potato turns to paste. A sip of beer washes it down but not without effort. "Pritchard ordered it? That Father couldn't be treated?"

"Doctor's wife heard Pritchard say it."

Weylan clears his throat. "I'm not sure what's worse, being killed by the poison, being kept alive to become a martyr, or being denied care to prevent it."

"All for money." If I don't start asking questions, I'll lose my thin grasp on my self-control, and I'll scream at Silas and start making mistakes. Changing the topic is the only way to get through it. "Railroad. What do you know about it?"

"You mean that Pritchard wants it?" Carlin asks.

Weylan leans back in his chair, his plate empty, glass in his hand. "We heard rumors about a strike."

"Here's what we know. It's not the whole of it, I'm sure. Pritchard was raking in the money. Last year was his biggest yet. None of that money made it to the workers. Prices went up at the store. He stopped repairing broken equipment. Last April, he stopped paying some vendors and started strong-arming others." Carlin looks at me, then past me. To the east. "Know that land they cleared?"

"Other side of where we lived? Yeah."

"He stopped paying the logger he hired to do it. Pritchard was that man's biggest customer. Cut him right off at the knees. Nearly put him out of business come June. Then he said he'd cut off his coal supply if he stopped clearing that land."

"What does he want the land cleared for?" Weylan asked.

"More mines," I say.

Carlin winks. I was right. "Their arrangement turned into a barter. Coal for wood. But Pritchard wouldn't deliver on time. That lumber got bills and workers to pay. Pritchard finally had him pinched so hard he cried for mercy. Bought the business out from under him, but for far less than he would have paid if he'd just paid the bill. Now Pritchard's running a lumber company. He's doing it to other vendors too."

Weylan snorts. "He probably says it's good business sense."

"It's like you know him." Carlin leans back too. His eyes are red-rimmed and always damp. He dabs at one with his sleeve. "He has a plan. Started making sense back in the spring. He's picking and choosing who he puts out of business, and it seems they're all big customers of the railroad."

I gasp. "He keeps eating little fish until he's big enough to go for the shark."

Carlin waves a hand. "Exactly. If he can't starve them out, he destroys them from the inside."

"How so?" Weylan asks.

"There was some iron company he wanted his hands on." Carlin picks at his tooth with a fingernail. "So he hired a detective to cause strife among the workers. Tried to pit them against the boss and unionize."

"That's a kiss of death," I say. "Just the thought of a union nearly starts a war around here."

Carlin leans in now, eyes wide. "People say he did the same with us. Back when your father was still here. Brought in some detective to push your father along, hoping he'd go too far so Pritchard could make an example of him."

But then he got sick and died first. The weight of what might have been falls on me. Pushing me down. Burying me. My shaky breath doesn't calm my nerves, but looking at the ceiling keeps the tears from making a fool of me. That was how Pritchard would turn him into a martyr. I won't cry in front of Carlin. If I do, he might not tell me everything I need to know.

Weylan asks Carlin if he wants a second helping. Carlin refuses but we both accept another beer.

I finally get my breath under control and my words dislodged from my throat. "You think they're doing the same with the railroad? Forcing workers to strike?"

Weylan fills our glasses. "A strike would lower the value of the railroad and reduce the amount he has to pay for it."

Carlin nods his thanks. "If the railroad isn't running, vendors can't deliver. It all falls apart up here before winter. The workers will freeze and starve. They'll blame the wrong people. They always do."

"And he's hoarding money," I say. "He has enough on hand to buy it. This is awful. You really think he hired someone to lie about what my father was doing and make him out to be a criminal?"

Is that what happened to Carlin? I'm too embarrassed by my own curiosity to ask.

He puts a hand on the table. "We don't know for sure. It's possible. The thing is, there's no use pushing a rolling stone. People are so furious that if he did do it once, he won't have to do it again. This place is on the edge of detonating without his help."

Silence rises around us. Between us. A fog that curls and twists and obscures my vision. I gaze out the window, but it's dark, and there's nothing to see. I hate the way this place feels on my skin. Grit and stink that has nothing to do with coal or mines. It's noble work, like Uncle said. It's a beautiful coal patch town with good hearted people. But every bit of it has been exploited. The land, the trees. The men, the children. The heart of this place has been pulverized.

"I just want to get what I came for and get out of here," I say.

Weylan scrapes his fork across his plate, dredging the last of his potato through gravy. "How well do you know Silas?"

Carlin lifts a shoulder. "Not well. No one does. He's Pritchard's man. Uppity sort who don't make nice with the likes of us. Why you asking?"

It's Weylan's turn to lift a shoulder, and I know the look that flashes in his eyes before he lowers them to his glass, swirling the golden liquid around and around. He's making less of his question than he really feels.

"Oran asked me about him at the tavern. What the rest of his family's like. Seemed generally curious, and I kept it simple. Said I didn't know his side of the family well."

Carlin snorts. "You two are believable as relatives, though. Got that uptight collar look. Like you starch your breeches."

"Probably just small talk," Weylan says with a smile. He's no stranger to being told he looks academic and proper, especially among his friends at home. It's not his fault he looks the way he does. "I don't mind if he thinks I'm uptight. I enjoy being underestimated."

CHAPTER THIRTEEN

JULY 22, 1901

Kicking this little hunk of coal down the street and watching it skitter off into the overgrown weeds feels pretty good for a change. I thought I'd have to meander between houses and hide, but there isn't anyone out here. The road just kind of ends where they stopped maintaining it. It's just like I pictured from the way Oran talked about it last night. End of the street. Past the old barn with the roof caved in. The trees close in a little, and the ground is pretty green with some rocks big enough to turn your ankle hidden by ferns and untended vegetation. And then there's a break on the right, wide enough to be an old road.

If I'm guessing right, this is the path Oran and Carlin were talking about. Man, those two would give up national secrets in front of me, like I'm not even there.

I used to hate the way people underestimated me. Nothing came easy when I was young. I lacked my father's confident demeanor, inheriting my mother's soft eyes instead. People underestimated her too. She was quiet like a field mouse. She could scurry around, go undetected. She seemed to know everything about everyone without exchanging a word with them. She wasn't sinister about it, and she was far too compassionate to be good at gossip, which is probably how she came to know so much. People would tell her anything. She was one of those rare people who looked as sweet and kind as she was, with no artifice about her at all. Unlike my mother, I'm not afraid to use what I hear. Hell, maybe she would have, too, if the poison from this place had killed me instead of her.

It took me a long time to grow into my height, and all I wanted was to be smaller. Not to stand out so much. Around that time, Pine grew into his own slimy skin and started to become a terror, picking fights everywhere he went, and now that I look back on it, that was the thing that finally made me stand up straight. Being tall finally had a benefit.

And then Charlie came along. I wouldn't be in this town if it wasn't for her. I wouldn't live if it weren't for her. I'd still be my own shadow. A dried husk of the person I used to be. I thought I'd just be here for her, try to convince her not to do anything rash or too impulsive, because God knows I can't convince her to go home. Never did I dream I'd be working at a tavern while Oran and Carlin give away this place's secrets.

Something about me makes me seem trustworthy, and don't get me wrong, I am. But every once in a while, a piece of highly useful information lands in front of me like a grenade most men would run from. Maybe I'm dumb. Maybe I'm not risk-averse. But I pick it up and I carry it around until it's time to toss it back.

This particular grenade sits in a clearing in the woods. It has four good walls that are covered in moss, a sturdy door, and a brand-new roof. And that's interesting because a building this dirty way back here in the woods with weeds growing up in the ruts where carriage wheels used to go seems like it wouldn't need a new roof. It just seems like such a waste of materials when half the houses in town could use one. It sure could use new windows though. And today won't be the first time I've climbed in one.

Of course, the last time I did it, I knew the folks who owned the place. And we more than compensated the general store for the ink we took. But this time, I've come for what's rightfully mine. And I don't even like Pritchard. Certainly not enough to care about breaking into his un-abandoned building. This should be easy.

When Oran slithered across the bar all glassy-eyed and bragged about his friendship with Carlin, I wondered why he was telling me so much. Then he started asking questions about Silas, and I figured he wasn't sure he could trust me. Maybe he wanted me to tell him some information about the inner workings of Stoke that I don't have. He seemed overly interested in who I am and why I'm here, but I had nothing to say so he kept talking, and that's how I came to learn about this building back here in the woods where Pritchard buries his bones. Like a dog.

I lean against an old tree and take it in. This building is covered in green moss, so the new roof really stands out. It seems like this should be a bigger moment, staring down the shack where Pritchard keeps his toys. Just on the other side of those easily breakable windows is proof that he killed my mother. I won't know for sure until I have it in my hands, of course. The only thing you get from counting chickens before they're hatched is disappointment, but I can feel it. The way you can feel snow coming. The way a watched pot really does boil.

Patience is a virtue, and I'm all out of righteous morality. Silas might plan to move all of this so Charlie can dig through it, but I don't trust him half as much as she does. He might let her get her hands on just enough to hang Pritchard, but I want it all. There's a reason he didn't tell her about this place. It might be as simple as hiding the theft of the papers from Pritchard or legitimizing the way Charlie ends up with them, but I don't think so. There's a slime on that man that he can't scrub off.

I'm going in there after those documents, and once I have them—if I have them—Charlie and I can start to live. Make a life. Together.

A gentle breeze rustles the trees, and I root myself in the shade, my ears trained for sounds of life in the woods. So far, it's just me and a few chipmunks. A squirrel is pretty angry about my intrusion on his acorn hunt, shooting across the forest floor and darting up a tree. Clicking and barking. I take a lazy, meandering route on solid ground, avoiding the crunch of old leaves until I can see the door.

If what I overheard in the tavern is correct, this is a pretty strange place to store documents, especially when there's an administrative building where Silas is taking Charlie to work. If those men were right and Pritchard's lackeys have been hiding his personal papers back here, then Charlie might not find what she's looking for, and I have to eliminate that chance. Either Silas doesn't know the documents are here or he does. If he knows they're here, he could be hiding them for a reason. They might implicate him. They might be the big hook we need to catch a criminal. If Silas doesn't know it's here, Charlie may not find that evidence. I need to at least look.

Disturbing as few leaves as I can, I get closer to the door. I can see where a cart has been through here, and it wasn't that long ago. The leaves are flattened where the wheels ran over them, and the edges of the wheel depression are still crisp. The prints from hooves and the boots of a man with feet about my size trample the area around the door. It seems someone walked in and out an awful lot, and then left.

There's a large padlock on the door, and there's no use trying, but I tug on it anyway. The windows are old, and I have no trouble prying one open. Inch by inch. Wiggling it back and forth until I can fit my hand in. I pause and listen for any sound in the woods. With the window open wide, a hop, and some effort, I pull myself over the sill and right myself in a dusty room where motes flitter in the ribbons of light. It smells like an old tabernacle. Unpainted wood that swells and contracts in heat and cold. The sweat from yesterday's sun has gone damp with the morning air.

My footsteps scuff and echo in the shell of a building. There are no rooms, just four walls, three windows on the two longest. A door on one end. It really does remind me of a tabernacle. The floorboards are wide and dusty. Hunks of dried mud that fell off shoes are scattered about. Spider webs blow in the rafters, shimmied by the air coming in the open window, and there are clean patches on the floor show. Evidence of where the last visitor walked. And there are drag marks where boxes or crates were shoved toward the door. Whatever was taken from this place, it was heavy. And my best guess is that all that paperwork is either destroyed or part of Charlie's task.

In the far corner, sunlight lands at the feet of some crates. I know better than to disturb anything labeled "blasting powder," but I peek just enough to confirm the contents. I might lack a degree of risk aversion, but I'm not completely stupid. I've nearly been burned by Pritchard's blasting powder once before, and I have no intention of being tangled up with it again, so I leave the way I came, lower myself to the ground, wiggle the window shut again, and make my way back through the woods.

I'd been hoping to learn something worth telling Charlie about, but there's absolutely nothing of value there. Nothing worth interrupting her day at the store with anyway, so I head straight to the tavern a little early.

Part of me hoped to find a trove of information that I could bring Charlie back to, that we could skim together in fifteen minutes, fit into my bag, and take home on the train, but that was an ideal scenario. I wasn't naive enough to pin any hopes on that idea. I'm a little disappointed that the information Oran let slip was either incorrect or untimely. But when I emerge from the woods on the abandoned end of town and walk up the street past house number four as if I was just leaving for work, I'm fairly confident I got away with my snooping. At least until I walk in the door and find Carlin and Oran at the bar already, hunched over plates of eggs and toast.

I have clean glasses to put away before the day gets busy. I can sense the energy of a rough afternoon. I only took a few days to pick up the rhythm of this place. Morning always brings in a scattering of miners who aren't working underground that day, looking for a bite to eat and a place to gather before they head out to wherever they're going. Mostly it's people passing through on horseback until the early afternoon. Then the place swells with people who are all in a hurry, with miles to cover, eager for a drink or two and something to eat. The older men from town come and fill the tables in the back until the early evening when they stumble home. Then there are the folks who come to catch a train. They aim to be early enough not to miss it, but it's always late these days, so they pass the time at the bar, impatient customers with a lot of time to kill.

"Don't you two work?" I slip behind the bar and fasten the apron around my neck.

"Not today," Carlin says.

"What got your boots so muddy?" Oran asks.

My boots and my pant hems too, apparently. I should have changed my clothes.

"Get lost looking for an outhouse?" Carlin snorts at his own joke.

I take a dirty rag from the pail beneath the bar and wipe at my pant hem. The boots will stomp clean, but a muddy hem is a bad look. Most people won't think anything of it, but I do. And Oran does too, apparently. His fork is still in his hand, but it's resting on his plate, tines down. I can't tell if he suspects anything, but the longer we make eye contact, the more I wonder what I'd say if he asks me why I was eavesdropping on his conversations and nosing around. I didn't hear anyone back in the woods, but that doesn't mean no one's watching the place. I could have been seen.

"I got lost," I say. "Looking for a shortcut to get here. Found some old building tucked back there with a new roof. Heck of a thing."

That should cover my tracks well enough. He doesn't know I overheard their conversation last night.

The door swings open and a man with sandy hair and dark eyes leans in and calls for Carlin, who shimmies off his chair and grumbles about being interrupted when he's eating. This leaves me alone with Oran. I crouch down and focus on my hem while Oran sips his coffee.

"Putting a new roof on an old empty building really pissed off a lot of people," he says.

"It's not empty now." I keep my voice light. Innocent. Let the words rise up.

"What do you mean? You go in?"

"Nah." I shake my head. "Just peeked in the window. Couple of crates with labels that say it's blasting powder. Looked like a storage building to me."

"That explains the roof then. Powder's useless when it gets wet."

Carlin shuffles back in, complaining about incompetent people. Man owes him money, apparently, and isn't paying him back fast enough. I use the interruption to take the dirty rags back to the laundry pile and fill the bucket to mop the floor. It gives me a chance to take a deep breath and let them sink their teeth into a new topic. Plus, walking away makes it look like my morning discovery was as uninteresting as it turned out to be. Oran seems to have bought my story, and if anyone ever says they saw me back there and I have to repeat it, I have Oran to back me up. No harm done.

By the time I get home that night and Charlie shows up a short time later, I've mostly forgotten about that building in the woods with its new roof and the blasting powder.

"You cleaned your shoes." She joins me in the front sitting room where I've settled with a book, and she looks down at my feet. My shoes are so shiny they're reflective.

"Went for a walk," I say. "Didn't want to trample mud through the house."

She smiles down at me and asks what I'm reading, and the way the sun hits her hair and picks up little flecks of red reminds me of the first time I saw her at the train station in town. Sometimes I look at her, and I can't believe how lucky I am that she speaks to me at all. I thought it would be torture, being in this house with her, playing at being a married couple when she turned me down in reality. For now, at least. My head knows that once this is over we can start our real life together. But my heart wants it now.

She steps closer. Leans down to see the cover of the book. I hold it away.

"What's the secret?" she asks. She lunges for the book. Her laugh tingles my skin.

"No secret." I grab her waist and twist her around, pulling her onto my lap. "I just want you closer."

.

CHAPTER FOURTEEN

JULY 23, 1901

"I don't need coffee." I yank on my left boot, and I keep fumbling the lace. I hate running late. Weylan insisted on sleeping on the floor last night, which only made sleep more evasive. For me. He snored just fine. How he can work on his feet all day after sleeping on a pine plank floor is beyond me.

He leans against the oven in his dressing gown, a ribbon of morning sun shining in his eyes through the open back door and making him squint. He turns suddenly, snags two hard boiled eggs, and puts them in my hands.

"Breakfast," he says.

I shove them into my pockets and spin to face the little mirror by the back door. It's cracked in the corner, but I can see my hair well enough. A quick re-braiding, and I'll be ready to go.

"I'm tired of going to that store and not making any headway," I say, fighting with the end of my plait. "I will find Silas today come hell or high water. We need to make something happen."

Weylan sits at the table and throws his elbow on it with his ankle propped on his knee. His hair is a mess, and he rakes a hand through it, tilting his head like he always does when he's considering options, but we truly don't have many. I'm at Silas's mercy.

"Not that I want to linger here any longer than we need to," he says. His slow, lazy grin turns the tide within me, coiling in my stomach. "But I'm starting to enjoy it."

It isn't until I lean down and give him a peck on the head that I realize how easy things have been between us. Maybe it's being here, away from town, settling into a different place. Part of it could be that we're working together to make do and get by. Unlike all the distance from before, there's so little air between us lately. There's no room for the pressure I felt back in Maryland to marry him or set him free.

"We've found our own rhythm here, and I don't want that to end either," I say

He catches my little finger with his. "Get to work. The faster we find what we came for, the sooner we can—" He raises an eyebrow, teasing me, and I swat him and step out the door.

It's a beautiful morning. A little damp. Birds take off from a tree just ahead, showering the ground beneath with dew. As much as I want to get out of this place, and as urgent my need is to find Silas and ask when I can start making progress, my mind is consumed with the ghosts of Weylan's touch. Though I regret that Weylan slept on the floor, I don't regret one bit that he broke our pact not to make contact. It's good that we stopped when we did, but his touch set a match to everything I'd tried to suppress.

My mind goes back to him all day. The sounds he makes. The tangle of his hand in my hair.

The day is a slow parade of women buying thread and fabric, picking up jars of fruit and sacks of flour. No one pays me much attention, except to welcome me to town. A few tell me I look like my uncle Silas, which is mildly nauseating, and they offer their sympathies for Rhodri's loss. By the time the sun begins its slide down the sky, the evening rush of men come in, stomping sooty boots on the newly washed floor. A few of them wink at me, like single men are wont to do, as they buy their cigarettes and cans of dip.

One of them approaches my counter just before close, his lower lip jutting out, packed with brown sticky goo. He turns his head to the side, looking down, ready to hawk a gob of sick-smelling vile.

I shake a finger at him as if he's a child. "Do not spit that on this floor."

"You're Harriet, aren't you?" He flings open the door, spits out onto the porch and looks both ways before stepping back in and flipping the lock. "Silas's niece?"

It isn't a question. Not the way he asks it, abrupt but not confrontational. The air bristles around us, setting me on edge. I swallow hard and try not to look nervous, running my tongue over my eye tooth because I know I look angry when I do it, and I will not let him intimidate me.

He grabs an empty tin cup from a shelf, inspects the price tag, and spits in it. "I'm Oran. Oran Walsh. Carlin's friend. I know you know who he is."

"Yes. You work in the mines together." I draw the words out slowly.

"Where you from?" he asks.

I tell the same story all over again. Some small town in New Jersey

I've never been to. On my way west to teach, but the job is delayed. My husband and I are working to earn our keep.

His eyes are on me the whole time, steady, no emotion. "Don't know Silas well, do you?"

I raise my shoulders and my eyebrows. "Honestly? No. It was kind of my uncle to extend the invitation when he heard of the hitch in our plans. Seems it was mutually beneficial."

That elicits the response of raised chin. "Mutually beneficial, huh? You don't seem the teaching type."

"And what is the teaching type?" I stop myself before I touch the end of my braid. Teachers can be young. Blonde. Women. "You don't seem like a miner to me."

He puts the tin cup back on the shelf but picks it back up again when I glare. "I suppose you'll be staying longer on account of that rail strike."

I open my mouth to say *if it happens*, but I remember I'm not supposed to know about that, so I squeak out, "The rail what?"

"Oh-ho." He leans forward so far that I think he might tumble. "You don't know?"

"Clearly not." Panic rises in me, creeping hot up my collar. The questions that surge through my mind are very much real. I need all the answers at once, but I'm afraid the questions would say too much. "What kind of strike? No more trains at all?"

"No one has said a word to you about it?" He looks incredulous, as if I ought to know this. As if I'm negligent by not knowing. I suspect working at the company store, even temporarily, might seem to afford me some inside information into where the goods come from.

"I've not been here long, and I don't plan on staying. Why would they?"

Another lift of the shoulder. This man is so ingenuine. "Thought you'd want to see your way out of here if you could."

Unfortunately, all I see is an impending disaster. "So tell me, then."

He steps up to the counter with the tin cup in his hands. "Their union is protesting low pay and bad working conditions. Workers keep getting hurt laying rail lines."

Sounds familiar. "I know nothing about it. I need to leave eventually. Soon. And there won't be trains? I can't stay here."

I need to make a plan. A carriage or a horse. I haven't ridden a horse in years. Surely I'll remember how, if I can find one, but where? Oran's expression shifts to sympathy, and it seems genuine enough, the way it ripples his brow.

"Look," he says. "If you need to get out, you could always walk west. Down the valley. Or there are horses."

That perks me up. I don't have any memory of that. "Where are there horses?"

He points a chin to the north. "Stables up the road toward Freeland. They're Pritchard's, but if you need to get out…"

Alright. There's an option. Just knowing calms me a bit. It was stupid of me not to have an escape plan.

"With luck, Prichard will buy the railroad soon." He steps back from the counter, leaving the cup and its sludge in front of me. The stink coming off it makes me nauseous, and I push it aside. "Then this'll all be over soon, and you can get back to whatever life you have."

I huff. "It might make the trains run, but it won't solve anyone's problems. Not here." I rest my hand on the ledger. "Everyone in this town will suffer. They won't have access to food. Prices will go up. Everything here already costs twenty percent more than it does anywhere else, and everyone's credit is stretched as far as it will go."

Oran reels back, lifting his chin. "That won't last long. This place is a powder keg. Most souls here are ready to stand up to Pritchard in some way. There are plans."

He gazes out the window, his expression unchanged, and I get the feeling he's waiting for me to react or respond in some way, but what would Harriet say? What would Silas's niece possibly think? The more time stretches out between us, the thicker the air gets.

"There's gonna be a war." He opens the door and spits his wad of chew out into the street, wiping his chin with his sleeve.

"Will they hurt Silas?" It's the only thing I can think to ask to get him to say more.

He chews the inside of his cheek, either searching for words or considering whether he should let them out. Why would he even tell me this if he believes I have ties to Silas and, by extension, Pritchard? A chill trickles down my spine as cold as ice water. Finally, he rolls tension from his neck, and it cracks. I'm a little jealous.

He looks me in the eye. "You shouldn't be here. You need to leave before something bad happens."

"What could possibly happen?" I beg him with my eyes to say. "Please. What are people planning? What war?"

Volleying his gaze between me and the window and the empty street beyond, Oran clearly doesn't want to say, and I can't blame him, because Silas's niece would surely give away their secret.

"Why would you tell me any of this?" I say. "Unless you think I can stop it. Tell me what they're planning."

He inflates with an inhale. "You seem young. Whole life ahead of you. Carlin's a novice. He's gone off his rocker. Wants revenge for what was done to him. Seems he's taken a liking to your husband. I don't know all what was done to Carlin or how much longer people can talk sense into him, but he's got a mind for trouble."

"Oh." The realization comes on so suddenly, I have to sit. The stool wobbles. "You think… you think Parker is helping Carlin? He's not. We extended neighborly kindness to him. But after everything Pritchard's done to him, you can't blame Carlin for being angry. For years, men have tried to work peacefully with Pritchard, and he's only gone to great lengths to vilify them for it. All they wanted was good pay and—"

I clamp my mouth shut.

"You seem to know a lot for someone who barely knows her distant uncle."

"I read. A lot. I have a ledger in front of me. And I met Carlin. He doesn't exactly withhold information."

Oran seems to come to terms with what I've said, and just a new question starts to spill from him, carriage wheels crunch and creak up the street and stop at the door. The cart groans to a halt.

When Oran smiles, he seems like a different man than the one who spit chew in the tin cup I'll have to clean. He reminds me of the Cheshire Cat with a smile that appears out of nowhere, gleaming brighter than it should.

"Ms. Harriet, I'm not the persuasive type. If I were, I'd have me a lovely wife and a cottage by the ocean. Wouldn't be living on a cot in some family's back room. I might not look or sound convincing, but I'm not lying when I tell you it'd be a mistake for you to linger around here. You'd wish you'd got out sooner."

He pauses with his hand on the door latch, and when he smiles his teeth are so white, such a contrast against his sooty skin, that he looks like some kind of devil. He tips his hat to the delivery driver whose arms are full of crates.

I step on the porch and greet him and his helper, and I watch Oran shuffle up the street, his pant legs baggy and dropping below his heels.

"Filling in for Rhodri?" the delivery driver asks. "I can bring these inside for you, miss."

I thank him and roll a milk can over to prop the door as the help heaves bags over his shoulders.

"There's a railroad strike on now."

"I just heard. I hope it doesn't put you out much," I say.

"Not yet, but this could be your last shipment for a while, so make it last."

The two men make quick work of bringing in all the crates and barrels, and as they climb back into the carriage to leave, I stare at it all with my hands on my hips wondering what to do with it next. The labels are all marked for the store except for two small crates for the town doctor. I haven't seen that man since he came to our house and said he couldn't do a thing to help my parents. *Wouldn't* is a far more appropriate word.

I peel the top off the crate. Morphine. The same medicine he said was reserved for people better than my parents. That monster. The sight of it makes me want to throw them against the wall.

As much as I'd love to deliver it myself and tell that doctor how I feel about him, he'll recognize me if he comes here to collect these crates. I could hide them in the back, but that won't stop him from coming for them. I can't tell Silas because I don't know how to find him. I spin and circle, then fling the door open and call out just as the carriage pulls away.

"Driver!"

The cart rattles and groans as he brings it to a halt.

I need to think fast. "The medicines. They're for the doctor."

"Doc'll be by to get them." He tips his hat.

"But there's an emergency in town today, and he's waiting for these medicines." It's a lie, of course, but I hope he believes it. I let my desperation show, grinding my teeth as I unclench my hands. "The doctor's been waiting for days. Would you mind dropping these off at his office on your way by? It will only take a moment. Just leave them on the porch?"

I squeeze myself small, pulling in my shoulders. I hope it makes me look like I hate to ask. He considers me for a moment, then nods.

"I'll bring them right out." I rush back inside and lift a crate. The glass bottles rattle together. On second thought, I sit it down and dig my hands in, pulling out a bottle of the morphine and a few other bottles and little boxes of things that I can't identify but might be useful. I hide them on a shelf behind bars of soap, and then I rush the crates outside and heave them onto the back of the carriage, out of breath.

"I'm much obliged," I say. "I hope it's not too much trouble to drop it off. At this hour, he's out making rounds, what with emergencies and all, so it should be fine to leave it on his porch."

"That does speed things up, miss."

The driver tightens his grip on the reins, flicks his wrist, and the horses carry them away.

CHAPTER FIFTEEN

JULY 24, 1901

Between Oran and the delivery, I'm late walking home. Mulling over everything Oran said makes my feet heavy. Since meeting Carlin and Oran, the whole town feels even more sinister and hollow than before. You don't grow up near a coal town without knowing the earth's veins pulse beneath your feet. That, deep underground, men toil and haul, stripping the mountain of its blood and mingling it with their own for the sake of warming the world when it's cold. Everyone knows they're underpaid and the work isn't safe. But knowing men have been tortured as Carlin was, and knowing they're bent on revenge, makes Stoke look and feel less like the home I once knew. It had been cozy once. Home, despite its flaws. Now it looks a lot like hell.

Father had known plenty of dangerous men. I'd listened through cracks in the floor too often to harbor any illusion that Stoke's bravest weren't also its most vicious, but revenge on any scale is just as bad as Pritchard's way of thinking. Not when justice is at our fingertips. And being even loosely associated with anything Carlin's planning might just get us burned.

The night has a chill to it, and I pull my shawl around my shoulders as I approach the house, breaking into a near run. I can't wait to tell Weylan about all of this. The glass vials of morphine and whatever else I stole rattle together in my pocket. The lantern is lit in the kitchen, and my belly rumbles for a bite of dinner. I'm just a few doors away when a man strolls from the shadows of a vacant house's shrubs, sending my heart racing. I nearly fall when I stop.

Then his form becomes familiar. "Silas." I should have known.

He nods back toward the empty porch of an abandoned house. "We need to stay out of sight."

I sigh and search the shadows. At this hour the women are inside cleaning, and the men are dog tired. Every door across town is shut. But there aren't even occupied houses down here, and there's no one to see us talking let alone hear me scream. I follow Silas around the building, holding my hand against my pocket so the bottles don't clatter.

"You need to stop sneaking up on me in the dark," I say. "I'm going to put a bell around your neck." I try to sound light-hearted because I need to stay on his good side, but I allow myself to leer a little. "Can I get access to the files yet?"

"You go to the main office tomorrow." He steps back and peers around the corner, his eyes pinned on the street, but rather than wary, he looks rather pleased with himself. "It turns out that files had to be moved from a storage building, and it only took a few hours for people to complain about tripping over boxes. Everything we need is there. Meet me at the building at eight."

"What will I do? Will people be watching? What am I looking for?" Questions spill out of me. I put a cork in them when he puts up his hand.

"Start with all the unfiled papers first. All the crates that are in the way. Skim through them, and you'll get a sense of what is there. I haven't seen it myself, so I can't guide you much, but any debt files, Pritchard's correspondence, meeting minutes could be valuable. Take anything you want and hide it well. Remember. Eight."

"Hide it how?"

He doesn't answer. In two long strides, he's slipped between the mountain laurels, and he's gone.

"Silas," I hiss. I need to tell him about Carlin's plan to get revenge. Silas needs to know that something is being planned. Maybe he can stop it. But he's gone into the night.

"Damn him," I whisper to myself.

I'll see Silas in the morning anyway, and I can warn him then. Oran seemed confident that something would happen soon, but he didn't say it would be today. It could be all for the better that Silas disappeared into the night. They've already tortured Carlin once, and I'd hate for them to hunt him down. Before I put him in harm's way again, maybe Weylan can help me figure out a way to tell Silas there's a plan without giving away what I know.

I head for the house and Weylan, who needs to steer clear of Carlin from here on out and keep his ears open for any signs of coordination.

The light is on inside. I take the stairs two at a time and push the door open.

"I have news," I call out.

With a growling stomach, I pause with my hand on the door latch as men's voices reach me.

I inch the door closed and step into the sitting room. The light is on in the kitchen, but I can't see the table from here, and the room has fallen silent.

"Charlie?"

"Emmett?" I nearly trip over a chair on my way into the kitchen. It scrapes across the floor. "What's wrong? Who's hurt? How did you find us?"

"Everything's fine." Emmett puts both hands up and leans against the back door. "We have some news. Stopped at the tavern and ran into Weylan."

I turn to find Max and Vernon sitting at the table. They've been here long enough to eat a meal, judging by the dishes.

"It's nice to see you," I say. "Really. I mean that."

He rolls his eyes as I rustle his hair.

"Sit." Weylan pushes to his feet, dishing food onto a plate. "Dinner will get cold."

"It's only been a week," Emmett says. "You sound like you've been gone a year."

Max's laugh crinkles in the air. "You look like you've been a housewife for a year."

"Take notes." Weylan pretends to punch him in the gut as he puts a plate on the table for me, at the empty space between Vernon and Max.

It smells delicious, and I'm starving, but I'm also too nervous to eat. "Feels like a thousand years since we last saw you. What's the news? There's a railroad strike. Are you stuck here?"

"Not yet," says Vernon. "That's why we came."

"Bea is okay?" I ask. "The newspaper?"

"All fine," Vernon says.

"Here." Max reaches across the table for a rolled-up newspaper. "Ruthie sent this. Tomorrow's issue."

It's the retraction. "Well, we know they read our paper here. I wonder if I'll be close enough to hear Pritchard's reaction."

Emmett huffs. "You better hope that's all you're close enough for."

"No, this is what they wanted," Weylan says.

"It's close to what they wanted," I add.

I toss the newspaper aside. It's old news already. What I need to do is sort out this plan of Carlin's. I would love to do as he asked and print the stories of Pritchard's sins like we did Whitaker's, but I don't want to play into Carlin's hand or be associated in any way with his plot. And then there's the chance that Oran could be lying. It might not be true at all, and if he's intentionally trying to keep Carlin from talking to us, then I need to know why.

I'm dying to ask Weylan if he's heard anything at the tavern. It all swarms around inside me like angry bees in a shaken hive, but the last thing I want to do is set them free with Emmett in the room. I'll never hear the end of his *I-told-you-so* liturgy if it turns out Carlin is planning to do something explosive.

I stab my fork into the thick stew and pull out a piece of chicken. It's still warm.

"You're a lucky man," Max says. "Nothing to do but cook and clean all day while your girl does the hard work."

"I'm a regular homemaker." Weylan folds his arms and leans against the wall next to Emmett. "At least I'm useful."

The normalcy in their banter soothes the air, makes the house feel like a home. Half the tension drains out of my shoulders, but it looks like it's settled into Em. His eyes dart from the ceiling, the doorway, the floor. His elbows are tucked in, and he looks like he'd be more comfortable standing in the middle of an active volcano.

"What's wrong?" I ask him.

"It's just weird being here again. It feels different."

"I know."

"Why are you two wearing rings?" he asks. "Have you seen Sophie?"

I shake my head and swallow the driest piece of chicken to ever come in a stew. "No. Haven't seen her. I've been hoping she won't walk into the store, and I won't have to explain why I'm here. I move to the administration building tomorrow, so things will start moving faster. And the rings are to keep our story straight. I'm Silas's married niece, as far as anyone here's concerned."

Weylan lets out a huff of relief. "Tomorrow?"

"Yes," I say. "I have to meet him at the administration building first thing. But I still don't know why you're all here."

Vernon and Max exchange a look that's far more gleeful than the five-hour train ride calls for, and it takes a second for my brain to re-engage.

"Harrison!" I exclaim. "Did he win?"

"He did." Vernon beams, and I deflate back into my chair. He taps his foot. "The whole town is in rapture. They're planning a celebration."

"That's why we came." Max is the one who finally gets to the main topic. "That and the train strike. To bring you two home."

There's no way I'm going home just for that, but the news puts all thoughts of chicken stew out of my head. I reach across the table for the paper, tease Max for hiding the biggest story, and skim

Ruthie's article about it.

"Tell me everything," Weylan says. "What did Whitaker do?"

Vernon twists in his chair to face Weylan. "Whitaker lashed out. A lot. He hit rock bottom."

Weylan and I bombard them with questions that they answer in turns, filling in each other's details. Whitaker had barely campaigned at all, assuming he would win by a landslide, but everyone knows him well enough now they'd vote for a goose or a roofing shingle before they'd vote for him again. Then after Harrison won, Whitaker contested.

"All the ladies at church sat down and recounted the votes," Vernon says. "Several times. Whitaker lost."

Emmett jumps in. "He refused to leave the office. They called in everyone to get him to leave."

"Even his brother," says Max. "Clarence. The police went to his mother's house, but she's so addled she didn't know why they were there. She tried to give them those painted mermaid's purses she makes. Sweet lady, just couldn't help. Then they called on Finn."

"Finn?" I ask. "What could he do?"

"Finn actually went." Emmett snorts. "Whitaker didn't let him in, though. Regina went, too. She stood there glaring at the house like it offended her sensibilities. Smoke poured out of that chimney like the house was on fire."

"Everyone knew he was burning papers." Max cocks an eyebrow. "All that evidence gone."

"That's a shame." My heart sinks. I may have my sights set on a bigger fish here in Stoke, but I'd still been hoping to one day get my hands on proof that Whitaker had bamboozled the town.

"People just wanted him to leave," Max continued. "My father picked the lock and went in. He told Whitaker to stop acting like a baby."

Judging by the look on Vernon's face, it had been good fun to watch. Vernon's smile is as big as I've ever seen it. "I guess Whitaker realized it was in his best interest to leave at that point. The whole town's been laughing about it."

Weylan shifts his weight and looks at Max. "It's about time your father acted normal."

Max says he isn't so certain it'll last, and Weylan asks where Whitaker is now.

"He was homeless for a day," says Vernon. "Until his brother Clarence said he'd pay him to leave town."

Having met Clarence, I could easily picture the schadenfreude rounding his cheeks as he made the offer.

"Whitaker accepted that offer," Max explains. "On his way out, he said the whole town was ungrateful, and he'd build his empire elsewhere. Word has it he's a few towns over with an old friend."

"The suffragists won," I say. "Leta must be elated." They coordinated a wall of resistance around Whitaker, and they have the stories of all those women who lost family members to the poison in the water. It's hope on a grand scale. Women can change things if they want to.

Emmett pushes away from the door he's been leaning against. "I think you two should come home."

"Are you crazy?" I ask.

Vernon twists back around to face me. "The railroad strike is happening."

"I know. It will severely harm the people who live here. Oran—" I say. Weylan asks how I heard, and I finally have a chance to tell him about Oran. Unfortunately, I can't tell him everything in front of my brother. I don't want to hash this out with a crowd. "Weylan, Can I talk to you in the other room for a moment? It's important."

Max lets out a low but teasing whistle which prompts laughter from Vernon. It nearly drowns out Emmett's grunts and disapprovals which have nothing to do with me pulling Weylan aside and everything to do with the fact that I haven't heaped praise upon his plan.

Weylan follows me into the front room where I move to the farthest corner from the kitchen to whisper. He stands so close he has to look down at me.

"Oran said Carlin is hell bent on revenge against Pritchard, and the people who've been holding him back aren't able anymore. He says a war is brewing. Oran seems to think he'll do something big that could hurt innocent people. He warned us to leave. Do you know what Carlin's planning? You've overheard them before. Have they said anything?"

"No. Carlin hasn't said anything like that. He's very twitchy. Doesn't speak in complete thoughts."

Suddenly another dozen or so puzzle pieces land at my feet. Oran seems to know a lot about the railroad situation. He also seemed hesitant to talk about Carlin's plan, which clearly he knew more about than he was letting on. I still haven't figured out why Oran would want me to know the things he told me. If he believes I'm Silas's niece and could put a stop to it, why wouldn't he tell me the facts? There is also a chance he suspects I'm not who I say, considering the way he questioned me. And if that's the case, what did he hope to gain by telling me? All of this makes me wonder if Carlin's plan is as disastrous as Oran believes it might be. Is he planting information with me to see who we leak it to? Or it could be genuine, and the railroad strike could prevent anyone from escaping if something terrible does happen. If I don't say something, I might regret it.

It all seems like such a mess. I can't organize my thoughts at all.

Weylan's eyes dart between mine. "What are you thinking?"

"Everything. Too much. I need to focus on why I'm here." I clasp my hands and blow into my fists as if my hands are cold. "I can't think about Carlin." I can't worry about what he's doing or whether Oran has good intentions. I can only plow forward, get what I can from the files and leave. "This is my only chance to get actual proof that Pritchard is poisoning people. I'm not going to miss this opportunity."

"I hate this." Weylan lets out a long string of *nos*. "We've jumped into action before only to realize too late that we had blinders on. I just think we should slow down for a minute."

I raise my hands. "We don't have time to slow down. And we're too close to leave now."

His pursed lips give him a gravely serious air. After a moment of searching my eyes, he nods slowly.

"Alright," he says. "We stay. Now what?"

"We say thank you for coming, but we are not going home with you." I take his hands. "You can go, if you want, but I hope you won't. Please stay with me. I need you. I feel less alone with you here."

He squeezes my hands back. "Of course. I wouldn't dare leave you here alone."

It's a massive request. One I hope I don't regret.

"Alright," I say. "We stay."

"I'll listen closely to Carlin at the tavern." He nods, and I search his eyes for a hint of hesitation, but I find him as determined as ever.

"I think you should avoid Carlin. I don't want to get tangled in this."

"Of course." He presses his lips thin.

We're pulled back into the kitchen by three stern gazes, and the air is sharp edged when we rejoin the others. Weylan aims straight for the stove, jabbing at something in a pot, but I fold my arms and plant my feet.

"We're staying here."

Vernon speaks first. "Of course you are."

Max tugs at his long dark hair. "Can't say I blame you."

Emmett shifts his weight against the door, and it creaks. He picks at his thumbnail. The room is so quiet the click echoes off the walls. I refuse to look at him because he'll only say I'm being stupid or stubborn or some adjective I won't be able to argue with, so instead I rip at the over-cooked chicken on my plate. Not getting what he wants from me, he grunts. Then he huffs. Then he sighs. He reminds me of our mother, at the end of her rope over some mess we made.

"Aren't you going to say something?" he asks.

I drop my fork and let it clang against the plate "I already did,"

"We're staying, Em." Weylan shoots me a look over his shoulder. "We're going to finish this."

Max and Weylan talk over each other, and Emmett talks even louder, demanding to know why we aren't marching right back to Maryland this very instant, warning me that once someone finds out I'm here — and it seems inevitable — I'll be in types of trouble I can't even imagine. Weylan and I stand firm.

"You both could be in trouble." Vernon unclenches his jaw. "But if you're staying, take these." He digs in his vest pocket and tucks two tickets under my plate. "Just in case. The prices are changing every day. These are pre-paid, and they'll get you out no matter what it costs. But you need a train to use them, obviously."

Emmett leans in. "So you should leave now."

Weylan eyes the train tickets like a dehydrated man staring at a puddle, and Emmett makes a disapproving, defeated grunt. He leers at me. "If you're smart, you'll use them soon. Don't linger around this place."

"I'm not leaving until my task is done, but I'm not going to drag it out, if that's what you think," I say. "I know where there are horses, too, if there's an emergency. And thank you, Vernon. It's really thoughtful of you to come all this way."

Vernon raises a shoulder, the tips of his ears pink. I forgot how much he hates the attention.

Max checks his pocket watch. "I hate to do this, but we have to leave." He slides his chair back, rising to his feet and smoothing his pants. "It's a long walk if we miss this train out of here."

We say our goodbyes. Weylan follows Max and Vernon into the front room while I corner Emmett. Or he corners me, rather.

"There's something you're not saying," he accuses me.

I can't lie to him. He can tell. "Father's friends are still scheming, that's all I know."

He rustles my hair for a change. "Don't get involved. The less you know the better."

I can't tell him I already know a lot, especially because I'm not even confident about what I know. But saying goodbye to Emmett for the second time in a week is making me feel like I'm in a fog. Oran's warning seems real now, and it feels like the worst of the danger that always loomed on the horizon is suddenly here. It feels electric. A dark and dangerous storm has arrived and there's no longer time to spare or prepare.

I push him toward the door. In the living room, Vernon shrugs into a jacket and Max prances, antsy to leave. Emmett asks Weylan if he wants to ride back with them, and something sharp passes between them.

"You could come back." Emmett's lips are puckered, and his eyes lift in a challenging way. "You don't have to stay here."

Emmett is daring him to come with them, forcing him to prove his mettle.

"Not a chance." Weylan slaps his shoulder hard enough to set him off balance, but Emmett recovers and grips the back of the chair. "I'm not leaving your sister here alone."

"If you're staying behind, you'd better bring her back with you." Emmett's voice is flat and low. "Or don't come back at all."

Weylan nudges him to the door. "I won't leave without her."

Levity passes between them as they shake hands at the door. Weylan closes and locks it behind them. Lost in his own silence, he tidies the kitchen by lantern light.

"Carlin is an explosives guy, isn't he?" I ask. "Knows a lot about that kind of thing?"

"Maybe it's an empty threat," he suggests. "Surely Carlin is smart enough not to catch the whole town on fire?" He sounds hesitant, despite the optimism in his words.

I shake my head. "I'm not so sure. Is it wishful thinking?"

"I'm too tired. I could sleep standing up," I say. "And I have a little sewing to do if I'm going to look like I belong in an office. Tomorrow over breakfast, I'll tell you everything that happened with

Oran, and you can tell me everything about Carlin?"

"It's a date." He reaches over and takes the plate from my hands, and I take the stairs up the bedroom. This skirt has a loose stitch in the hem that I can fix in no time at all. I'd like to make the best impression I can, even if it's a false one. Before I slip into my nightclothes, I take the little vials of morphine from my pocket and slip them into the dresser.

I've never stolen anything before. Not like this. There was the ink from the general store, but it was for a noble cause, and we left money behind to pay for it. This was different. Impetuous. Vengeful. It could get me into a lot of trouble if anyone ever finds out. All I know is it could help some people who truly deserve it, and I pray it won't be us. Before I leave here, I'll have to find a way to get it to Sophie, so she can get it to people who need it most.

CHAPTER SIXTEEN

JULY 24, 1901

Weylan's still asleep. I tiptoe across the floor, managing to hit every loose floorboard as I go. Then I slip into my mended skirt and pair it with a simple linen blouse pleated at the waist line. With my hair piled on top of my head in a poof, I blink at myself in the mirror. I look much older with my hair this way, like a teacher or a shop lady. Not at all like Charlotte Morris, but that's fine, because I only need to look like Harriet.

Behind me, Weylan shifts in bed, rolling over and tossing his hand on my pillow. He looks at peace in his sleep. I don't want to wake him, so I move down the stairs on the edges, sparing him from the house's creaking bones. I gather a mid-day meal of cold meat and bread and take it across town, heading down and avoiding the rest of the workers. Silas had said to meet him at the administrative building, and he is right on time, standing at the short end of the wood-clad building. The solid rectangle is three stories high with windows all around.

The door at the building's corner leads to a flight of stairs which we take to the second floor. He barks instructions at me the whole way. Don't talk to anyone. Keep my head down. Don't make eye contact with people.

A long, narrow hall pockmarked with doors ends at a windowless one. Just as I open my mouth to ask if his lack of faith in my own sense of self-preservation was making him regret bringing me here, he opens the door. Behind it bustles a flurry of activity.

People rush in all directions, paper and boxes in their hands, talking to and over each other in so many words it's hard to isolate just one. The space is bright, lit mostly by two walls of windows, with desks lined up in rows. There must be order among all the chaos, but to me, it looks like theater, a tightly choreographed dance routine of madness.

We proceed through the office, turning right, where we face a wall lined with wood filing cabinets broken up by some office doors. And there are boxes everywhere and stacks of paper. Teetering heaps of it.

I must look overwhelmed because he extends an arm as if he's about to give me instructions, but he says, "This isn't all yours. But there is so much for you that no one will notice if you take your time."

He waves me up to the front desk, a heavy metal hulk covered in office gadgets. The woman behind it rises and extends a hand.

"You must be Harriet. It's nice to meet you," she says with a grin so wide the apples of her cheeks make her eyes narrow. She reminds me of Regina, and I trust her just as much. "We've heard nothing about you from your uncle, I'm afraid, but if you know how to sort pieces of paper, you'll do just fine. I'm Edna Fazio. Let me show you around."

Silas makes a show of wishing me a good day, vowing to check in on me. It's hard to force my face into the kind of gracious and grateful smile one might expect a niece to display at a moment like this. He puts his hand on my shoulder as he passes to leave, and I struggle not to shiver.

Edna doesn't seem to suspect a thing. She's overly friendly and verbose, talking with her hands, but she's the only one. Every person we pass looks like a shell of a human. There's little warmth or geniality among them. But I'm not here to be sociable, anyway, and the isolation will make it even easier for me to find what I'm looking for.

She weaves between desks. No one looks up. "You're Silas's niece, you say?"

"Um, yes ma'am."

"On his sister's side?" she asks. But it isn't a look of curiosity she gives me. Suddenly the suspicion is written all over her face, in the lilt of her grin and the corners of her eyes.

My mind reels. I don't even recall Silas's last name or what he might have told her, but it stands to reason we'd have different last names. I try to come up with something I can commit to, but there's only an instant, so I shrug and pretend I misunderstood. "Family is so complicated, isn't it? I see so little of Uncle Silas. It was kind of him to make room for us like this, and I'm so glad I can earn my keep. Is this what he needs me to file?"

There's a flicker of mistrust in her eyes as she turns to the towers of mess. "Indeed. And aren't you lucky to have so much to do. It can be a difficult place to work," she says. "There's a lot of competition here to please the boss. Don't worry, though. You'll never see him.

He never steps foot in this building. That's what he has Silas for. But you'll be judged on your looks by the rest of these men and, if I were you, I'd be rather prudent about who's attention I courted. I see you're married?"

I spin the gold band around my finger. "Yes, ma'am." The lie sounds foreign. "Going on a year now."

"That will help. A young woman like you would be swallowed whole by these monsters." She looks me up and down, arrives at a decision that exhausts her, and waves at me to follow her. "Come. I'll introduce you. Then they'll leave you to the work."

The offices along the outer walls have window views of the breaker, where boys pick rocks and hunks of dirt from the coal as it comes down the conveyor. The offices are occupied by managers of all types of boring things. Mining engineers. Bookkeepers. They're perfect carbon copies of the same man over and over, slicked-back hair and a starched collar, a shirt too white for the scenery. Their eyes start at my face and drift down my form and return again with a smile or a smirk. One or two I recognize from my father's days, but I only ever saw them from great distances. I've changed even if they haven't, and they could never recognize me the way Carlin and Oran did because they're a different class of human entirely. They're the vinegar to our oil.

When Edna finishes the lap of introductions around the building, we stop at the wall of boxes, crates, and papers. There must be thirty cabinets, each four drawers high. I'm surprised the floor doesn't buckle beneath the weight of them. They're all solid wood with brass handles and little paper tags. They nearly span the length of the office, except for the breaks in the middle where they flank closed doors. It could take me a lifetime to find evidence in here.

"How is all this organized?" I ask.

Edna shows me how to find the account numbers on the documents. "Other than that, I don't have much experience wading through these papers, but you'll find your way, I'm sure. I'll leave you to it," she says. "We'll be grateful to have you sort as much as you can while you're here."

What I can't figure out is why Silas would have me file all of this together after they'd put so much effort into keeping it apart, but that's not for me to decide. For all I know, he intends to burn it all to the ground once we've brought Pritchard to his knees.

Silas had suggested I start with the boxes, but I needed to know where to put things and what type of information I might stumble upon. Left on my own to file, I open the cabinet drawers one by one. Accounts are in the cabinets on the left, correspondence is filed by company names, in alphabetical order, in the cabinets on the right.

The accounting files I skim through are mostly payroll, mundane orders for supplies and various inventory items. I make a leap for the W drawer first thing, but there's no Whitaker file. That would be far too easy, anyway. So I take my time digging through the boxes, filing papers, familiarizing myself with the company names for the rest of the day.

Nothing of importance makes its way to the surface by the time people rise from their desks and stretch. With so little progress, it would be easy to sink into despair, but Silas never promised the evidence would be easy to find. The papers are as disorganized as I should have expected them to be. Yet I still can't help feeling down.

My feet are killing me when I check the time, so instead of saying goodnight to Edna, I take the shortest path back to house number four.

I beat Weylan home, as I assumed I would. It'll be some time before he gets home from the tavern, so I start a dinner of quick rolls and vermicelli soup with vegetables I salvage from the garden. Just after it's done, Weylan enters through the back door and reels me into his embrace, spins me around, and we gaze into the soup pot together, his chin on my shoulder.

"This smells delicious. How was your day?" he asks.

"Exhausting. Disappointing, if I let myself think about it. I'm finding my way around the files, trying not to be obvious that I'm looking for something. Tomorrow will be a better day, now that I know where things are. I can see Pritchard's house from where I'm doing all the filing. That's motivating."

We talk while we eat. Weylan fills me in on everything Carlin said at the tavern. Nothing new, and nothing of note. Then we chew over Oran's warning about a war on the horizon, and I try to recall every detail of what he said yesterday, to pick it all apart for clues. Picking it apart only leaves us with shreds. So many people hate Pritchard and all he's done. Men have lost lives and children to the mines and the poison in the water. They've lost fingers and feet because of awful working conditions. They've faced cruel punishment, far crueler than their crimes warrant. And all the while the Coal and Iron Police intimidate people with their presence.

The conversation puts a damper on our dinner. We clean up and go to bed early, sticking to opposite sides of the bed as if our rule had never been broken, the wall between us never breached.

The next morning, I arrive early for work. The sunny morning and the light breeze put a spring in my step. Today will be the day I find some evidence. I just know it. My hands are dry from all the paper, but I cheerfully set about my task, trying to memorize file names and the companies Pritchard does business with. The morning flies past, and just as I discover the board of director records, my empty stomach grumbles. I don't even know what a board of directors does, and the letters swim on the page, but my gut says something is here. Unfortunately, my gut also says I'm hungry, and I'll be better suited to remember what I read if I'm not so famished, so I pause for lunch. While I eat, a dozen men in clean suits file into the doorway nestled between the cabinets. They don't even look at me.

I don't know a lot about these types of men, but I do know there's a direct correlation between how much money they think you have and the amount of attention they're willing to give you. It gives me an odd sort of pleasure to know I'm nearly invisible.

I rush through my lunch and return to filing, keeping my head down as I listen. But the men aren't making much effort to be quiet. They talk in voices loud enough for me to hear through the closed door without straining. I can't tell if they're managers or the board of directors whose papers I'm skimming, but they seem tasked with cruelty.

"He's lagging in the mine, and he will have his pay cut starting Monday."

A shuffle of paper and the pronouncement of a familiar name. Royer. I went to school with a boy named Royer. He'd been meek and quiet, but his father had been among my father's allies.

"He isn't paying his bills. Pritchard wants him lashed. Basement prison, no food for a weekend."

A whole weekend without food. Decided in a second. By people who sit in an office. I hold my breath, listening for disagreement. No one bothers to protest. My stomach churns as more paper shuffles behind the door.

"Mancuso. The Coal and Iron Police propose breaking his finger for the theft. Pritchard signed off on it."

I gasp along with the rest of the room. The Coal and Iron Police are supposed to protect company property. Surely, they can't be expected to overlook theft, but breaking a man's hands could ruin his family.

"Nels is a maniac. I'm not ordering this. I know Mancuso's sister. He's not a bad man or a drunkard."

"He's one of those Molly Maguires, and Pritchard wants to make an example of him. Put them all in the Frank Morris pile."

The Frank Morris pile? What does that mean? Father wasn't a Molly Maguire. The Mollies were Irish immigrants who fought back. They were accused of collaborating over a series of murders. Many think they were wrongly accused. They were hanged for it, and some of them were innocent. There's no doubt the violence never should have happened, but Father wasn't a Molly.

"Frank Morris was not a Molly," the first man says, as if he read my mind. "It's not right to pin that nom de guerre on men who didn't earn it."

Another man huffs. "They didn't have to hang Frank Morris. He took himself to the grave."

I squeeze my hands so hard my knuckles crack. They're wrong. Pritchard killed him. There's no other way of saying it. Father didn't take himself out of the fight. The fight stole my father.

"The Coal and Iron Police are here for a reason. This uprising could have been worse. By making sure the workers realize those benevolent societies, or whatever they call them, do more harm than good, we've avoided a lot of bloodshed." The man pounds the table.

"They're Mollies. Every man who speaks out is a Molly. Every man whose crimes threaten to derail the peace is a Molly. They're Morris men, and they're dangerous."

A new understanding settles in my stomach, mixing with my lunch and making a sour slurry. It sounds simple enough to slander one man to keep him in line, but these are real people with families and lives, and they're ruining all of them. And he's ruining my father's name and legacy by associating him with something violent, and that's not who my father was at all. Perhaps John Kehoe started a riot that turned bloody, but my father only ever stood on a crate to urge men to lobby for their own welfare. He never asked for violence. I know this with every fiber of my being, and anything Carlin or Oran, or any of these men, have to say otherwise is simply not true.

"Nels is a maniac for employing that Pinkerton detective. He'll push those workers too far, and we'll all regret it."

There's a mumble of disagreement, and I wish I knew what it meant. A Pinkerton? I've never heard of such a thing. I scan the little paper tags, find the drawer that would hold such a file, and find nothing. As murmurs of agreement ripple through the room, I confirm there's nothing under Morris or Frank either.

The conversation turns against Pritchard. The time he accused a man of trying to unionize, burned him and hauled him twenty miles out of town, abandoning him in the heat of summer to walk back on his own without water. The time when he erected gallows and marched three men to them, making them plead for their lives before pushing them to the ground where they lay with their hands bound in ropes. It's so brutal the papers in my hand shake.

"Something needs to be done about Nels," someone says.

"By who?"

There isn't anyone. Even the governor bows to his whims. He has his very own police force, for heaven's sake. The silence on the other side of the door grows thicker than the summer humidity, and their hopelessness seeps out from under the door. It makes me wonder how many of these men would join Silas in subverting Pritchard if they all knew. That, alone, gives me hope. If there's resistance in rooms like that one, among men with stiff collars and gold watches on chains, then there's hope.

In the meeting room, papers shuffle. Chairs scrape the floor. I leave my filing on top of the cabinet and make my way to the privy, so they won't know they were overheard. Eye to eye in the mirror with the part of me that just wants this to be over with, I yearn for a way to connect with one of those men. Surely at least one of them would be willing to help. In a dream world, I could take all this evidence back to Maryland, sort through it, let a lawyer build a case, and every single one of those men would corroborate the evidence and testify. That's a big dream and a lot of *ifs*, but these are the people closest to Pritchard who could help me end this thing. I must find out who they are so I can write to them one day if I need to.

First, I have to find that evidence. And figure out what a Pinkerton is.

Once I'm sure the room is empty and the men are gone, I return to the files, this time with more resolve. I flip through the board of director minutes but quickly realize there's little of value there. It's merely a series of bland reports on repairs to the coal breaker, ventilation work, promotions for shift managers, and orders for new tools. But just as the day is about to end, I discover a folder labeled *DEBTS*, directly before the one labeled *DIRECTORS, BOARD OF*.

Inside that folder are typed invoices to builders with notes in the margin. Pritchard instructed him not to pay, to starve out the company until he can bankrupt them. Pritchard asked what the accountant thinks companies would be worth. And there are pages upon pages about the railroad, estimating its worth and who he needed to choke to get his hands on it.

"How's your filing going?" Edna's voice behind me sends my heart into my throat. I shove a page into the folder and cram it into the drawer.

"Well. I've made some progress, though it barely feels like it."

"It seems you have. Two whole boxes are empty." She peers into one of them, giving me a side-long glance. "Those men certainly can be loud, can't they? I hope they don't distract you from filing."

Something dark flashes in her eyes, the hint of a hidden meaning in her question, but she looks down before I grasp it.

"They're no bother." I set my stack of unfiled papers aside. I can finish them tomorrow. "They're too distant for me to hear. Little more than mumbles behind that thick door."

"What a shame." If she's relieved that I can't overhear them, she hides it behind exaggerated disappointment. "I know what happens in there, and I was hoping for some good gossip."

My laugh is genuine. "Oh, if I did hear anything, I couldn't possibly say. Silas would have my head, wouldn't he?"

She lets the rigid exterior slip. Her eyebrows arch, her eyes dart to the side, and her grin is undeniably cheeky. "Silas would never know about a little idle gossip."

That night, Weylan and I sit at the table under the gas lamp, and it's like old times as we inspect Edna from every angle. Every head tilt and narrowed eye. Each hand motion and grin. It takes some time for Weylan to come around because he hasn't met her, but before we go up to bed, I'm nearly convinced I can trust her. She isn't the stern woman she seems, and I don't think she's manipulating me. I think she's complex. Curious. Unconvinced that Pritchard and his board of directors are the hero corporate overlords they think they are. She wants to know what's happening behind that door, and whether she truly trusts me or not, the door is open just enough for me to find out why.

CHAPTER SEVENTEEN

JULY 26, 1901

The next morning, I step over a rut in the street on my way to the office, and trudge along the edge of the road, dodging crab grass that stretches out into the rocks. My feet and shoulders still ache from the long day standing and crouching at the cabinets, pulling open heavy drawers with sticking slides. My fingers are covered in paper cuts. But I know the drawers and my way around them now, so even though my feet are dragging, I'm motivated to get back to my search. And to Edna.

Pritchard's grand house comes into view just before the crest of the hill, gleaming white with a big front porch. It has a high-peaked roof and a church-like air, with brackets and woodwork that remind me of a doily. It's too much, like it's trying too hard to sugar coat the rot inside. In any other place, it might be awe-inspiring. Beautiful, even. But here it's a mockery.

A group of men passes, miners running the opposite way. They head toward the mine, stragglers who don't want to face the wrath of the managers. The latches of their metal lunch pails clanking as they pass. One of them slows and whistles at me, and I keep my face down, biting back the urge to glare at him in case he recognizes me.

I take the path to the office, tug open the door, and rush up the stairs. Edna is at the desk just inside the door. We exchange a friendly greeting, and I'm back at work, carrying a bundle of papers as I skim through the drawers so it looks like I'm filing, but I'm scrutinizing the contents, lingering to get a good sense of the companies and people in Pritchard's orbit.

Most of what I see is worthless, so I skim through the Ls and Ms and Ns. I lose track of time until approaching footsteps send me diving into the unfiled papers, making myself small, so I fade into the scenery. The men close themselves behind the door again, and I position myself near it, hoping to hear what they're saying, opening and closing drawers as quietly as I can. They're focused on extremely boring things like bills to be paid and supplies to be ordered.

I file a stack of correspondence and reach the back of the drawer to find a blank folder. No label at all. Inside are copies of letters with handwritten notes in the corners about checks that were sent. One hundred dollars to a man named Lester Morgan, the letter signed by Pritchard, pledging his support. A stack of more just like it follows, made out to men whose names and businesses I don't recognize.

The letters share the same tone. Thanks for favors. Offers of aid. Notes to bookkeepers demanding they not pay certain invoices.

And a letter to the railroad renews an old offer to bail them out of their worker welfare troubles. My hand slicks with sweat, and I wipe it on my skirt.

I perceive no lightening of your burden any time soon, and it would be in your best interest to accept my offer before your railroad decreases in value.

This is it. And there are ten more letters like it of varying lengths. It's not enough on its own to bring Pritchard down, but it's an incriminating piece of a larger puzzle. I can't take them yet, though. Not while those men are still in the conference room. I push the drawer shut, and it grinds on its track.

A hand lands on my shoulder. My heart leaps into my throat, and I stifle a yelp, but I jump and turn to find Edna behind me.

"Good work," she says. "We should have lunch."

I can't truly turn her down, so I give the brightest and friendliest grin I can while my hands still shake, and I follow her to the small table where office workers sometimes dine. I brought with me some leftover rolls with cheese and fresh beans, and I snap off the ends while she tucks into deviled ham on bread, and she tells me about the office and the people, the work they do here.

"You and Silas aren't familiar?"

"No, I'm afraid." It's an easy thing to admit. "Distant."

That's an understatement. I pick at my food, hoping it looks as if I'm making nothing of the conversation. If anyone will divulge secrets over this meal, it needs to be her.

She takes in a short breath and clamps her mouth shut. Glances around her and does it again. She leans forward, and I match her, but only by a degree. I need her to say something. I practically beg her to ask the right questions and give the right hints, so I can know if she's part of the resistance against Pritchard or not.

She opens and closes her mouth like a fish out of water until she inflates with a breath and likely a bit of courage. My heart thunders, and I smile, urging her on.

"Does Silas have you looking for something?" she asks.

I let out a small gasp and lean back. "Whatever do you mean? No. He just has me filing. What would he want me to look for?"

Her coy smile spreads. The fine lines around her eyes deepen. "Oh, you can tell me."

I snap the end off a bean and let it fall onto the table. "What makes you think so?"

"A niece who looks and acts nothing like him just happens to come through town while tempers are at their tipping point, and after moving all those files out of the office in Pritchard's house, he moves them again? Puts them here because the place where they are is just too damp even though it got a new roof three months ago. And for a temporary worker who doesn't have anyone to impress, you could move slowly, but you're going through those boxes like there's a lit fuse behind you, and you didn't start at the beginning. You're looking for something, Harriet. What is it?"

I could tell her. The words tingle my tongue. The truth wants to spill out of me. My body aches for an ally who will help me find what I couldn't possibly know exists. But I can't say a word.

"What on Earth could Silas have me looking for?" I ask.

She lets out a laugh so controlled and quiet that I'm impressed. "Whatever will let him take control of this place."

"Pritchard would hate that, I gather. And you report to him."

Her eyes darken in an instant. Her jaw clenches. It happens too fast to be contrived. She says, "I report to myself." And I believe her.

More than that, I now need an ally. If she's noted all that about me, other people may have too.

"Is it obvious?" I ask.

She softens, and her shoulders round. She picks up her deviled ham, but she doesn't take a bite. She holds it out like cash she can exchange for something good. "It's just obvious to me. I hear a lot."

"I can tell." I glance around, to be sure no one can hear. The office is nearly empty with men away for a mid-day break. A few men are gathered in a distant corner, loudly discussing their plan for a baseball game.

"How do you feel about Pritchard?" I ask.

"He's a monster."

"I'm looking for files. Can you help?"

She places her sandwich on the embroidered napkin she brought with her. "My heart is in it. But not my neck."

CHAPTER EIGHTEEN

JULY 27, 1901

The morning dew glued grit to my shoes and it stuck with me all the way to the office, so I wipe my feet just inside the door. Edna jumps when she looks up, digs through the scattered papers on her desk, and waves an envelope at me.

"This was under the door for you this morning. From Silas, it seems."

"For me?" My name is on the envelope in a rudimentary scrawling. My name—my fake name— is spelled with only one R. *Hariet.*

My curiosity is bigger than my patience, so I rip it open and skip to the end. It's signed as being from Silas but the handwriting is not at all what I would expect from him, and the wording sounds nothing like the way he speaks.

Get yur work done early to-day and leev before noon. Tell no one you got this note.

I flip it over and hold it up to the light. There doesn't appear to be a hidden meaning in it, though it's certainly not from Silas. Carlin? Oran? If there were something to know, they would just tell Weylan.

"Is everything alright?" Edna asks.

"Yes. All's well." I fold it back along the crease and tuck it in my pocket. There's no hint of familiarity to her demeanor, which bodes well for what passed between us yesterday. Both of us can keep secrets, it seems.

My shoes aren't clean yet, but I would rather defile the rug than draw suspicion by lingering. Besides, I have to figure out how to discreetly collect as many papers as I can, get them to the lavatory, and shove them into the lining of the massive pockets I sewed into this skirt last night.

All morning, as I dig through the files, the note worms its way through my thoughts. It occurs to me that it may be a warning from Carlin or Oran, and perhaps I ought to heed it. I could feign an illness, but that would delay my work at best or make me look suspicious at worst. People have seen Weylan speak with Carlin at the bar, and anyone could have seen one of them drop off the note. In the end, I just keep working. Faster. Setting aside papers until I can slip out the door with them.

A rumble of distant thunder barrels at us. It rolls over us, and I turn to the windows. Most people do, satisfying that deep human need to know what's coming. The sky has taken on the earthy green hue of a coming storm. It makes Pritchard's white house look gothic. There's a flurry of activity on the side of the house, where workers are replacing a window. Silas climbs the stairs, pausing to talk to a man on the porch. I imagine he's there often. When I was a child, I used to wonder what it was like inside that big white house, but I don't envy him for his proximity to it now.

The first fat drops slam the ground and pound the window. A big fat drip picks up coal dust and slides to the sill, dredging through the silt.

I turn back to my work, ready to file a stack of Pritchard's dry correspondence with the Pennsylvania National Bank, because I feel the need to make it seem as if I'm making progress. Suddenly I see a gap between the wall and the first cabinet that I had not noticed before. There's a bag jammed in the crevice. It's old and worn with dinged corners and a handle that's cracked with age — the old kind that looks like a doctor's bag. The brass hinge is dulled by a layer of dust, so no one's used it for some time. Just the place to stash my growing pile of evidence, but it's wedged in tightly. I glance about to be sure that everyone's returned to work, and I yank it out. It's empty, thankfully, so I toss in the thirty pages I've seized so far, and shove it back in place with my toe.

The bank letters require me to open a drawer that's been stuck for two days, so I sit cross-legged and wiggle it from side to side. It budges a centimeter at a time. It slowly opens, and I find the folder. Inside the drawer, page after page is more of the same. Boring correspondence. Invoices and receipts. There's nothing of note until I unstick two folders and the word Pinkerton jumps out.

The first folder contains copies of letters back and forth. In one, Pritchard asks an employee to send a check to the Pinkerton Detective Agency for two hundred dollars to see "the thing through." Another he received references suspicions of dangers that must be thwarted, and a promise to provide a list of operatives by courier.

Another letter vows to attain power over the minds of the men and to unseat the leading spirits of the Active Labor project by enticing them to act in a manner of disregard so egregious they'd be punished to the fullest extent of the law and serve as a deterrent.

A deterrent.

My face burns clear up to my ears. When I overheard the men in that office talk about coercion, forcing workers to commit crimes so they could make examples of them, it seemed distant. Just a tale. The Molly Maguires were hanged in this way years before I was born, but holding the paper in my hand that ordered it to happen feels like touching their very deaths.

Pritchard sat in the house outside this very window and wrote a letter to hire a detective agency to position men among the workers, to influence their thinking and cause them to commit crimes just so he could hurt them.

Like the very air I breathe, I need to know their names. Who were the men he intended to harm? Was Carlin among them? My father? With so many people milling about in the office, I don't have time or space to read all the pages and study the dates to see if my father and his friends were involved, but it stands to reason Pritchard meant to pin a murder on my father.

This alone could unseat Pritchard. Sweat beads on my forehead. Heat creeps up my neck. I can't let anyone see me this flustered. I'm not supposed to read any of this. Swallowing the ire, with my head down, I gently remove the pages and set them aside. Slowing my breath and returning to the boxes, I find an entire stack of Pritchard's correspondence bound in twine and tied with a bow, like it's a present just for me. Within the papers are organized by the other party in the communication, so I have no trouble at all finding Harrison's name. It pleases me greatly to see that Harrison returned a check and an attempt at bribery with a polite *no, thank you.*

The breath that came so quickly before completely escapes me now. Blackmail. So much of this bundle is blackmail. I resist the urge to clutch the pages to my chest. It's the proof to back up Leta's claims. It's the verification I yearned for. I resist the urge to shove it in my pockets and run for the door.

Instead, I stand and stretch my lower back, scanning the room. Typewriters clatter away. People scratch at paper with pencils. Someone cranks the handle of the big cast iron adding machine and it clicks and clacks. No one pays me any mind, so I move swiftly, collecting the pages, stuffing them in the case, and wedging it back into the crevice with my toe.

Now to figure out how to get that bag out of this office. I could linger at the end of the day. Come in early and sneak it out to Weylan.

Suddenly, without any warning, the air severed and splintered. The last of my thoughts fractured, soaked up by the swelling fireball outside the window that exploded into a blinding light, carried on the loudest sound I've ever heard. It's so very bright. Orange at first. Then red. Then it glares white as snow as everything that Pritchard is, all he owns—his gingerbread house that masquerades as a church, his papers and comforts and lies—it all turns to shards.

It seems to take forever, but it can only be a piece of an instant. A fragment of a moment.

Lightning, I think. *It hit the chimney and the whole house exploded. No, that's not right. That doesn't happen.*

All my senses are overcome by the sharp shatter of glass and deep cracking fracture of stone and wood launched into the air by the roaring bang, and it all fades away behind the ringing in my ears.

The building shakes beneath my feet, robbing me of my knees. I crumble. Duck. I cover my head with my hands as glass sprays all around me, peppering my skin. It stings and burns.

Time stands still. All I can think of as the sky turns to shreds is that time when I was about seven years old, and we took the train to the beach. The sun glittered on the water, turning the horizon into a blinding line of white. A blast of wind had picked up the sand, transforming the world's most delicate softness into shards of agony.

I might be screaming. I'm not sure. Then a large piece of the wall to my left caves inward, and I do know for sure. My throat burns with my own voice, but I can't hear a thing beyond the ringing in my ears. My voice is cut off by the dust and debris filling the air. Suddenly I can't breathe.

The air is dense, thick with a silt as fine as flour. Blasted with shards of glass, I scramble to my feet. The force of air through the hole in the wall swirls my skirt. My chest rattles, and my throat throbs as, along with everyone else, I run for where the stairs might be. People scramble over desks and chairs, splinters of lumber, and giant rocks. We're all coated in black soot and gray ash. Bits of wood and glass cling to our hair and clothes.

The stairs are dark and hot, but it's easier to breathe here, and we stream out the door to another world entirely, one that's untethered itself, spewing its insides all over the outdoors. Glass and stone and wood from Pritchard's walls and roof. Things that might have been porch railings. All of it obscured by an annihilating fog of everything that man owned.

The people scatter, walking or running east toward their homes. Others head for the mine entrance. I don't even want to imagine a collapse. Mouths are open in silent screams, their voices lost behind the ringing and throbbing pain in my ears.

It seems as if hours go by before the world returns, before enough ash and brick and wood settle for me to see clear across the street. A group of women tumble and flail over debris, heading for the skeletal wooden coal breaker. It's still standing, and it appears fine, but if I had a son or a husband there, I'd run for him, too.

"Lucky no one was on the street," a woman says, covering her mouth with her arm. I swallow hard and rub below my ear. At least I can hear again, even if the voices sound very far away.

"Men were working at Pritchard's," I cough out. "Replacing a window."

A man just ahead of me looks over his shoulder. "Not anymore."

The sound drops out again, like someone covered me in the densest of quilts. Silas was there. I take a few steps toward the house—what's left of it, anyway—but the man pulls me back.

"Where are you going?" he demands.

"To help," I exclaim.

"No one survived that." The woman loses her balance stepping over what might have been a door frame. She puts her arms out to steady herself.

"I can't just stand here when I'm capable of helping," I say.

The side of the house where the men had been working on the windows is now a gaping hole. The whole wall is gone, blown across the span of lawn and out toward the thick line of trees that served as a buffer between Pritchard and the town. I can see clear into a second story bedroom, but nothing makes sense up there. There's no bed or bureau, no little dresser or nightstand. Tattered wallpaper flutters in the wind.

The back of the house fared much worse. There's so much debris and none of it makes sense. It's like someone held up the house like a dandelion puff and blew on it, scattering the beams, the furniture, and the slate tiles from the roof. Small fires smolder among the wreckage, a few taking light.

A wet gurgling sound reaches me, and the horror of realizing someone survived all this rises in my throat.

"Silas?" I spin in place, looking for the source of the sound. To my right. I stumble my way through the debris field, tiptoeing and wedging my feet onto the small patches of earth so I don't trip. My breath catches on my courage when I see a patch of blood-streaked white hair. I move some boards and make some room for my footing, and sure enough, it's Pritchard. He's alive, but barely.

How he didn't die is a… I won't say it's a miracle. Rather, it's a mystery. His chest must be crushed flat underneath this wood beam. It's as thick around as me. There's no way I'm strong enough to move it. Besides, there's so little room between it and the ground, that he won't be alive for long.

His neck strains and his chin wobbles like he's going to vomit, but blood comes out. Thick. Red.

The earth around him is staining red, blood mixing with the soil, seeping around the rubble and soaking into the debris. Paper and wood and pieces of Pritchard's miserable existence all ground up so fine they're ash.

He turns his panicked eyes to me, and he knows. He knows who I am. He knows I've been here.

I could tell him that it's not my fault, that I didn't cause this explosion and wouldn't have wanted it. I could tell him that he'll be fine, that men are on their way to help. That the doctor will fix him up. But I don't want to lie to him because he doesn't deserve the comfort.

He sputters and spits. Blood sprays from between his teeth.

"It's such a shame," I say. "I have morphine, but it's not with me."

Would I give it to him if it were? He denied it to my father.

His eyes are wide or wild. Not like Father's, where when he clawed at the life being dragged from his body. Pritchard is pleading, and I haven't anything to give.

"I hope I'd be the kind of person who would show even my worst enemy whatever mercy they ask for. I'm not that nice, I suppose, because I'm just glad the morphine's not with me so I don't have to decide whether or not it would be wasted on you."

I stare at him for a time. No more than a minute, I guess. Seems a lot longer than that, the way time does when it stretches out because you know what you're seeing means something and you're trying to untangle it from the rest of the moments and hold onto it. My arms tingle and my head is fuzzy so I know I'm in shock, and the whole scene is the most gruesome thing I've laid eyes on since that time Father shot a deer when I was a child. But I can't stop looking because later, when I have a chance to sit with Pritchard's death in silence, this might mean something to me.

The strain drops from his face. From his neck. The blood doesn't gush with his pulse anymore. It trickles like the flow of a drought-stricken creek taking with it the chance for justice I'd been fighting for all along.

The world seems to rise up again with the shout of men's voices at the side of the house. The smell of this place is horrid, burnt and sour like nothing I've ever experienced before, and it makes me heave, but my stomach is empty so it's all for naught. I fumble my way in that direction in time to see them lift Silas's body. A man at his shoulders, two men at his feet. His arms flop in an unnatural way, almost as if he were an over-stuffed rag doll.

I round the house and make it mere steps into the street when I see Carlin. What's left of him, anyway. He's no longer whole, and most of him is covered by wood boards and chunks of plaster and lathe. His face is turned away, and I don't need to walk around him to see his eyes because I'll be haunted forever knowing he caused this. He did this to himself. He should have been in the mine. He had no business being here. The note came from him, I know it now, and I didn't listen. I didn't figure it out and try to stop him.

Little shouts go up and men gather to collect the pieces of their friends and fellow workers, their neighbors and families. I ought to feel something, but I don't. Maybe I'm too full of ash, and it's soaked up all the tears.

The doctor has arrived, high-stepping through the debris. There's a futility in the way he pauses and rakes the back of his hand across his forehead. Like trying to plug a break in a dam with a cotton ball.

"Blasting powder is the only thing that would do this." Edna appears at my elbow.

"And one very aggrieved man." I look down at Carlin. At half of Carlin.

Behind us, little boulders tumble and skitter from the office building, from the wall where I was just standing. I know I'm lucky to get out of there alive, but I can't feel it. I should be furious, but I can't feel that either. All I can feel right now is the gaping hole of loss in my chest that's shaped like a doctor's bag full of the proof I came so far to find. It's all gone now. And what good would it do anyway? Pritchard is gone. Silas is gone. And any chance we had to grasp justice lies in splinters at my feet.

CHAPTER NINETEEN

JULY 27, 1901

I can't leave Carlin alone. Weylan is out there somewhere, but God knows where. It feels like the world has been shaken inside a jar, and everything is scattered in a million directions, blasted into tiny pieces and tossed about like stars in a night sky. I need to get to him just as much as I need to stand still, but I can't leave Carlin alone. No matter what he did, he endured more than any man should, and I owe it to my father and the people who care about Carlin not to leave him alone. Weylan is out there, though. As soon as I get the attention of two men who bring a make-shift stretcher to carry him away, I walk off empty handed, without the evidence I came to collect.

I move as fast as I can on wobbly knees back in the direction of house number four. Carriages rush in every direction, toward the mines, toward the coal breaker, away from Pritchard's house and the devastation. People run and trudge in every direction, dodging each other. Men with fire buckets and women, wild-eyed with fear, run toward the disaster. They pause to grasp the ash-covered men and women running away from it, begging for information. Was it their son? Their husband? People emerge from the houses, clinging to doorways, peering through the gaping wounds where windows used to be. Shutters dangle from houses. Shattered glass glazes the ground.

I reach a point where I don't have to cover my mouth anymore, but the smell is strong. It churns my stomach and chokes my lungs. Sour smoke with a hint of sulfur. If thoughts were bees I'd have a swarm, and the only thing keeping me calm is knowing that I can't do a thing until I find Weylan.

The day feels like it's been an instant and the length of a war at the same time. Without the aid of the sun, which is obscured by smoke, I have no idea what time it is, but Weylan is probably at the tavern. If I turn left and slip between the houses, I can get to him there, but he may have joined the surge of people heading toward the disaster or gone back to the house.

Suddenly, one voice cuts through the ringing in my ears, and I turn as Weylan emerges between houses.

"You're safe," he says. "Thank God."

He grasps my shoulder. I squeeze his arm. We cling to each other in the middle of the street. He smells like wood and lye soap and tavern. Months seem to go by before he pushes me away, holds me out at arms-length, and I want to tell him everything all at once, but the mere thought of putting all the thoughts together makes me so very tired.

"Did you feel it?" I ask.

"Glasses flew off the shelves. Shattered everywhere. The men went running to find out what mine shaft it was. Did you hear?"

"Hear?" I still can't quite hear. "It wasn't the mine. It was Pritchard's house. Carlin did it. The house exploded. They're all dead. Pritchard. Silas. Carlin."

I remember the note in my pocket, and I put it into his hand. Disjointed as it is, the story tumbles out of me. As much of it as I can gather together, anyway. The note. Carlin. The wall caving in. Glass and rock. How someone said it must be blasting powder. The bodies and parts. My face is wet, and I wipe the dampness away when I finally get the words out about the evidence I found.

"I found proof of blackmail. And Pinkerton is a detective agency. They were hired to create trouble."

He takes my chin and turns my head, dabbing at a speck of blood with his sleeve. He says I have a cut, but it's small. Taking my hands and turning them over, I notice for the first time that they're covered in tiny cuts.

"Come on," he says. "Let's get to the house, and you can tell me again."

He wraps his arm around me, covering my head with his hand, and I realize I'm not crying. It's raining. Heavy drops pelt us, and we rush toward house number four.

"The medicines." I have to raise my voice over the rain. It crackles among the leaves, splats and splatters on the ground. "Morphine. We have to take it to the people who need it."

"Charlie." He sounds exasperated, but compassion threads through it. "It doesn't sound like anyone survived that. We need to clean up our trail and leave this place."

That's the decision made, then. He's right. Silas is gone. Pritchard is gone. There's no telling who would step into the void. If anyone knows who we are and why we're here, we could be in trouble. There was no reason to linger.

He steers me up the stairs and through the front door.

"I need to go back. I must get that bag."

He says nothing. Weylan is in his focused mode, and I appreciate it because my vision is clouded by the memory of Carlin. His head turned. The unnatural angle of it. Weylan leads me up to the bedroom, throws his suitcase on the bed and starts heaving clothes into it without folding a single thing. He tells me to change, and tosses me a skirt, and I find a matching blouse, but the smell is in us now. It might just be a part of me forever.

"I need to get the bag," I say again.

"What bag?" he asks.

"I put evidence in a bag." The muck in my lungs is starting to give way, and I fall into a coughing fit. "We need it." Each word takes effort.

He has me by the shoulders, his head tilted down to look me in the eye. "You just told me the wall caved in. You're not going in there."

I cough and stomp my foot to protest but it feels more like wiping off my shoe.

He huffs and goes back to packing. "How will you explain walking through town with a bag full of documents anyway?"

"Train," I say between lung-clearing hacks. When will we catch one? Should we try? I can't get the words out, but it doesn't matter because Weylan knows just what I mean.

"Shit." He throws a shirt on the pile.

Suddenly, I remember. "There are horses. North of here. They're Pritchard's."

He blinks at me, inflating and deflating as he calculates. "With a suitcase?"

Not an easy ride.

"There is one train," he says, checking his watch, "leaving the station at four. Visitors passing through mentioned it at the tavern. It might be packed with people trying to flee. Is it better to stay until then or try to leave now?"

"If we walk all the way to the stables, and the horses aren't there, we won't make it back in time. Can we make it to the next town?"

"Not on foot. Not in time."

"We wait for the train, then."

We make our way downhill and wait on the station's porch, in a narrow wedge where heavy drops of rain that plunge from the eaves and trees can't reach us. Puffy little birds emerge, shaking off the damp, calling for their mates. The sound of hammers boarding up the houses staccatos off the hillside, and we wait with half a dozen other travelers under the station's eaves as rain pounds the roof and slicks the rails. My clothes are soaked. My hair is soaked. Weylan looks like he dragged himself out of a lake. He holds the suitcase by the handle, and my hands are empty so I twist the ring around and around my finger, because I ought to be holding that bag of documents.

I fight back the lump in my throat again. I can't read Weylan. His eyes are fixed on the rail line, his knuckles white, and he shivers. No, he shakes. Quakes.

"Are you alright?" I ask.

He turns to face me, white as a sheet, his shoulders quivering. "I'm not."

I've never heard him admit to such a thing. He's always been the tough one. The one with a protective layer of bark. But now grief and anger twist and contort him into someone new.

"Carlin did this." He says it one syllable at a time. Like it's too much for his mouth to process. "With blasting powder. People died."

"I know." I kick at rocks that made their way onto the platform, nudging them back into the rain.

"I did this for my mother. And you. And now—" He doesn't say more.

"Let me go back for the evidence. It wasn't that bad. I'm sure I can…" There's no use continuing, because the light has gone out inside Weylan. This is what true hopelessness looks like on a man. Part of me wants to leave him here with our bags, run back to the office and see if I can find that bag, but if I'm delayed I could miss the train. And I can't bear to leave him like this. It's better if I stay. The truth is, that building won't stand for long anyway.

When the train arrives and carries us off, it will all be over. It will all have been for nothing. It won't matter if Leta finds proof that politicians accepted bribes to hide the poison in the water because there's no one to hold to account. All that matters is that Pritchard hired detectives to turn his victims into criminals and murderers, and I'll never know if my father was a target. I will be haunted by the ghosts of that mystery and the sight of Carlin for the rest of my life.

Finally, the golden light of the coming engine glows on the tracks. It's a long train. I've never seen so many cars lined up together. Probably because of the strike, making up for lost time when they don't run. We slip into an empty car, and the train doesn't stay for long. We're barely in our seats when it lunges down the track again.

"Tickets?" I ask Weylan. His hands are on his knees, one finger making a lazy circle around and around. He stares at the floor.

I dig in his bag and find the tickets, passing them to the conductor when he comes around. The man punches them and looks between us, tips his hat, and moves on onto the next car.

Once we settle into our seats, I rub at the pain in my chest. I can't tell if it's from all the grime I breathed in or from all the pain and shock.

He leans his head back and shuts his eyes. A tear finds its way to his temple, and he wipes it with the heel of his hand.

I feel like my brain is full of dust motes, but I ought to say something. "I'm sorry I couldn't save the documents. I should have grabbed the bag, but how would I have explained it? I don't know what I was thinking."

"How many people died, do you reckon?" he asks.

"Pritchard. Silas. Carlin. I saw four or five men replacing a window." A window Carlin probably broke in order to set the blasting powder. And then he lingered to watch his handiwork. "I don't know who else."

"No one at the office building?"

I inhale, but it's shaky. "I think a woman broke her arm. I don't know."

His face twists and a sob curls from his chest. "This is my fault."

"What? No. Carlin did this."

"I could have stopped it, but I didn't. I told Oran about the blasting powder in that building in the woods."

"What building?"

He doesn't seem to hear me. He just makes that little circle on his knee and gazes through the floor. "Oran told Carlin what I said. This is my fault. If I hadn't gone into those woods, and looked in that building, I never would have known. If I'd just cleaned the damn mud off my shoes, Oran wouldn't have asked me about it. Then Oran wouldn't have told Carlin, and this wouldn't have happened. How do I fix this?"

"What building?" I grab his hand, try to stop the circle. He flattens his fingers beneath mine. "Tell me."

The story falls out of him in snipped words and short phrases, and finally I understand. "But this isn't your fault. You didn't force Oran or Carlin to do anything. Carlin chose this. He was intent on doing this long before he met you."

"How do I fix it, Charlie?" His eyes are filled with desperation, his whole body tense with despair of helplessness. "How do I bring those people back? How do I get my mother back?"

It's a plea from the depths of his soul, and I have no idea what to say.

Too many emotions, too many questions, drift through my mind to grab any one and hold onto it. They flit like dust in a stream of sunlight, flickering and fading.

The train doesn't blow its whistle as it pulls through towns in the breaking rain. The car rocks us both into a welcome numbness, a break between worlds at war. Behind us, the trail of destruction is long. Innocent lives have been lost. Justice denied.

Outside the train window, the rain disappears, and in its place, the thick, lush growth of summer paints the land green along the tracks. Yellow bursts of mustard grass dot the field beyond. The sun picks up gold in the fields, throwing its light on the raindrops gathered on the shrubs and wilds along the tracks, sparkling like diamonds.

"Oran."

The name escapes me like an uncaged bird, flitting into the

sunlight. Weylan seizes it, and in an instant I wish I hadn't said it because I can see the panic of the same realization bloom inside of him.

"I never trusted him," he says. "I should have kept my mouth shut."

"He was the Pinkerton mole. He pushed Carlin to do this." Maybe he didn't have to push very hard, but he nudged a broken man past the point of no repair.

CHAPTER TWENTY

JULY 27, 1901

The train pulls into the North East station just before dinner. My stomach doesn't seem to know the time. I should be hungry, because I haven't eaten a thing since the morning, but I'm not. I'm stuck. Suspended. A vegetable trapped in aspic. It seems audacious of the clock for it to continue ticking off the minutes after the world exploded, and I just want to claw the day back, keep time from trudging on while I make sense of what happened, but there's no way to make sense of what Carlin did. There's no way to untangle death and destruction and innocent lives lost from the revenge Carlin needed more than he needed his own life.

Several times I had tried to ask Weylan if he thought there was such a thing as a just war and if he thought justice could truly result from one, but he was far away and deep in his trace. His body swayed with the roll of the train. I'm not sure I'd have liked his answer either way, so I gave him his space. But now the door creaks and grinds when the conductor heaves it open, and the sound of outside comes flooding in. People laughing. Footsteps. Carriage wheels.

I hunch to glance out the window. "The station is full of people."

Pennant banners strung along the eaves flutter in the breeze, and it feels like the Fourth of July. Children crouch by the station door, playing with jacks, and a group of women laugh together, turned upwind as their hair takes flight.

"What happened?" Weylan asks with the dream-heavy voice of a sudden awakening. Suddenly I realize we won't share mornings anymore. I never had a chance to pack up and say a proper goodbye to the make-believe life we've been living.

"Election," I say. "This is for Harrison."

"Right. I forgot."

It seems incongruent. The whole world should be different, changed by the chaos we walked through. But not like this. I'm dizzied by stepping off the train into a sunny world that sways in festive air when I can still smell the smoke on me and I can still see Carlin when I close my eyes.

We collect our things from the conductor and walk together to the place where we must part. Weylan to his home, me to mine. This feels like an ending, and I'm not sure why. It isn't just that our time in town was cut short. There was, yes, a certain joy in playing at the future we hope to have, and the ending of it is bittersweet, but it's more than that. Weylan is different. Walking beside him is like being in the company of a stranger. I don't know what to say.

"Do you want to come over for dinner?" I ask. "I can cook. We can tell the girls everything that happened. Bea will want to fill you in on the newspaper."

"I don't…" His eyes dart between the clouds, to the river beneath the bridge, up the street where the storefronts are kissed by the evening sun. He wears no expression, but he seems three inches shorter, as if life drained out of him. "I don't want to eat dinner."

"That's okay. I'm not hungry either. What will you tell your father?" I ask.

"Trip was good. Got some business done." It comes out so fast, I know he's rehearsed it.

"Do you want to talk about it before you go? We could sit on that rock back by the river."

"No." That comes out fast, too. "I need to get home."

The word *home* lands somewhere deep in my chest, the way it lingers in the air between us. His home isn't my home. After everything we've just been through, I wish it was.

"Oh. I almost forgot." I twist his mother's ring off my finger and hold it out, pinched between my fingers.

"I need some time." He takes the ring and slips it in his pocket. He wears no expression, and his eyes aren't focused, but if they were, he'd be concentrating on a spot of the hard-packed dirt road about six feet behind me.

It knocks the wind out of me. "What do you mean? From the newspaper? From us?"

"From everything. I'm serious, Charlie. All of that was my fault, and I need to figure out what to do."

He starts to turn, and I grab his arm. "There's nothing to do."

His cheeks get splotchy red and his mouth twists in a way that emulates a smile, but he isn't being friendly. He wants the conversation to end, and it does when he walks away.

"It wasn't your fault," I say in his wake. "You couldn't have stopped it. Carlin could have already had all his supplies. You have no idea where he got that powder from."

The words aren't empty. I'm not saying it to make him feel better. It's the truth. Carlin was intent on doing this one way or the other, but Weylan doesn't even seem to hear me. He doesn't even look like the same person. His gait is short and tight. As I watch him go, he straightens his spine and I can see him put on the mask he'll wear for his father. If I'd had any idea that this would happen and that he would blame himself, I never would have stayed in Stoke. He was only there because of me. After we learned of the railroad strike, he could have left with our friends, but I asked him to stay. Emmett taunted him, yes, but I'm the one who begged him to stay because I wanted him there. If anyone deserves to carry any blame, it's me.

When he's out of view, I rush home, praying I won't encounter anyone I know on the way. Luckily, I don't. All of Main Street seems alight with voices floating out open windows and shoppers bustling in and out of the stores. At the apartment, everyone is in the kitchen. They jump when I enter, asking a hundred questions. Bea trails behind me to our room where I toss my bag on the bed and start to make piles of my clothes, but nothing is clean. Everything smells awful.

"There was a fire," I understate the story when she wrinkles her nose at the smell. "I'll have to clean the bag, too."

"I can't believe you stayed alone in a house with Weylan." She says it as if I joined a kitten killing cult.

"Nothing happened, Bea." There's no sense leaving these foul clothes on my bed, so I gather them in my arms. The whole room will smell. "I'll tell you everything you want to know when I'm done washing this."

"That must have thrown him for quite the loop," she says. "The way he's suffered for wanting to start a life with you."

"He's a changed man, Bea." In more ways than one.

Over the course of dinner, I tell them everything, starting with Silas stumbling out of the woods behind Sophie's house all the way to Weylan walking away with his mother's ring in his pocket. I leave out the part about Weylan blaming himself, though. The demon that plagues him may not be real, but it's still his to contend with. After a bath and a good meal, he'll see that it isn't his fault. Nothing he could have done differently would have prevented what happened.

"You didn't get the evidence?" Ruthie asks. Turkey dangles from her fork, poised in the air.

"It's all gone," I say, peeling dark meat off a leg with my fingers. "It's over. All of it."

* * *

The next day, it truly feels like it's all over. I get some of my frustration out by finishing my laundry. Yanking my clothes off the line and having the sun on my face wakes me up a bit. It's a Sunday and the girls scatter, running off to church and lunch with their families, leaving me alone to iron and sit by the open window. To write down everything I remember from Stoke, preserving my memories before they cloud.

Afternoon sun bakes the street, and I slog through it on my way to Weylan's. No one answers the door when I knock.

He doesn't show up at the newspaper on Monday morning either. Bea seems skeptical when I tell them Weylan needed time to deal with things he missed since we've been gone.

"He was gone for weeks," Bea says. "The newspaper is his biggest priority. What could he have to do that isn't accounting?"

203

"It hasn't been weeks. It's a week and a few days." Ruthie corrects her without looking up from her pencil sketch. "That's worse, frankly."

Hazel leans against the counter. "You'd think he'd be chomping at the bit to get back here."

I couldn't argue with them any more than I could explain his absence. He should be here, but he always gets quiet and keeps to himself when he has a lot to think about.

"He has a lot on his mind. I'm sure he'll be in later." My desk feels foreign, like it shrank while I was gone. I tug open the drawer to pull out a pencil. The drawer reminds me of the filing cabinets in Stoke, though, and a grief for something I never had that I can't quite quantify coils in my chest.

"You know, I bet he's doing what I did," I say. "Writing everything he remembers."

Bea sits on her desk and shoves her pencil in her loose bun. "Well, let me tell you what Mother's been up to."

I lean forward and try to listen as they lob stories at me, cannonballs that bounce off my stern. The suffragists are in a state of elation over Harrison's win, plotting their next move to gain even more support in the state for suffrage. They're sending speakers all over and raising funds to subsidize candidates for the state house and senate. The day goes on like that, with all these reasons I should feel hopeful, but my mind is on Weylan as I try to tell myself it's fine that he's not here even though it isn't. So on Tuesday, once it's well past time for Weylan's father to be down at the brickyard, I go to his house and knock on his door again. And his bedroom window. If he's home, he's not answering. After sitting on his porch for a few lost and lonely minutes, I realize there's one person I can confide in without breaking Weylan's confidence, so I cut between houses and cross the train tracks and make my way to the brickyard. It isn't Weylan's father I'm after, but Emmett.

"No, it's fine that you've been back for days but haven't come to tell me anything," he says when we round one of the outbuildings for some privacy.

"Sorry." I wince. "I had to get all my memories down on paper before they got mixed up. It was traumatizing. There's a lot I need to tell you about, but I have to find Weylan. Have you seen him?"

"No." Em steps back. His hands are covered in an orangish sand. "Why haven't you seen him? What do you mean, it was traumatizing?"

"The abridged version? Something bad happened and Weylan is blaming himself for it, and he said he needed some time to himself, but it's been days, and—"

He cuts me off. "Leave him alone. Men don't want to talk about that kind of stuff. If he says he wants to be alone, that's what he wants."

"But... Is Weylan's father here?" I ask.

"No. He's in Philadelphia. I have to get back to work." He looks over his shoulder as if proof of his claim is after him. "Look, you got back days ago and haven't had a spare second to tell me what happened?"

"I promise, you don't have time to hear about it right now. I'll come to your place after work and tell you everything." If he comes to ours, I'll have to leave things out.

He says *fine*, but it's not. I'm not leaving Weylan alone. With nothing to lose, I knock on his door again, and of course there's no answer, so I head for the train station to see Vernon. He's sorting mail at the post office window but hasn't seen Weylan since we got back.

"This isn't like him, though," I say. "To disappear for days."

Vernon's chin puckers and he shrugs. "Who knows. He's probably got a lot to do. He's not big on relaying information people need to know sometimes. He might have gone somewhere and forgot to tell you."

Max agrees with Vernon, when I run into him by the bridge. "You know how he is. He gets a wild hair to look into something, and he runs off for a while. Probably came up with some wild idea at three in the morning and took a train somewhere to investigate."

"But Vernon hasn't seen him," I say.

"He works inside. He doesn't see every train."

That much is true, and I admit it.

I head back to the newspaper office, taking the long way down Main Street. Their complete lack of concern doesn't make me feel any better. They don't know what happened in Stoke. They didn't see the daze he was in or how low he'd been brought by guilt. It feels wrong that he's not answering the door, and perhaps they're right and he did come up with some idea and ran off to investigate. It's true that he does like time to himself when he has a lot to think about, so maybe I do need to let him come to me.

Enough occupies my mind to fill the walk to work. Justice is gone. That path is overgrown and weedy now. We'll never be able to see it come to fruition.

Mannix's house comes into view. The last time I saw him, he was furious with me. If he knew the truth of all we'd just done, he would scream, but I have to see if Weylan's been there, so I take a chance and knock. And I wait.

"Why are you knocking on the door?" he asks when he opens it shoulder-wide. "You always tap on the window."

"I don't know. Because you were mad at me, I guess. I have a question. It won't take long. Have you seen Weylan?"

He blinks at me as if I've asked the price of pie in Spain.

"You're busy," I say. "I don't mean to bother you."

I take a step back and turn to leave, but he clears his throat and I actually hear him removing his glasses to clean them. "I'm not that busy. Come in. I owe you an apology anyway."

"You don't," I say, but I follow him inside and around the corner into his office. Sunlight splashes over the books on his desk, and I'm reminded of that lawyer in Washington D.C. and how full of hope we were back then.

"Where did you last see Weylan?" Mannix asks, as if he's a glass of lemonade I mislaid.

"More like when. It was days ago. We went to Stoke." I look down at my hands. "I know it was dumb, and you don't want to know about any of it, so I won't burden you with it, but something awful happened there that had nothing to do with—" I cut myself off, but Mannix waves his hand in a circle, urging me on.

"The story won't be complete if you don't tell all of it," he says. "Out with it."

"You'll yell at me and tell me I've done childish things, and I already know all of that." I close my eyes and let the sun paint the inside of my eyelids a luscious pink. Then I stand. "You haven't seen him, so I should go."

"Sit." He points his pencil at the chair.

"If you haven't seen him—"

"You need my help finding him. Charlie, just tell me what

happened."

I shut my eyes. "Weylan knew where there was blasting powder in Stoke, so he told one of my father's old friends about it innocently. But that man used it to blow up Pritchard's house and it killed several people, and Weylan blames himself. It's not his fault. That man was intent on doing it anyway. But Weylan thinks he could have stopped it. And now no one has seen him."

"What did you expect to happen?" He asks coldly. Flat. It's not the reaction I expected at all, and it throws me back down into the chair. "Did you think I would fix it? Make it all better?"

"Well, no. I don't know, really. I don't want anything. I just wondered if Weylan had been here. Because you're the person I always go to when I'm stuck because you're always…" The adult. The one who knows how to handle things. "You take the emotion out of hard things and make them sensible."

"It's up to you to do sensible things, Charlie." He stacks his books and lines up the corners so they make a perfect tower. "I understood how you wanted revenge, how you came to seek justice for what happened to your family and your home, but going to Stoke and learning where blasting powder is located is incredibly irresponsible considering what happened last year. People just don't stumble into risky situations like you do."

"Leta does," I squeak.

"But these are different extremes." He counts on his fingers. "You yelled at Whitaker in the street. You got into a fight with Pine and someone stabbed you. You fought with Finn. You got embroiled with Pritchard. Again."

"None of that was my fault," I say. Though it was. "Okay, it was. But I have explanations. I ran into Whitaker on a bad day. Pine picked a fight with me. He shoved me and his friends taunted me at that dance. Finn was abusive to Emmett. And I had all the evidence in my hands that Pritchard was blackmailing people and hired a detective to embed himself with the miners and force them to do violent things just so he could make an example of them, so it isn't like I'm wrong. It wasn't evidence of the poison, but it was just as bad, and now all that evidence is gone. My intentions were good."

"Then where is Weylan?" he asks far more calmly than I am. "And what do you have to show for all that effort?"

"I have nothing to show for it, but that's not my fault, and I don't know where Weylan is, but I need to find him. I know I made some dumb mistakes, but we did what you asked. We looked for evidence. All those victims in Leta's papers deserve justice, and there's none left. The scientist is dead. No one knows where his work ended up. All our chances are gone, and Weylan blames himself. He just wanted justice. He lost his mother, and he wanted someone to pay for that. I need to find him, and that's all that matters."

"Do you think he's in danger?"

"I don't think so. Everyone in Stoke who was a danger to our effort is gone now, unfortunately."

"There are no quick fixes. Likewise, there are no quick ends. You may think it's over because Pritchard is deceased, but the efforts he put in motion don't stop that easily."

He sighs deeply, and I'm pretty sure it came from his toes the way he curls over his desk. His fingers land on his books and he tilts his head to look at the spines. I'm reminded of that Washington lawyer and how he went right to his wall of identical books in search of something relevant and somehow managed to pluck just the right one. I yearned for that kind of magic, for my brain to be full of all those solutions, but Mannix isn't as confident as that Washington lawyer was. The way he strokes the stack of books, it's almost like he wishes a genie would emerge and make this all go away. We might be at odds, but we're even on that count.

"I understand how you got into this situation, Charlie," he says. "You've seen the personification of justice? Lady justice wears a blindfold so she remains unbiased as she weighs the case in front of her. But that same blindfold prevents her from seeing other things too. Like the pain in her periphery, other courses of justice, human ache. You may not want revenge anymore, but your search for justice may have made you blind to other things. I have not seen Weylan, but if I do, I will let him know you're looking for him."

In a sudden movement, he scatters his stack of books one at a time, flipping them open to marked pages. He flails his glasses until the arms unfold and he winces them back into place on his nose. He doesn't usher me out of his office, and he doesn't need to. I already know I'm on my own.

CHAPTER TWENTY-ONE

JULY 31, 1901

Charlie has knocked on my door eight times since we got home, and if I answer, I'll just end up telling her the whole truth. That's the last thing she needs from me.

The leaves from that tree scrape my bedroom window every time the breeze blows, and I count the casualties over and over. Three or four men replacing a window. Carlin. Silas. And Pritchard. All dead. Plus, the woman broke her arm, Charlie said. God knows how many other people broke bones, needed surgery that will leave them worse than if they never had it. Fighting infections. All the medicine reserved for people richer than them. All because of me. All because I gave too much information to Oran, who wasn't who he let on to be at all.

It isn't just letting slip about that blasting powder that comes back to me over and over. It's bending down to rub at the mud on my hem. Choosing to distract them with the truth of what I'd seen so they wouldn't make up bigger lies in their head. And worst, I keep seeing the way Oran looked over at the Coal and Iron Police before Carlin came in and sat down beside him that last afternoon before the explosion. There was a knowing between them. A familiarity that no other miner had shown to those men. It lasted half a second, but it was there, and if I'd been looking the other way, I would have missed it.

The thin line of his lips. One half curled in a smile. Shooting a glance over his shoulder as they passed. And the slightest nod from that short officer. It was so quick, and it sent a jolt straight down my spine. Then when Carlin and Oran slithered off their stools and scuffed out the door, I waited until those four policemen were three sheets in the wind and offered them a round on the house.

You know, for keeping the place safe.

I asked them if they knew that Oran fellow because, I'd said, he seemed like he'd had a bit too much to drink. And they said they had him under control because he was one of theirs. A Pinkerton detective. And I asked what the heck a Pinkerton detective was, and that's when the clock started ticking down.

I may never know why people divulge their secrets to me. Usually, it's a good thing. But right at that moment, I'd wished no one ever spoke to me at all. I can still hear the clink of the empty glasses as I stacked them together and set them on the next table.

"What's a Pinkerton detective?" I'd asked.

That shorter officer set down his drink and ran his wrist under his nose and said Oran was as good as a spy. And the man across from him said he was better than that because he put ideas in those miner's heads. Then the short one laughed. Cackled like a bird. He said at least something was going into their heads. They all laughed with him, and I tried to match their enthusiasm by just more than half so I didn't look as offended as I was. Then, as the crescendo faded, one of them—I can't remember which—said there would be a revolt soon and then a hanging.

"Make an example out of them," I'd said.

Then Oran would be paid what he was worth for riling them up and having them hanged. And I'd wondered in that moment what the price tag would be for something like that, especially from a man who didn't like to pay his vendors. But that would be a question too far, so I carried the empty glasses away, and just after that, I made my biggest mistake.

If I were thinking the way Charlotte needed me to, I'd have kept my focus on Oran and this Pinkerton situation and told her everything that night, and she would have lined it up with what she learned. Instead, I started thinking like a newspaperman. I wondered what Pritchard intended to do after hanging a group of indignant workers. What was his endgame in this chess match? He could already buy the railroad at a reduced price because he'd destroyed their customer base and competition. That wasn't it. Maybe he intended to intimidate the workers who might form a benevolent society and angle for better pay. There were plenty of signs he was doing just that. Maybe he was trying to send a signal to his opposition downstream. People like Leta and all those mayors. And us.

If I hadn't focused on that for so long while I washed those glasses, letting all those distractions get their claws in me, I would have told Charlie about Oran being a mole. I would have seen that Carlin was a lit fuse. But I missed it because I was looking at the wrong thing.

Carlin didn't know about that blasting powder until Oran told him. That's when Carlin's whole demeanor changed. He wasn't shifty. He didn't look over his shoulder. He wasn't jittery or self-conscious. He took his hat off at the bar. His foot didn't bounce. His voice was low and easy. Oran knew just what he was doing when he told Carlin about that blasting powder, and some little part of him must still be human because he tried to warn Charlie. He told her this place was a powder keg and that the workers had plans. He tried to warn her. And we would have put the pieces together, and I could have stopped Carlin, if I'd been thinking about Oran instead of what Pritchard wanted in the end.

Out in the sitting room, my father's footsteps creak. The front door opens and milk bottles clank together. He comes back down the hall and stops outside my door. His shadow makes two dark dashes in the ribbon of sunlight, and I resent that he returned last night from whatever business he attended to. My ears train on all his sounds, and his puttering splits me in two, trying to drag half of me into the day and out of this room where at least I know the walls can hold me.

"Are you feeling better? Do you need anything?" Father's voice echoes in the narrow hall. "There's milk in the kitchen."

I clear the fog from my throat. "I'm fine. Starting to feel better. Getting up in a bit."

"Leave a list on the counter if you want me to collect something from the market for you."

The front door opens and closes again, and my father has left for work. I can't get away with claiming I have a stomach bug for much longer, so I take a bath with hands that don't feel like they belong to me, towel dry my hair, and I put on a suit. If I try to look like myself

I might feel like it too? It doesn't work.

The front porch is bright. Too bright for my eyes. I sit for a second on that old dining room chair and I wait for them to adjust.

Mannix's office is only a few steps away, right where Main Street starts, and I find myself standing at his front door, knocking on it with the same sort of disoriented out-of-bodiness that carried me here.

Mannix looks shocked when he opens the door, eyes wide and wild, chin tucked in. "Charlotte's looking for you."

"I know. Can I come in?"

He holds the door open and waves me to his sitting room, which is strange because I've never seen this half of his house before. The walls are papered in dark green with blue flowers everywhere. The furniture is a light-colored wood. There's a table under the window with a pink lamp, and half a dozen books. I feel like I've fallen out of the sky into a foreign country. I start to ask if we can go to his office because I'm comfortable there, but it doesn't matter.

Mannix sits on a red upholstered chair, and I take the one opposite.

"Charlotte has been here," he says. "She told me a bit of what happened, but I'd like to hear your version of things."

He sounds more like a parent than a lawyer, and I can understand why he'd be frustrated with us. We're pretty stupid, Charlie and me.

"There's blood on my hands." That's all I can say because my mouth goes dry and my throat closes. Panic rises in me again, like it has the last few nights. The feeling of needing to claw the air, something huge and hungry chasing me, and I can feel its hot breath on my neck, and I'm trying to catch up to something that's slipping away. I'm grasping for something just out of reach. A lever or a wheel that I can pull or spin to make it stop, but the *what* is just as impossible to define as the darkness that swells up out of the ground, swallowing me whole.

Now that I've said it out loud, I know why I'm here.

"I can't see Charlie anymore. I don't want her to see me ever again. I caused it. Then I could have stopped it, and I didn't. I threw away my own chance to get justice. I ruined all Leta's hard work. Charlie wanted justice more than anything, and I took it away from her. From all those people who suffered. When they realize it, they won't want me around. People died, and I can't live with myself. I need to turn myself in."

Mannix chokes and coughs. Grasps the arms of his chair and raises his rear a few inches, sitting down again with his knees pointed to the door. "To who? Have you been charged with a crime?"

"No, but I should be. Innocent lives were lost. I helped cause it, and I could have stopped it, but I didn't. The Coal and Iron Police will look for any accomplice of Carlin's they can find to get justice for what happened to Pritchard. They had a man on the inside. His name is Oran Walsh, if that's even his real name. I'm the one who told him where the blasting powder was. There aren't many people there who know our true identities, but we have no idea how loyal those people will be, and waiting around for Pritchard's private police force to come looking for us is misery. What will they do to Charlie?"

Mannix is thoughtful. With his elbows on his knees and his fingers laced, I know he's trying to reason with me, but I don't want to keep explaining this. I need to get out of here.

"Those things don't sound like crimes, Weylan."

"It doesn't matter. They were going to force men to commit

crimes just so they could hang them. They aren't going to play nice with us."

"I'll help you figure out what to do." He glances around the room, his eyes snagging on books. He chews a lip and shakes his head and goes on to the next. "Every man needs to run away from himself at least once. That's what my mother used to say."

"Running away sounds like a good idea. For years. Forever."

Mannix rises slowly and goes to a shelf on the far wall. Among the brass and pewter candlesticks is a small, lacquered box with painted flowers on top, and he lifts the lid and extracts a key, closing his fingers around it.

"If you're serious," he says, turning to me, "I have a place you can go for a while. A lighthouse."

"A lighthouse? I was thinking Scotland."

He doesn't hear me. "It's been in my family for some time, and the caretaker left. It's empty right now which is dangerous for ships."

"I don't know the first thing about running a lighthouse."

Mannix tucks the key into his vest pocket and smooths the plaid fabric over his belly. "It's not that it's difficult. It's a lifestyle. You're smart. You can learn."

"You won't tell Charlie where I am?"

He sighs. Looks out the window. "It's cruel. She loves you. You can't avoid her."

"She will resent me, Mannix. She won't at first, but she will eventually, and it will tear both of us apart, and I can't take any more. She deserves to be happy."

Mannix rolls his neck and waves his hand as if thinks this is a short-lived thing. That I'll forget it. Get over it. No one gets over being a murderer by way of negligence.

"For now," he says. "I agree for now."

I stand. "Then I'll go."

We arrange to meet at four in the morning, before the sun comes up. Mannix says there's no way to communicate from out there. No postal service. No telegram. I do as he suggests and spend the day making arrangements, writing notes, packing my things. My clothes are rolled so tight the case barely shuts. With no idea what one ought to wear while operating a lighthouse, I choose outdoor things. For mucking a stall. Feeding chickens. Being outside in the rain.

My father is gone again, down at the tavern to celebrate Harrison's win with some friends and talk through what happens next, so I take the note I wrote for Bea and step into the darkness.

I rile up a few dogs as I take the long way to the newspaper office, and I can't help remembering leading Charlotte this way the first time I took her to see the press. I reach the point where she'd slipped in some mud, and she took my hand, and my heart aches for the people we used to be. For how easy things were then. I could tell she didn't want to touch me when I offered to help her steady herself. I thought I repulsed her. Never dreamed she'd fall in love with me.

I shake my head and crack my knuckles to rid myself of the memory, but it comes back with a vengeance when I step in the back door of the newspaper office.

It's only been two weeks since I was last here, but it feels like a lifetime. Like a different man last grasped the doorknob to my office. Inside, it's the same. I don't need a light because the moon shines through the windows well enough. Bea has used the desk, but it's tidy. I glance at the ledger and see Emmett's handiwork. They've done calculations every other day, and placed an order for ink.

The press room feels like a scene frozen in time. Like an old photograph of the moment I brought Charlie here and asked her to run it with me. Moonlight lands on the sharp edges of the press, the way I saw it the first time I brought her here. The way the lantern light made it seem to dance until I put the globe on the lantern and lowered the wick. I wanted to impress her so badly. For her to trust me. The newspaper was never her passion, not as much as the truth was, the way she could use it to hold people to account. But that's what the newspaper needs. Someone who cares about the truth. Between her and Bea, this place will survive.

Winding through the desks, I can make out the ghosts of the daytime. Hazel had dragged her chair to sit across from Bea and left it here. Ruthie painted something and laid her brushes out to dry.

I push all the chairs back under the desks, leave the note I wrote to Bea on her chair, and I slip out the way I came.

I barely sleep, so I have no trouble joining Mannix at his barn before dawn. I expect to climb into his little Duryea, but he has two horses and a mule he declares to be too stubborn for the trip but essential. We ride the back way through town and follow the road down the peninsula. The land narrows as we thread through the woods. Clusters of houses fill the air with patches of smoke and the scent of burning wood. At times, sunlight gleams off water to our east and west, blinding in its intensity.

Eventually, the land flattens out. The trees give way to grasses. The road becomes a path, and the path narrows before it curves to the right. It's only been an hour, perhaps, since we left town, but as the field gives way to open sky, sweeping land that opens to a cliff over the bay, and a beautiful cottage attached to a lighthouse, I can't help but think it might as well be Scotland. Mannix lets out a string of apologies. It's dusty. Closed up for a while. Not very modern. I tell him it's beautiful because it is. When he says it's isolated and doesn't feel welcoming, I tell him that's what's beautiful about it. To me, it's freedom.

There's a small barn and a chicken pen, and a finger of land that juts out over the bay. This is the place where the rivers connect, the North East River from the west and the Elk River from the east. I'm at the top of the bay, and I can't believe I've never seen this view before.

The house is two stories and white with a porch and black shutters. It's been shut up for a while, so it smells damp and hot, but with some airing out, it'll be comfortable. There's furniture. Some chairs and a settee with one large curved arm sits against the wall, covered in pink upholstery. The kitchen has everything I need.

Mannix shows me how to clean the lenses and wind the clocks, how to trim wicks and use the fog signals. Weather readings are done on a schedule and recorded in a log book. All of these things look easy to me and Mannix has no reservations about my ability to get them done. I make plenty of notes because I'm fairly certain people will die—more people could die—if I don't get this right. He promises to deliver fuel along with some chickens and various supplies and, just as the sun reaches the top of the sky and the shadows pull back into tiny puddles, he apologizes for needing to take both horses, but he leaves the mule and returns to town, leaving me alone with myself.

It's not the ending I thought I'd have. There's no Charlie. No justice. No light shining on the truth. It's just me and this cliff and light reflecting outward to boats so they don't lose on their way. Like I lost mine.

I'd wanted to find whatever tainted the water and killed my

mother so I could make it stop, and I got what I wanted, and I learned the truth. But now that I have the thing I yearned for, I realize it was never going to be enough because justice is impossible. There's no way to get back a life once its lost, to glue the past back to the present and make it whole again. And the consequence of all that trying hurt those people in Stoke. They'll never be whole again either. I couldn't blame them for wanting justice of their own, and if the police are looking for me, I deserve whatever punishment they think I should face.

I walk out to the edge of the cliff and look down at the rocks and the water. It's one hell of a drop. The breeze that washes over me is a hot one. Damp. It smells like rivers and rocks and fish. I step back and head for the house.

I took more lives than the ones I lost by not stopping Carlin, and nothing can ever repair that.

CHAPTER TWENTY-TWO

AUGUST 1, 1901

The sun sears the morning dew off the grass, and the moisture hangs low. It makes for a hot and muggy walk to the newspaper office. Hazel fans herself with an old newspaper, and Ruthie lags behind. Mrs. Weaver, gardening in bare feet and a house dress, hands us over-ripe tomatoes as we pass her fenced yard, and we carry them to work. They're near bursting, their skin smooth and shiny.

Bea holds it up to her nose and takes in a deep breath. "You were in bed when I got home, but I saw Weylan's father last night. He was at Harrison's party."

"I thought he was away," I say. "Did you talk to him?"

"No, he slipped out before I could. I asked Harrison if he knew where he went, and he said he got in late on the train and wanted to get to bed."

"Well, that's good news of a sort," I say as we cross the road. "If Weylan doesn't show up here by nine, I'll go down to the brickyard and force him to let me in to see Weylan."

"I'll walk with you if you want," Bea offers. "Moral support."

I dig the newspaper key from my pocket. Bea gave it back to me after I returned, but it feels like she ought to be the one with it. The newspaper is more hers than mine, in some respects. She cares for the ledger and ordering the supplies. She loves its words and its mission, the people it reaches, the lives it records. It isn't that I fail to share her passion. I do. It's that I've been so distracted and negligent. It almost feels rude of me to step into Weylan's shoes after Bea has done so much.

"I might take you up on that offer." I unlock the door. "I'm afraid of the state he'll be in."

"Someone's been here." Hazel pushes past us and goes to Bea's desk. "I left my chair right here at your desk, Bea. It's been moved."

Ruthie enters last and weaves around us to her own desk, snatching up her yellow paint. "My brushes are moved."

"Charlie?" Bea holds up an envelope. "It's Weylan's handwriting. It was on my chair."

The lettering is unmistakably his. She waves it at me, a little ominous flag, and I snag it. The small, slanted letters are in his handwriting. Without a doubt.

"It's addressed to you," I say as I give it back.

Ruthie rummages beneath her things. "There isn't one for me."

"Me either." Hazel spins and folds her arms. "Your desk is clear, Charlie."

She's right. There's nothing on or under my desk. Nothing on my chair. He wrote to Bea and not to me, and suddenly I realize he's gone.

"Why did he only write to me?" Bea muses.

"And why isn't he here?" The words rasp out of me.

Her eyes are on me as she opens it, and she reads quickly but it still seems like it takes forever. Ruthie tells her to read out loud, and Bea swats her away.

"Come on," Hazel barks.

She shakes it at me. "You read it."

"Out loud, please," cries Ruthie.

"Fine." I unfold the letter. His handwriting hurts my heart.

Bea locks eyes with me, and I wish she could impart all of it with one look so I wouldn't have to feel the words sink into my bones one at a time. She doesn't tell me to take the letter away, to read it in private. Instead, she nods and urges me on, and that's worse somehow. It means Weylan's letter is impersonal. As cold as his eyes were when I last saw him.

"Bea," I read aloud. "Please take care of the newspaper so Charlie is free to do what she needs to do. She will still own the newspaper, but there should be money enough coming in to hire Emmett to keep the books and work with vendors if you encounter any trouble. I have faith that you all can carry on the good work we have done. I am proud of all of you. Thank you for everything. Sincerely, Weylan."

I throw the letter on the desk. What is this task he thinks I need to accomplish?

"It sounds like he's leaving," says Ruthie.

"It sure as hell does." Hazel snags the letter and flips it over, back and forth, like there's hidden meaning in the paper that wraps all the way around.

Bea sits. Hard. "What does this mean?"

"He left," I say. My bones feel it. He's not in town anymore, and I have no idea where he could have gone. Or why. What he hopes to achieve by leaving.

Pacing isn't enough. I'll lose my mind if I don't come up with a plan. "I need a minute alone."

A chorus breaks out of *certainlys* and *of courses*, and I go down the hall to Weylan's office, because it's the only place I can think of to go. I close the door and press my back against it, but Weylan isn't there to greet me this time, to flirt with me and say this is a dream of his. This time, it's my worst nightmare.

CHAPTER TWENTY-THREE

AUGUST 1, 1901

I stand with my back against the door, nausea cranking my stomach into a hard ball. He's gone somewhere and left no note for me. No word about where. How long he'll be gone. I always worried I would lose him, push him away with my inane belief that I couldn't live until I dealt with death, but now he's gone. Truly gone. And it sure did sound like he meant forever. I feared this for so long, a shattering goodbye that would push Weylan into the past along with everything I am and love, making the promise of our future unreachable. This isn't exactly what I feared. It's far worse.

All the things we did together come back to me in flashes. Stealing ink from the five and dime store. Coming here for the first time in the dark of night. The way the lantern light highlighted the reverence in his face when he looked at the press. How he surprised me when he bought this place. When he asked me to marry him, and I said *yes but not yet.*

I was so stupid. I should have said yes. Immediately. Now and forever.

The tears come hot and fast, and I lose my footing. Weylan's desk is cool beneath my fingertips. The chair, not unlike my life, is molded to his shape. It accommodates me when I pull myself up to the desk, squeaking out in greeting or minor protest. I don't know which. I scatter the items on the desktop. There's no note. Not on the chair, not in the drawers, not under or in any of the Baltimore Suns, the Philadelphia Records, or the Saturday Evening Posts that he lovingly hoards. Not in the drawers either.

Nothing stands out except the victim statements collected by the suffragists. It seems like a million years ago Leta brought them here. The act of going through them, learning their curves, these lives interrupted.

Losing our chance at justice is impossibly hard. Knowing I can never prove what killed my parents and could have taken Emmett is only the tip of the spear. I can never hold Pritchard accountable for what he did. There is no way to close the wound in Weylan's heart or anyone else's. I can never help all these others find that same justice.

Every morning, I wake and get one instant of peace before the sword plunges deep into my chest. For days, I've been barely existing, wandering around in a fog, trying to figure out what to do next, because Weylan would emerge eventually with some new resolve and we would get through this. But I cannot bear that we have lost this fight, and I have lost him. I don't know how to make my own peace in a world where it's been denied. Carlin chose to seek his own bloody, eternal revenge, stealing resolution from Weylan. From me. From countless other people. He took innocent lives to achieve that one selfish aim. Now that Pritchard and Silas are gone, the cruelty just gets handed down along with all the other company assets to the next man who comes to power.

But if cruelty passes down, love must too.

We may not have justice anymore, but I still have fight left in me even if Weylan doesn't. And I still have love to spare. I need to use it to find him. Dammit.

The hot tears slide down my cheeks and wipe them with the back of my hand and dry my hand on my hip.

I have been helpless for far too long. Unable to save our parents. Losing our home in Stoke. Coming here. And I've been so hopelessly wrong. Refusing to let Emmett become his own man. Trusting Silas and staying in Stoke. Being so bullish. And now all these victims Leta and the suffragists spoke to on their endless quest for equality told their stories for nothing. They're out there now, clinging to threads of hope, and it's all gone. They're powerless all over again. I will never see the scorched earth of Stoke. I will never witness a new town rising from its ashes. Workers who thought they were coming here for something better only ended up in water that could take their lives, and they will never see the freedom promised to them by the hope of this country.

Wrongly, I'd believed I needed that justice before I could live, but that was a lie I told myself to keep from living. To try to stop the gap from widening between the person I used to be and the person I couldn't picture myself becoming. All that time, I'd been turning into someone new whether I liked it or not. And suddenly I understand Mannix's statue of Lady Justice and that blindfold she wears. I let that fear blind me to anything I didn't want to see. I wore that blindfold of justice so I wouldn't have to see the life that would have made me happy. But not anymore.

I run through all the places Weylan might have gone, but I can't think of anywhere he'd rather be than here at the newspaper. When things are at their worst, he's always here. At this desk.

If I were to make a big pile of all the *whys*, I still wouldn't know what was in his mind. I know what's in his heart though. He's not running toward anything. He's running away. From himself, from the blame he believes he needs to carry.

Suddenly, my heart clenches, and my lungs stop taking in air like that time I fell out of a tree when I was younger and lost my wind.

There are other things to run away from. What if he's running from the law? What if they are after him and he had to flee? It would explain why he only wrote the one note to Bea. Perhaps there wasn't time to say more.

I'd like to think if Weylan's father saw or heard anything, that he'd find me and let me know, but he's gone so often and knows so little that he may not have understood what was happening. I have to talk to him. The wall between Weylan and his father is made up of thousands of bricks of grief, held together with the mortar of silence, and it's time to break it down.

This will take an army.

I push the chair away from the desk, fling open the door, and dash down the hall. I can't do it all on my own anymore.

Bea is seated at her desk, tapping her pencil against a paper. Ruthie is leaning over her shoulder, one hand on her hip. Hazel's face is curled up in thought.

They all turn to face me when I say, "I need help."

"It's about time you asked." Bea holds up a piece of paper. "These are all the people Weylan knows. We can—"

The door to the newspaper office opens, and that shard of light pierces the floor. My heart does gymnastics and sticks the landing in my throat. It seems to take forever for a foot to appear, but it's attached to a skirt. Not Weylan. The hope that he would walk in the door is eclipsed by my cousin Sophie following the ribbon of sun, my aunt on her heels.

"Sophie! Whatever are you doing here?"

They're both out of breath. My aunt appears far less frail than the last time I saw her. She's always been all bones and sinew, but strong as an ox. Two bags dangle at her sides, her shoulders bowed by their weight. She drops them to the floor and fumbles for the seat Hazel pushes beneath her before she lands on the floor. Snagging a newspaper off the edge of a desk, she fans her neck. "This town is quite adorable. You haven't done it justice."

"Thank you, I agree…"

I'm cut short by Sophie's launch across the room to grasp Ruthie's hand. "You must be Bea. It's so nice to meet you, finally. I've heard so much."

"That's me." Bea stands and her chair scrapes the floor. "I've heard so much about *you*."

The girls embrace, and my worlds collide. The earth has shifted, sliding us into one chaotic pile. Greetings and introductions fly about, and I can't get a question in among them all. The terror of their visit is swept aside by Sophie's exuberance, shaking hands with Ruthie, laughing about her mistake. She finally turns to me, and though we saw each other mere weeks ago, she squeezes me as if it's been ages.

It's then, I notice the two suitcases she dropped by the door. Four heavy bags? "What is all this? Are you here to stay?"

She shakes her head. "We can only stay a few hours. We told

father we've gone to Philadelphia. I have no idea what it all is, but a woman named Edna brought it to us and said it's very important."

CHAPTER TWENTY-FOUR

AUGUST 1, 1901

Four heavy bags full of papers. Four. That's at least four times the amount of paper I set aside before the blast, and Edna sent all of it here. Weylan's father will have to wait, because the key to bringing Weylan back is in these papers.

The bag where I squirreled away my findings is scuffed and worn, and ash cakes the folds of the leather, but it's the same bag. I throw it on the counter and it lands with a thud. Sophie heaves another up beside it, and in an instant, all four bags are opened.

The sight of the papers I scavenged from the administrative building makes me dizzy. I never thought I'd see any of this again. All of it smells of smoke, and it's so very disorganized.

"What is all this anyway?" Hazel asks. Bea steps up my right. Sophie on my left.

"Clues. Hints. Proof," I say. "I never even had a chance to read it all. There were people coming and going, and I couldn't stop long enough to read, so I shoved anything that looked useful in this bag.

It was tucked between the wall and the filing cabinet. Then the blast happened, and half a wall caved in, so we decided not to risk going back. Edna must have known somehow. But I only had this one bag."

And it's the smallest of them. I don't know what's in the others.

"Edna scared me half to death when she knocked on the door." My aunt, still seated, fans herself with a newspaper. Her legs are stuck straight out, skirt pulled up to her knees. "I thought something happened to one of the boys."

"Did Edna say anything?" I lick my pointer finger and flip through the pages. Bea will positively die when she sees the check Harrison returned to Pritchard with the note that says *no, thank you.*

"She didn't say much." Sophie tilts her head, watching the pages as they fly. "I opened the door to see a woman with a suitcase, and I thought our house was a strange place to try to catch a train. She asked if I knew how to reach you, and I almost said no. Who knows what kind of madness the new coal people are trying to pull? But she said those papers were really important to you. One look, and I knew they were important, so I said I could. She said it had to be done immediately."

The blackmail files are all here. It's even in the same order I stuffed it in the bag. Another seems to be full of Pritchard's correspondence, in some loose alphabetical order. Harrison's note and returned check are in the middle, among the Hs. It's like finding medicine for a fever. Ice cream on my tongue on a hot summer day. I pull it out and slap it on the counter in front of Bea, who gasps and holds it up to the light.

I spin to face Sophie. "What is happening in Stoke?" The questions start falling out of me. "Who's in charge? What are the police doing? Is there word on who caused the explosion?"

"How do you know about all that?" My aunt drops her newspaper fan to her lap. She's about to chastise me, and I've earned it, but I need answers first.

"It's a very long story," I say. "I'll tell you as I go through all this."

I take in a sharp breath and share a sidelong glance with Hazel, who opens another bag and sticks her head in. She breathes deep and coughs.

"We need to air these out before the whole place reeks of smoke." She extracts a stack of pages like they might explode if she handles them too carelessly.

"There's good news, I suppose." Sophie and I each pick up another bag. She extracts the contents, lifting out stacks of pages and slapping them on the counter. "They're switching to strip mining."

"That's fantastic," I say, "but only marginally better."

"Fewer fires. Not so many collapses." My aunt's words soften on the ends, dropping down with the weight of heavy sorrow.

Sophie tilts her head to glimpse the pages as I flip through them. "The new operator is some man named Hudson. He says they're building new houses soon."

"Making promises he won't keep." My aunt is right, of course. I wonder if my uncle sees it now, if the tide among Pritchard's apologists has shifted at all.

"I've never heard of Hudson," I say. "Who is he?"

"An outsider." She continues. "The whole town is in misery and fury. Funerals on top of each other. I couldn't bear to go. I simply cannot stomach any more rumors and gossip and worrying. Your uncle says word in the mines is that Pritchard hired someone to frame people and make them seem bad so he could justify what he was putting us through. An old friend of your father's was found in the rubble, and they think he did it."

I catch the sarcastic remark before it leaves me. Gossip, indeed, but it's rooted in the truth. I want to say Carlin's name. I want to feel the way it curls off my tongue. I want it to drip with acid as I let it go. The compassion I felt for Carlin having endured more than a man could bear has collided with the betrayal and animosity I feel at having lost the chance at justice. I clamp my jaw shut rather than say something I might regret.

All I can do is focus on the evidence in front of me. I splay my fingers on the counter as the weight of all this paper lands on me. I can use all this evidence to stop the next coal boss from being just as evil as Pritchard. But Weylan comes first, and I need to bring him home now. If I can find the Pinkerton papers in all this mess, I can prove to him that this wasn't his fault.

"Help me go through these and find anything to do with the Pinkerton Detective Agency."

Ruthie asks what I mean. Hazel asks where to start.

"There must be two thousand pieces of paper here," Bea says. My aunt's laugh sounds like a chirp, and she says it's at least three thousand. She carried half all the way from Stoke, and she ought to know.

I empty the last bag onto the counter. "It will take forever to make sense of this. But I have to show Weylan it's not his fault."

"What's not his fault?" asks Sophie.

"I'll tell you everything while we look."

"We're going to need more help." Hazel steps back and takes it all in, hands on her hips.

My aunt rises to her feet, shimmying her skirt until the hem hits the floor. "Let's see what we can do."

Bea pushes away from the counter. "I'll go get Emmett and Vernon."

"Vernon's not at the post office," Hazel says. "He doesn't work on Thursdays."

"He's fishing with Max," Ruthie says.

Bea leans back to peer at the clock. "That's in the opposite direction. It'll take a while."

"Not if we divide and conquer." Ruthie snags her straw hat off her desk. "You get Em and Vernon. I'll get Max."

"We're still going to need more help if we're going to get through this today," I say.

Bea turns to Hazel. "Can you get my mom? She's at the market."

"Of course." Hazel races out the door behind them leaving me and Sophie and my aunt to begin to untangle it all. The jumbles of paper seem impossible to put into any kind of order. Pritchard's letters were mostly contained to one bag, but everything else is madness.

"We can make heads and tails of it all later," I say. "For now, I'm looking for anything with the words Pinkerton, Detective Agency, and the name Oran Walsh."

There's no better way to start than to dive in, so I grab a stack and try to put on blinders against anything that isn't what I'm looking for, but the temptation to read is strong. All the while, I tell the tale of meeting Silas at the outhouse and staying at the other end of town, how I accessed all these papers and did my best to uncover the truth. My aunt and Sophie aren't as shocked as I expect them to be. My aunt, in fact, thinks it was perfectly predictable.

"Just like my brother," she says. "A bull on a mission."

"But how will all this help?" asks Sophie. "Publishing it in the newspaper won't force Hudson to treat the workers any better than Pritchard did."

"There's a lawyer in Washington who took a lawsuit about clean water all the way to the Supreme Court," I say. "He's willing to help us build a case."

Sophie smiles right away, but it takes my aunt a moment longer to come around. With the shake of her head and a hint of disbelief she says, "A real lawyer, huh?"

The door swings open. Hazel hurries in with Leta behind her. Regina slips in with Susan on her heels. A small handful of other suffragists tumble in the door, and they marvel at the size of the room and the antiquated press. The sight of Regina sends a shock through me.

"What do you need us to do?" she asks.

I begin to make an introduction of the aunt who couldn't take us in and the woman who did though she didn't deserve to, but I stop short. We don't owe each other anything anymore.

The women listen as I explain what we're looking for: references to Pinkerton, Detective Agency, Oran Walsh. I tell them how important it is to keep the papers mostly in order.

"I'll never remember that," Leta says.

They prop open the door, roll up their sleeves, and take stacks of pages. I take some paper and one of Ruthie's paint brushes and paint the words we're looking for, then I fasten it to the wall.

"This," I say. "Any time you see those words, set the paper aside."

"What will you do with it when you find it?" Leta asks. She knows Weylan has been in hiding, and she covers her mouth with her hand when I tell he's left us with only a note. Finding Weylan could be harder than finding the papers, but I can't let that slow me down.

Evidence first. Then I'll talk to his father. He's out there somewhere ready to be brought home. I can feel it in my bones.

It isn't much later that Vernon arrives with Max. They leave their fishing poles in the corner and declare themselves free of fish scales without even asking why they've been asked to search through these papers.

Max steps next to me and takes a stack. "I still haven't seen Weylan."

"I know. He left." It's hard to hear the truth in my own voice.

"Does this have something to do with it?"

I nod through a sigh. "Weylan likes facts. He'll come back if I can find him and show this to him."

Emmett flies in covered in brick dust and sand with Bea at his side. "What the everlasting hell?" His eyes land on Sophie and our aunt, and before a word is exchanged, I can see the same shock play out in him that rattled me so deeply. Our two worlds have collided, and it feels like an earthquake. Emmett clamps his mouth shut, but I can see a wild sense of adventure starting to flare in his eyes as he rushes across the concrete floor to greet them.

Behind him, Weylan's father fills the doorway.

"Have you seen him?" I ask.

He nods. "He's at a lighthouse."

"What lighthouse?" I've never seen a lighthouse anywhere near here.

"I have a confession to make." He places a hand on my elbow, and steers me, gently, away from the counter.

"This is making me nervous," I admit. Weylan's father and I speak so infrequently. He's never around, always hopping on a train or rushing from one place to another. "I've never seen you look so serious. Is he alright? Is he injured?"

His eyes soften in an instant. "He's fine. Well, as fine as he can be, considering how disconsolate he is. I want to apologize for not being around more."

"I don't think there's anything you could have done—"

"No, I mean to say that I have been absent on purpose. I cannot sit still in grief. It drives me to motion. I think you understand that." He looks at me, imploring me, begging for my agreement or kinship.

"I do know what you mean. I cannot sit still."

"Weylan is not like us. He shares our need for action, but he can sit still in it. Unlike him, I cannot sit in that house or be in this town for any length of time because it's full of the past. The ghosts. When it isn't the past appearing all around me, it's the future I can never have. I've been gone so much of these last two years, that I didn't realize Weylan needed me."

"Well, to be fair, sir, he rarely needs anyone."

He looks at his shoes. Folds his arm around his middle and steps back. "He said he had a stomach problem. I sent the cook away, so she wouldn't catch it. He said he'd feel better soon, then he left a note. Did he leave you one?"

I glance over at Bea, who flips through papers alongside Sophie and Emmett. "He left a note here, yes." I can't bring myself to admit that he didn't leave one for me. "You saw him? You said he's alright?"

"He is. He didn't want to see me at all, and he wants to see you even less, and that's how I know you'll be the one to bring him back. I need to help you do that. Tell me what you need me to do."

* * *

Weylan's father settles at a desk beside Max and takes a heap of papers from the bag. Vernon explains how they're sorting it all. Voices have always carried in this brick and concrete room, but all the low talking and rustling of papers seems deafening. The girls work at the counter with Emmett, my aunt, and cousin. Vernon and Max have a sizable pile of papers to sort into four smaller piles. And Leta and Sarah, Regina and the two other suffragists have pulled tables together over by the printing press where they make quick work of Pritchard's correspondence.

"How will you get to him?" Bea asks. "The lighthouse is far."

"How far?" I ask, situating myself at the counter and taking a pile of banking records.

"Down the peninsula," Max says. "All the way down."

"Mannix will take you," Weylan's father says. He moves a few pages from his unsorted stack to a pile in the middle.

"I'd go talk to him now," says Emmett. "We saw him on our way up from the train station. He had a cart and some of Otto's horses. He might be heading out."

I can already hear Mannix say how irresponsible it is of me to have all this paperwork, that Edna could easily divulge that we have it, that the whole of the Coal and Iron Police could descend on us all. The line between being a journalist investigating a story and being a victim in search of justice is so blurred it's not even visible anymore. I'm not ready to hear Mannix say it's impossible or too hard. I just want to find the proof that will convince Weylan this isn't his fault and take it to him.

Bea leans down to see past Em. "We can pull all this together. You should go."

Emmett elbows me. "Tell him to come down here. We can use all the help we can get."

"If you're walking back toward the station, we should join you." My aunt places her finished stack at arm's length, against the wall. "It's a long train ride back."

Sophie tugs my sleeve. "Walk with us."

"Go on," says Leta. "Say a proper goodbye and let Mannix know you have all of this evidence. He'll be glad to hear it."

I can put off talking to Mannix, but I don't want to miss seeing my family off safely. There was a time I wouldn't have let this paperwork out of my sight, but everyone has this under control anyway, and one less set of hands for an hour won't change anything. My hands are dry and my fingers are black so I wipe them on a rag and promise to return as soon as possible.

As I walk through town with my aunt and Sophie, I point out places I've come to know well and too well. The school. The road to Regina and Finn's. The bridge where Emmett and I first saw a fish kill. Our goodbye at the station doesn't last long before they're off again, heading north, leaving me on the platform with half a dozen travelers just passing through.

I hesitate at Mannix's back door. I don't want to knock it only to hear the thousand reasons why all the proof in the newspaper office is awful, how it's irresponsible of me to have it, but a small voice in my head says it's worth enduring just for a moment. Just to let him know that justice is within reach after all. In a heartbeat, I straighten my spine and square my shoulders, fill my lungs with some clean air, and I knock.

Mannix looks tired, which throws me off balance. I expected stiff and stern or the cocked-eyebrow exasperation that demands I spit out what I have to say. But if I'm not mistaken, there's a little relief in the motion of his hand as he swings the door wider. Almost as if he expected me. He asks me to come in.

"Sit." He motions the chair on the other side of his desk. The office is warm in the sun. Dust motes flitter in the light. "Weylan has gone to a lighthouse."

"I heard. His father came to see me." I grip the arm of the chair and lean forward, shortening the distance between me and Mannix's words. "When did he go? How did he get there? Will you take me to him?"

"I just returned. That lighthouse has been in my family's purview for years. He's safe for now. He's distraught, but this may be good for him."

"Safe? From what? Is he in trouble? When can I go to him? The police in Stoke—"

He raises both hands, patting the air, calming the space between us, but it's not helping my racing heart at all. "There was no specific threat. Not as I understand it. But the Coal and Iron Police don't operate under the typical rules of law. Pritchard was allowed by the state to hire his own police to enforce his own set of rules. They operate without impunity."

"I know." I can feel my pulse behind my eyes. "You don't have to tell *me* that."

"He was so insistent…"

"There was no threat? What did he say? Tell me everything he said to you. Please. You know he tells his father nothing. He didn't leave a note for me. Is he coming back?"

His tight little shrug and his head shake, which is more like a shiver than anything else, infuriate me. How is it that he has nothing to say?

"Weylan feels responsible for what happened," Mannix says. "He wanted to get away, and I had a place. I don't know when he'll return. From the sound of it, he doesn't intend to. He took the importance of running the lighthouse very seriously."

"So that's it? He's just abandoned the newspaper and left all of us behind."

He tilts his head one way then the other, as if weighing the issue. "That kind of task can be healing for a man. Or a woman. He may return yet."

"Will you take me? Please?"

"Yes, but—" Chin tucked, he looks uncertain. "I should warn you that he preferred to be alone. Weylan is a shell of himself right now. It won't be easy to bring him back here. You can't force him."

"But I have proof he's innocent. Once he sees it, he might change his mind."

Mannix takes a sharp inhale. He sits up straighter. "What do you mean, you have proof?"

Every word I choose with care, knowing any one of them could land on Mannix's bad side. Once he knows the whole of it, I lean in again and wait on the edge of my seat. Everything about this feels enormous and life-altering, most of all for Weylan, and the time it takes Mannix to formulate even a stroke of his chin in response drives me further from sanity.

"Bring the papers to me," he says.

"No. I'm not ready to let them go just yet."

"I can help you go through them."

I shake my head. "They're at the newspaper office. Half the town is helping go through them. You can help if you'd like. Right now, we're looking for the Pinkerton papers, so I can take them to Weylan. It will take some time to make sense of the rest, then I'll deliver them to that lawyer in Washington, but I'm not letting it go until I've read it all. Will you please take me to Weylan?"

Chin in his hand, he looks so tired when he says, "We'll leave very early in the morning. Be here at four."

CHAPTER TWENTY-FIVE

AUGUST 1, 1901

My feet are killing me when I return to the newspaper office. The mood has lightened since I left, and the suffragists seem intent on making Weylan's father laugh. He's a handsome man who hates attention as much as his son does, and it's easy to see where Weylan gets the red splotches on his cheeks.

Ruthie, Bea, and Hazel are only halfway through the banking files. Emmett works with them, rifling through pages next to Bea. Every once in a while, he pauses, squints, extracts a sheet and sets it aside. Vernon is seated at Ruthie's desk with a stack two fingers thick doing the same thing. Max is at my desk, reading a page like it's homework, tapping his foot, chewing on a pencil.

Meanwhile, Leta, Regina, and the others have emptied the entire bag of Pritchard's correspondence and sorted it into five tidy stacks.

"Found another Pinkerton reference." Regina passes a page to Leta.

"Excellent work, ladies." Leta hands it to Sarah who slips it into the bundle, declaring them in order by date. "I do have to run and get dinner ready, but we have all your Pinkerton references right here, so you can take these to Weylan when you're ready."

"Really?" The stack of perhaps fifty scraps and sheets of paper contained letters and receipts. I'd been hoping there'd be more.

Sarah holds them out to me. Only weeks have passed since I first saw these papers, yet it feels like five years. It's all here. Pritchard hiring the agency, ordering checks to be sent to them, letters asking them to speed up their work, dig deeper, push harder. I clutch them to my chest.

"Did you read any of it?"

"A little." Regina twists in her chair. "He was an awful man, wasn't he? He talks about ways to push workers into making mistakes so he can punish them. All to increase productivity. Terrible. But we found something you might want to read." She points at the pages I clutch to my chest. "It's not good news. Read the last three pages. I do need to go now, because Finn will have my head on a platter if I don't make my way back soon."

It's a letter. A carbon copy of something Pritchard mailed to the Pinkerton agency. It's almost two-a-half years old. In it, he instructs the agency to pin the murder of a man on Frank Morris.

In the moment it takes me to process whether this means anything to me or not, if it changes anything in my life, I realize it doesn't. It might have if I'd discovered it a year ago or even perhaps last month. But by itself, the letter is meaningless. Pritchard is gone, and I already suspected he'd tried to manipulate my father. His death may have prevented his hanging, but knowing changes nothing.

"I'm very sorry," Regina says as she stands. She pushes her chair under the table and gathers her shawl. "Your father was a good man, and he didn't deserve it."

"It makes me feel better, I think. Vindication." I place the papers back in the stack. "Thank you for everything."

She places a hand on my arm and says she owes me, though she doesn't. Then she slips out the door with the others.

Hazel looks up from the counter, where she's working elbow-to-elbow with Ruthie. They seem to have a system.

"Did you see Mannix?" Hazel asks.

"Yes. I'm going to see Weylan in the morning."

Vernon tilts his head back and says, "I never think about that place. It's the perfect spot to hide out for a while."

"Who owns it?" Max asks. "How did he even find out about it?"

Weylan's father stuck a paper-cut thumb into his mouth and then examined it. "Mannix's family owns the lighthouse. Way the hell out there."

Everyone seems to know where it is except Emmett and me. It's dour. Lonely and isolated, Max says. None of the others have ever been there. But everyone agrees that it's hardly the place you'd send someone if they had a severe bout of the doldrums, let alone someone who bore the weight of innocent lives lost. But no one knows the place is there unless they've seen it by boat, and the house is too far from the water for anyone to see him there, so the arrangement works in Weylan's favor. Even if you did see him from the water, you'd have to scale a cliff face to reach him unless you knew which sandy cove to disembark upon. In some ways it sounds perfect. Quiet. Peaceful. Nowhere near the Coal and Iron Police. If Max does make it sound a bit like *Wuthering Heights*.

I take a stack of papers to Hazel's desk and wiggle my toes in my boots. Lord, my feet are killing me.

"Good luck to Weylan," Max says. "I hope he enjoys chopping firewood."

"Hopefully I can convince him to come home tomorrow." I intend to stay with him until he agrees, no matter how long it takes, but voicing my doubts of a fast victory out loud would only court dissent. There's no way Weylan's father would support us living alone out of wedlock for even a day, and what he doesn't know about Stoke won't hurt him.

Weylan's father stands and stretches, examining his thumb. "I should go too. Dinner plans. Let me know how it goes tomorrow, Charlotte. It seems your long war is almost over."

Sometimes I'd wondered—dreamed even—about the moment I would know it's truly over. Topping the list of my imagined scenarios was a dramatic moment in court where a judge with a deep voice would read a verdict and Pritchard would be hauled away, struggling against his chains, declaring he'd get his revenge on us someday. That would be the moment life would begin, but life doesn't always change in big explosive moments or shattering losses. Sometimes, apparently, it's as simple as paper.

I say as much to Weylan's father when I walk him to the door. "I suspect my father would have felt the same. After all the violence and threats, it's strange that paper is what undoes the villain."

"Weylan is lucky to have you," he says as steps outside and he walks away. "You're well suited."

"How will I get all this to that lawyer in Washington?" I wonder aloud, turning back to Bea and the girls. "I've imposed so much on Mannix, and I have to get to Weylan."

"Give it to Mannix anyway." Bea cocks a shoulder as if it's

obvious, but she doesn't realize just how awkward things have been between Mannix and me. Ruthie and Hazel agree. Everyone does, all at once. It is the obvious solution.

"He did offer." I hate to assume he would go through all this and try to understand how the pieces fit together before sending it away, and if the lighthouse is that remote, it would be impossible for me to reply very quickly if the Washington lawyer needed help putting it all in context.

"I know it's getting close to dinner time, but once we're finished here, I could write down some notes to help connect this evidence to the statements Leta collected."

"This is all fairly organized." Ruthie brushes stray hair from her eye. "For the most part, similar things were already together. Leta went through Pritchard's correspondence. It was mostly in alphabetical order, then by date. This pile is banking, sorted by bank. He had several banks, apparently."

Vernon lays his hand on a towering stack closest to the printing press. "This is all that's left to sort of the railroad files. I haven't skimmed through it, but I'm sorting it by date. When it's done, you could easily match it up to bank records and his letters."

"There are some papers that we couldn't categorize. They're over here," says Max. Luckily, it's not much.

"You might make better sense of it all than we did," says Bea. "And there's not much left. I thought it would take longer when I saw how everything was thrown in the bags, but it must have just shifted in transit. It was pretty organized."

"Leave it to Edna," I say.

I start to say they can all go home, that I can get it from here, but Ruthie simply turns around and continues to dig through the pile of miscellaneous papers. Vernon and Max dive in to help. I step next to Hazel and help with the last of the railroad files.

It's late afternoon when we finally finish, all of our work arranged in five bundles and tied up with string with a small set of pages that don't seem to fit in any of the other categories. As visual representations of accomplishments go, it doesn't seem like much, considering all the effort and time it took, but it's here. It's done. It's the culmination of all my wanting, the reward for all the risk. It's exoneration that secures my father's memory. It's vindication of my mother's suspicion that the water was tainted and we shouldn't play in it. It's undeniable proof that the pain and the loss and the darkness I've lived in are real. But it's also a doorway. The threshold to the future that I thought I couldn't have. Weylan waited so long for this, and now he's not here to enjoy it, so I can't either.

"I'll get Mother's papers off Weylan's desk." Bea walks off, down the hall, her footsteps louder than usual in the quiet. She returns with the witness statements her mother collected with the help of the suffragists, and Hazel offers to type up whatever summary I want to write because she can type as quickly as she can think. Her typewriter is a heavy beast of a machine that she has to bring from a shelf across the room.

"How long do you think you'll be at the lighthouse?" Bea folds her arms and leans back against the counter. It's the same poise she takes after we've set up every issue just before it goes to print, when she asks what we missed and what stories need following up, but this time the work is done.

"Mannix made it sound like it will be hard to convince Weylan. Both Mannix and Weylan's father said he's not himself anymore. He didn't want his father there at all, and I'm the last person he wants to see. I suspect I might be there for a while."

"We should form a plan, just in case." Bea looks a little like her mother when she holds her chin up and glances at Emmett, ready to take charge. I have an affinity for the serious version of Bea. "We could get by for a while without Weylan, but if it's going to be long term, we're going to need help. We need muscle to lift this paper. And there are advertisers who just don't respond to us because we're women. I'm sorry, but it's true."

"Then Emmett can help," I say. "Weylan's father will understand. Just explain what you need to do. Give Emmett my pay while I'm gone. Take my part of rent out of the newspaper money, so you don't have to cover my share."

"I'll always help. You know that." Something passes between Emmett and Bea, some hint of an affection that's more than two casual acquaintances. The intimacy in the meeting of their eyes belies their excitement of working together, and I would comment on it, but Emmett realizes I noticed and his cheeks go red. I'll embarrass him alone, and not in front of his friends.

Max pushes a chair out of the way so Hazel can put the typewriter down. It makes a clacking, clunk sound when it lands on the desk.

"We can go on like we did when you were in Stoke," Hazel says. "I'm ready to type when you are."

"What can we do to help?" Vernon asks.

Ruthie dives into the witness statements. "I have an idea. We can go one by one through the witnesses, and match them up to the evidence. It won't take long."

I leap for the first one. "That's a great idea. We can cite the evidence like it's a research paper."

Vernon laughs. "Thank God someone paid attention in school."

CHAPTER TWENTY-SIX

AUGUST 1, 1901

It's late and dark out when we finally finish. We place three of the heavy bags by the door. On top, Bea places all the witness statements Leta collected. I add the recollections I dictated to Hazel. Then Ruthie adds the summary of allegations we've been able to compile over the last few hours. All this paper makes me feel adult, though I hope the lawyer doesn't laugh when he sees all this. The feeling of having missed something big along with a thousand important tiny details is inescapable, but it's all in one place now, which is a miracle. I never could have done this so fast alone, and I say so.

"It was actually fun." Vernon wipes his hands on a clean rag. We're all ink-stained.

Max agrees and reaches for the rag when Vernon is finished. "It felt like detective work. I bet the bonfire's still going on down at the park, if you all want to go?"

"What bonfire?" asks Ruthie.

Vernon shoves his hands in his pockets. "It's Pine's birthday."

Hazel snorts. "I don't want to go to that."

"He won't be there." Max throws the rag at Emmett, and it hits him in the chest. "He came up with the idea and moved off to wherever with his father when they lost the election. I have some moonshine to take."

"I'm beat," Em says. "But I'm in."

Hazel tugs Ruthie's sleeve. "We're going. Don't argue."

I feel lighter all of a sudden. Weylan is safe. I have enough to prove to him that he didn't cause that explosion. Everything will work out.

"I need to pack for the lighthouse, though." I don't even know for how long.

"Oh, come on, Charlie." Bea nudges my hip with hers. "One fling before you head out."

"I suppose." There's nothing left to pack but the Pinkerton papers, so I throw the old doctor's bag onto the counter and open it wide. It's strange to think that Pritchard once used it to shuffle papers between his house and the offices, and it may have once carried an order that would result in my father's hanging. Now it can deliver absolution to Weylan. When I shoved papers into it back in Stoke, I hadn't noticed the interior pocket. It runs the length of one long side and has a single snap clasp which is undone. Inside is a small book, bound in black leather, that I hadn't noticed before.

"What's that?" Emmett asks.

"Not sure." A slip of folded paper falls out when I open the cover, and I see my name in block letters. Ruthie scoops it up before I do, and she puts it in my hand.

Please deliver to Charlotte Morris, North East Record, Maryland. This book contains the contemporaneous notes of Oran Walsh. Please read the last entry first.

"I can't." I put the book down, throw my elbows on the counter, and press the heels of my hands into my eyes. Nothing less than a confession and explanation can be in Oran's book, and whether it exonerates or implicates Carlin, I'm not ready to read it.

"Can't what? What is it?" Em reaches for the book. "Holy Jesus on a unicycle."

"What?" Bea rushes to his side. Hazel peers over his shoulder. Vernon and Max abandon their inspection of the printing press.

"Is it bad?" Ruthie stands back, hand at her throat.

Emmett holds the book out to me with a question in his eyes. I push it back at him. "You do it."

"Out loud?"

"Yes, please!" exclaims Bea.

The book is small, about five inches high and four inches wide. The pages are unlined, covered in sharp slants and wide loops. Upside down, I can tell that his Fs and Es are curly. Emmett finds the last entry, dated July 28. The day after Weylan and I left Stoke. It feels like a thousand years ago, but it's only been days.

Emmett reads. "Some days ago, I believed Parker, who I now know is Weylan, to be a spy. A man planted by the railroad to infiltrate the coal operation. I wasn't certain, but I informed Nels Pritchard of my assumption and he ordered me to keep an eye on Weylan. Once I had proof of Weylan's attachment to the railroad, I would order the Coal and Iron Police to arrest him. But we needed a reason, so I intended to manipulate him into committing an offense, much like I had done with Carlin. I was, fortunately, unable to complete that mission."

"I knew it," I say, mostly to myself.

Emmett goes on. "I questioned Weylan, asking whether he knew Silas well. Then I asked the same of you at the store. Your elusive answers left me feeling more confident that you were not who you claimed. When I asked Silas about the new young woman who took over for Rhodri, he made a mistake. He said he hired a young couple to work in town. When I told him you introduced yourself as his niece, he was neither confused nor outraged. He appeared annoyed and resigned. He stated that he believed you might actually be Charlotte Morris, daughter of Frank Morris, come to cause trouble."

I pound the side of my fist on the counter. Not that it matters with Silas dead and Stoke irreparably changed, but he sold me out. He could have caused me harm. I shouldn't be surprised. There's a reason I never trusted him.

"Sorry," I say. "Go on."

Emmett takes a breath and reads slowly. "That's when Silas admitted he knew I wasn't a miner. When I said I was surprised that Pritchard would allow you to enter town, Silas grew more furious. He said he'd been watching me because I seemed out of place. He'd investigated me, as I was investigating you, and he'd discovered my employment by the Pinkerton Detective Agency, hired to root out worker coordination against the company. I told him I was pleased to report even more corruption, as I suspected he had brought you in to undermine Pritchard and take control. I never informed Pritchard of Silas's intent, and he died unaware.

"That same day, however, likely to avoid the consequences of his own scheme, Silas informed Pritchard that you were in Stoke. I was at the tavern when a police officer slipped me a note. Pritchard requested my presence. He suggested I harm you. Killing, quite literally, two birds with one stone. But harming a woman was taking things too far, so I tried to warn you without unmasking myself by leaving a note with Edna in a hand you might mistake for Carlin's. Then I tried to steer Carlin to the least harmful course of action."

"Oh my God." Bea grasps my arm. "He was going to kill you."

"Of course he was."

Emmett leers at me, but keeps his *I told you so,* to himself. He taps the book and continues. "Carlin grew suspicious of me around that time. He had accelerated his plan to cause an explosion that would kill Pritchard in the wee hours of the morning on a day when no one else would be harmed. Instead, he lured Silas to the house, to meet with Pritchard. He tried to lure me to the area as well, to meet with him, but I refused. Carlin set off the blasting powder, ending his own misery. I deeply regret informing him of the blasting powder Weylan found, as it sealed those innocent fates."

"There you have it," Max whispers. "That should convince Weylan."

Ruthie pats my shoulder, and I cover her hand with mine. We'll bring him back. I'm sure of it.

"Keep going?" Emmett asks.

"Please," I say.

"As the debris settled on the disaster, I searched for you and Weylan, not knowing what to say. Perhaps I would have told you about Pritchard's threat or told you who I was. Either way, I found you at the station, but with others present, I could not confront you. When I returned to the administration building to assist with helping the injured, I found Edna. Having watched you closely, I knew you were acquainted, and I informed her of my true identity and yours. I don't know why. Desperation, perhaps. Revealing the truth to gain firm footing during uncertainty. My job there was done, after all. To my surprise, Edna reluctantly admitted she knew your secret."

The thought of Edna digging through rubble, helping search for the injured and survivors, broke my heart. "Poor Edna. She was kind to me. She'll be traumatized by this forever."

"I lingered for a few days, hoping to find and obliterate evidence of the work I'd done. Edna found me the next day. She said the company files were destroyed and scattered when the building finally collapsed overnight, but she found, in the rubble, the bag Pritchard moved papers in. It was full of documents she believed you had hidden. While sifting through the rubble, she was able to secure additional files. Fortunately, the cabinets contained the files in the collapse. Edna asked if I would assist in delivering them to you, so she would not be seen with them, but I refused. I did, however, ask to include this letter and my notes. Perhaps your newspaper can put an end to the types of cruelties committed there."

"We will have a good time trying," Ruthie says.

Emmett flicks the paper in the air. "There's more."

"Long winded, isn't he?" mumbles Vernon.

"Thank God for it," I say. "I wish I'd known all this sooner."

"I cannot say this strongly enough," Em reads. "The Coal and Iron Police are coming for you. The workers viewed Carlin's crime as a tragedy but also as a leap forward for the worker movement. The C&IP are still under orders to extinguish the last flames of Frank Morris's legacy. Word has spread among them of Weylan's contact with Carlin and your presence in town. Weylan is in particular danger." He flings the note outward at me. "Do you see now?"

Emmett's last words ripple out around the room. No one says a word, we just glance at each other. Em and me. Bea and Max. Hazel and Ruthie.

"I'll be gone longer than I thought," I say.

Suddenly the room erupts with protests and declarations.

"You can't bring Weylan back here," Bea says, tapping my arm with her elbow.

"No, I don't think I can. They can't prosecute an innocent person, though, can they? The truth is right here in Oran's little book. We even have documents to prove Oran's claims. We have letters and receipts."

"Don't you understand?" Em leans in, fury lighting his eyes. "They don't care. They will come after you and Weylan anyway. They will protect themselves by coming to destroy this evidence. It's only a matter of time before they find out you have it."

I take him by the shoulders. "That's why we have to get it to that lawyer. We're finally steps ahead of them, Em. I'll go to that lighthouse and stay there with Weylan, and we won't come back until the law can protect us."

Vernon pats the twine-bound stack of Pinkerton papers. "There was a copy of a resignation letter from Oran Walsh. It was in the miscellaneous papers, and we put it with the correspondence. That backs up his claim that he quit his work."

"I wonder where he is now?" Ruthie ponders. "We might need him to testify."

"We'll find him." Hazel takes the book from Emmett, flips through the pages, and hands it back. "What do we do with this?"

"Give it all to Mannix, I guess," I say.

"You seem calm." Em loads the papers into the old doctor's bag and tosses Oran's book on top. "That's never good, when you're calm."

"I am calm. Everything that was once confusing now makes perfect sense." After all we've been through, how far we've come, I would have a right to be angry, if I were. Pritchard isn't even here anymore, and he's still tormenting us. But I'm ready to live my life now. "I just want to get to Weylan."

Bea lifts a bag, bending her elbow and raising her arm so it fits behind her shoulder. Hazel lifts another, listing to the side. Max reaches the third bag before I do.

"What about that pile back there," Bea points with her chin.

"Oh, no. It's those random pages that didn't fit anywhere else," I say. "I'll get them."

They're scattered and as I reach to pull them together, my eyes land on a handwritten page. One word jumps out.

Mercury.

I pick it up. Turn it around. Hold it up to the light.

Bea drops the bag. "What is it?"

A man has visited neighboring towns professing to be a scientist, claiming his work has detected Hydrogen Sulfide in the air around Stoke and arsenic and mercury in the water.

My trembling hand shakes the paper, flickering the light behind it.

It has come to our attention that he may have reached out to you.

My skin tingles, my mouth dry. This is the man Weylan saw talking to Whitaker at the train station. It has to be.

We would urge you to contact us at your earliest convenience if he has made such claims, as our extensive studies have proven otherwise, and we are undertaking legal means to silence this slanderous and libelous attack on our profitable and beneficial industry.

Pritchard saved a draft of the handwritten letter he used to coerce mayors into suppressing evidence of his poisoning. The language is so similar to the letter they sent to us here.

Representatives from our company will be visiting your town soon to offer our reassurances and to secure your confidence in our operations.

The list of recipients reads like a map of towns downstream from Stoke.

"Are you alright?" Emmett asks.

"No?" That's the last thing I say before the world goes dark and the floor crashes into me.

* * *

"Are you sure you want to walk all this way?" Bea sticks to my side like glue, walking between me and Emmett.

"I am. I'm fine. I just fainted, that's all."

"Promise me you'll eat something before we go to the bonfire," Bea says.

"Of course." I'm starving, now that she mentions it. We skipped dinner, organizing all those papers. "I'm just hungry, I guess. And I can't believe our luck."

"I can't believe it's almost over," Max says from a few steps behind.

We round the corner to Mannix's back door, our delivery too precious to risk being seen. Habit leads me around the back, I suppose, and I feel bad knocking at this late hour. There's light inside his office, so I feel a little better when he answers, though he's clearly exhausted, and I've intruded on his night.

"I'm sorry to impose." I motion behind me, where my brother and our four friends stand with four bags at their feet. "We sorted all the evidence I told you about earlier, and it seemed like a lot to carry by myself in the morning so—"

"Bring them in." He rips off his glasses and for the first time in a while, he doesn't appear annoyed with me.

I tell him about the summary I wrote and show him the book of Oran's notes. I read to him the warning about the police. We all agree that the Coal and Iron Police have no jurisdiction in Maryland, and it won't be easy for them to reach us here by legal means. It's the illegal means they'll leap to first, so the best course of action is for me to go to the lighthouse, too, and isolate there until the massive gears that run the machine of law begin to turn. Eventually, lady justice will balance her scales, and we can return. As for the bonfire, what Mannix doesn't know won't hurt him.

He glances into the bag, at the contents, like we brought him a casserole and promises to safeguard it all until he can get it to that Washington lawyer. Then he ushers us back out into the night where we stomp down his stairs and walk down the middle of Main Street.

Hazel loops her arm through mine. "I can't believe you're just letting it all go."

"It's time." I shrug. "None of it matters anymore. I've done everything I can do. The only thing that matters now is Weylan."

Gas flickers in street lights and in the upper windows of the shops. The metallic ring of an old piano ruffles the air. Camptown Races. Vernon skips ahead.

"Where do you get all that energy?" Em asks.

"Dunno. It's a nice night. Not too hot. There's a bonfire. We have moonshine and no one to tell us what to do. I'm just in a good mood,

I suppose."

Despite Pritchard and Silas and the explosion, Weylan being gone, the police threat, and the legal battle ahead, and despite the uncertainty of what will be, I know one thing for sure: there's room for joy. For a long time, I thought I couldn't have a drop of it until I finished this fight, but I'd been so very wrong. There's joy on the horizon for me. There's joy for Weylan, and I'm going to help him find it. And from the looks of the way Bea laces her fingers through Emmett's as they walk ahead of me, there's joy for them, too."

CHAPTER TWENTY-SEVEN

AUGUST 2, 1901

I'm up before the sun, eager to get to Weylan, but with a pounding headache. At least I had the foresight to pack my bags before drinking moonshine at a bonfire. Max had guessed the lighthouse is about an hour's ride away by horseback, though he'd never been there himself, and I hope the crisp air will clear my head a bit because it will be a long, miserable ride otherwise.

"Is it time?" Bea whispers.

"Yes." I pull on the skirt I laid out at the foot of my bed. "Don't get up."

"I want to say goodbye again."

"We said goodbye a dozen times last night. You should sleep." I haven't the heart for another long hug.

"Alright," she says, "But only because I don't want to cry again."

"You only cried because you were sloshed."

I can hear her smile in her voice when she agrees and reminds me to take the last of the peaches because they'll just go bad if I don't. I promise to write as soon as I can and beg her to send letters with Mannix when he visits. At the last second, I remember the coal duck I made in Stoke, and the little coal lion. They sit on the windowsill with my netting needle and the old mermaid's purse with its seascape painting. My father had carved the lion as part of the circus menagerie he gave me when I was a child, and though I know it will be here when I return, I'd rather carry it with me instead. One comfort from home won't weigh down my journey.

Just before I slip out the door with my bags, I add the over-ripe peaches to the satchel of treats, and I step outside. The dark overtakes me, wrapping its arms around me, as I walk up Main Street to Mannix's house.

There's something odd about being awake at this hour, just on the wrong side of life. All of it — the doorway-sweeping women and the shop-keeping men, the children playing in the street and the dogs in the windows who bark when we pass — all of it just stopped and wrapped itself in a cloak of darkness. It will wriggle free again when the sun arises. Life will shake off the morning dew, rattle its bones, and make its noise, but for now it's still. I can feel its eyes on me as I walk up the steps to Mannix's back door. The light is on inside.

"Tea?" he asks, a little bleary eyed.

I leave my bags and step inside. "No. Thank you."

He offers me a bite to eat before we leave, and I decline on account of my wobbly stomach. The bonfire is less to blame than the anticipation of seeing Weylan for the first time since we stepped off the train. Though I've kept it at bay, it begins to swallow me as we make our way to the horses tied to a cart at his barn. It's laden with crates.

"I keep thinking about the Coal and Iron Police," I say, watching him load my things onto the cart. "Are you sure we're safe?"

He yanks on a strap and shoves at a box. The contents rattle, but otherwise, it looks secure. Even so, he yanks on the strap some more.

"You're doing the right thing by staying away for now," he says. "No one here will leave a paper trail leading to you. We'll let you know when the coast is clear. I'll come up every week or so and bring correspondence and supplies. The most important thing is to help Weylan. He's not well."

"Do you think it will be hard? I haven't seen him since we got back. You know more than I do about his state of mind."

"Charlotte?" He points to the seat beside him, and I climb up, careful not to trip over the hem of my skirt. The doctor's bag from Stoke is already on the floor, and I wedge it between my feet. "I hope that he is happy to see you, and that he's undergone some drastic transformation in the last few days, but don't get your hopes up for a warm welcome."

Mannix pulls the carriage down the drive, past his house, and he turns left. Main Street is empty but people will flood the streets soon, sweeping their porches, opening their stores. The newsstand, the pharmacy, the little fabric shop. Bea must have gone back to sleep, because our window is still dark. Leta and Mitchell's house is still dark too. I should be glad and relieved that no one sees us go, but I feel like I'm leaving behind all the people I care about, trading them all for an indefinite isolation at the farthest reaches of the earth.

At the end of Main Street, where the road gently curves to the right at the park, the street narrows and aims south, down the peninsula. There's nothing here but wild land and hints of water beyond the trees on either side of us as the peninsula narrows. I've never been this far out of town, and I've never been this alone. I don't have Bea or Leta or Emmett. I'm on my own this time, with the most important task I've ever been set to.

"Is it truly that isolated out there?" I ask as we take a corner. Glass bottles rattle in the back. "Max says it's miles from anything."

"It is. No neighbors. No noise. Just you and your thoughts. It's idyllic, really. If you enjoy the quiet."

There is joy on the horizon. I simply refuse to believe that all of this had been for naught. When Weylan learns that Oran took the blame for what happened, he'll see that it wasn't his fault. That nothing he could have done would have changed Carlin's mind at all. Knowing the truth doesn't bring back the innocent lives that were lost or the anguish that Carlin suffered, but knowing will help Weylan claw his way from beneath the shame he doesn't deserve to carry. Maybe it's the invisible sinew that ties us together, but I know I can reach him.

CHAPTER TWENTY-EIGHT

AUGUST 2, 1901

"What is she doing here?"

Weylan steps off the porch without using the stairs. It's not a big drop, but it's enough to jar the knees, though he takes it in an easy stride. His arms are folded, and blotchy red creeps up from under his beard, a sign of a strong emotion on his part. Though I can't quite define it, I'm starting to have one of my own. I've never seen him with a beard or with his shirt untucked and his pant legs rolled up like this. Dots of mud cake his shins. There's a deadness in his eyes, slowly being lit by his fury, and I have to take a step back and remind myself not to take it personally.

I hadn't expected a warm welcome. His father had warned me. But I also hadn't given a lot of thought to how I'd be received. Mannix had said Weylan wanted to be alone. I guess I thought he'd take one look at me, be overwhelmed by his own ambivalence and be as stoney faced as he was when we parted ways last week. Instead, the closer he gets, the more irate he seems.

"I told you I wanted to be alone. I don't want visitors."

Just as Mannix heaves my bag off the carriage, I squeak out, "I'm not visiting."

"What is that supposed to mean?" he barks back. "You're not staying here."

"We've had some news." Mannix pushes a crate of bottles into Weylan's chest. Twice. Finally, Weylan unfurls his arms and accepts it without giving it a look.

"I don't want news," he said. "I want the opposite of news. What do you mean, you're not visiting. You're here, aren't you?"

I pick up my bag with one hand and the doctor's bag of evidence in the other and say *I'm staying* at the same time Mannix says *she's staying*, and Weylan follows me onto the porch, bottles clanking.

"Do not go in that house." He sets the crate down.

I spin to face him, but he's facing off against Mannix instead. "I'm doing fine on my own. I do not want her here."

Mannix rubs a spot between his brows. "The chickens got out."

"One chicken. The same chicken. All day, every day. That's why I'm a muddy mess. I don't need help with the chicken or the lighthouse, so she can leave." He aims a thumb in my direction.

There's a weathered old chair on the porch with white paint peeling off in shards that will stick to my skirt, but I sit anyway. "I'm not leaving. What happened was not your fault. Oran admitted to everything. He was the Pinkerton detective Pritchard hired to push the workers into committing crimes, and he pushed Carlin too far. I have all the evidence to prove it right here."

He blinks at me as if it means nothing to him at all, and I don't know how he could have forgotten in such a short period of time.

It's only been a week. His face goes soft, his jaw slackens. His eyes focus on some inward place, and all the fury and feeling seems to drain right out of him. He walks past me as if I'm not here, and he goes into the house.

"I told you." Mannix pats my shoulder before returning to the cart for another armful of supplies. "He'll be hard to reach."

The screen door slams behind Weylan, and the creak of the hinge rings in my ears.

"Kitchen is on the left." Mannix heads that way with a basket of vegetables.

The front door opens to a narrow central hallway with stairs leading to the second floor. The walls are wainscotted on the bottom, painted white but dingy with age. They're papered on the top with blue stripes and little blue flowers that are far too cheery for this cold welcome. I peek into the sitting room on the right. The walls are cream on top and deep red on the bottom. It's sparsely furnished. A blue sofa and matching settee, two blue embroidered chairs. A few little tables. A bookshelf. A fireplace. All covered in a layer of dust. It isn't like Weylan to live with dust.

I find him in the kitchen on the left with Mannix. The kitchen is much cleaner with shelves and cupboards and a wood burning stove. It's antiquated, but sunny, and there's a coziness to it that feels safe and warm. The only sign that Weylan has used it is the little trail of cinders beneath the stove door. At least he's eating.

He leans against the window sill, biting off a hunk of venison jerky, turning his head and yanking at it like a feral dog.

Getting through to him will be a lot harder than I thought.

"Weylan?"

He says nothing. Just rips off chunks of meat. Chews and chews.

"The Coal and Iron Police are after us. We brought a note from Oran that I want you to read."

The door slams shut again, and Mannix drops a bag of blankets at the bottom of the stairs.

"It's like he isn't even in there." I have no qualms speaking about Weylan in the third person.

"I know." Mannix motions up the stairs. "I can show you to your room."

We each have our own, which is a great relief, and there's a large lavatory and a cabinet full of supplies. Everything from soaps to shoe laces.

"Just in case," Mannix says. "I try to come once a week, but you never want to go without."

I make my bed while he leans in the doorway.

"It will get better." I tuck the sheet under the edge of the mattress. "We can take opposite schedules with the lighthouse. Perhaps if he gets more sleep, he'll come back to us."

"Let's explain it all before I leave. Then he can blame me instead of you for the fact that you're here. It might make the next few days easier."

It takes a bit of coaxing to get Weylan to sit at the kitchen table with us. The ripe peaches Bea sent prove too good to ignore. He doesn't look at either of us, but he does take Oran's little black leather book when Mannix pushes it in front of him. His eyes move across the pages, and he flips through the book, but he makes no indication that it meant anything to him at all.

"Weylan, this proof that it's not your fault." I lean across the table and touch the corner of the book, nudging it closer to him, willing him to hold it in his hands or say something. "It wasn't your fault.

Oran pushed Carlin to do it. And he knew it was wrong, because he tried to change course at the last minute. It was so brave of Edna to get this to us. For my cousin and my aunt to bring it to the newspaper. It's a miracle that we have all the evidence, and Mannix will take it to that lawyer in Washington, and we can go home soon. But none of it is your fault."

He doesn't hear me. The words just wash right past him, across the kitchen, and out the window.

"It isn't over." Mannix does his best to fill in the pieces, explaining all the legal doors that are open to us now that all this evidence has been collected. He's as calm and patient as ever. Instead of feeling overwhelmed and lost in the conversation this time, I actually understand what he's saying, which feels like a lot of progress for someone who spent the last year as angry as I've been.

"This is everything we hoped for, Weylan." I try to touch his hand, but he pulls back, laces his fingers in his lap and blinks at the table.

Mannix leans back and extracts his pocket watch from his vest pocket. He checks the time and clicks it closed again. "I should go. I have an appointment this afternoon, and I have to get this cart back to Otto."

In a sudden jolt, Weylan's on his feet. Then he's out the door and across the pasture in a few long strides. I wince at the door slam.

"Something broke in him," I say. "I've never seen him like this. He's far worse than when we parted ways at the station."

"His father says he's never *been* like this. But he admits to being absent and not seeing a lot."

"He said the same to me, too."

I promise to do my best. To give him space and hope he comes to me. Like trying to lure a feral cat indoors from the cold. We say our goodbyes as I help Mannix carry his empty bags, boxes, and baskets out to the cart. He waves one last time as he steers the horse around the little barn and down the path that leads back to town.

I find myself alone in the sun, dry grass under my feet. The edge of the peninsula is some sixty paces from the house. That's a guess. I don't count. The land is open down here, giving a clear view of the bay on the horizon, except for clusters of shrubs on the periphery. Boats bob on the water, and I have no idea how a lighthouse works, but the weight of the responsibility slowly presses down on me.

The shrubs on my left rustle and shudder, and Weylan emerges with a chicken in his hands. Her skinny little legs dangle.

"Lady Peckington Von Bolter," he says.

"What?"

"She likes to run. Her name is Lady Peckington Von Bolter."

It's hard not to smile at that. "Makes sense to me. Good name."

"I'll take the night shift." He holds Lady Von Bolter out away from his body and carries her to the pen. I follow, a puppy at his heels.

"We're on opposite schedules?" I ask.

"Yes. So I don't have to see you. I told you, I want to be alone."

It stings, but he wants it to. He's pushing me away, and I can't let him. "Let me take the night shift," I offer. "You can't be alone in the dark all the time."

"I don't sleep. It doesn't matter." He opens the gate with his foot, and a dozen chickens scatter. "This is my home, not yours. You get days. I get nights."

"You'll have to teach me what to do."

"I'll show you once." He closes the gate and faces me as if he'd never been close at all. Like all those days in the newspaper office, sitting in the gazebo at the park, going for long walks, sitting on the rock by the creek, and being in Stoke together for days, falling asleep in each other's arms had never even happened. We're strangers.

He blinks and looks down at his boots. The tether between us stretches and frays. I'm afraid a strong gust of emotion might sever it.

"I like the night," he says. "I like the boats on the water."

"Alright. But if you ever want to trade."

He turns and walks away from me, and I scamper to catch up. "Will you please speak to me for a minute? Just one minute." I grasp his arm and spin him around, and his cheeks redden again. I've already broken my promise to myself that I'll let Weylan come to me. I might as well shatter this silence between us while I'm at it.

"You haven't cleaned the sitting room," I say. "And you have a beard."

"Indeed."

"I'm doing this all wrong." I press the heels of my hands to my eyes until I see stars. "The Coal and Iron Police are after us. Or they will be soon. There's actual danger out there, but maybe the new coal boss will be a better person than Pritchard was, or maybe the government will rule that it's not okay to poison the water. Things will get better. They have to. We can't stop living."

"People died, Charlotte."

The use of my full name, instead of *Charlie,* sends me back a step. He never calls me that.

"But it isn't your fault," I say. "You could have printed the location of that blasting powder in the newspaper, and it still wouldn't have been your fault. Carlin was intent on doing what he did. Oran was tasked with pushing him to do it. Several people knew that powder was back there."

"But I didn't stop it." He jabs his finger into his chest.

"How would you? What would you have done to stop Carlin? Do you think you could have reasoned with that man?"

He launches toward the barn, where a small mule grazes, and in an instant, he's yards away as if I weren't there at all.

Someday, he will emerge from this shame-tinted grief, this shell he built around himself. He'll laugh at something small. Joy will find some small crack and force it open, pry at it with its hard fingernail and chip away the edges until light gets through. He'll realize that when times are terrible, and the world seems stacked against you, that you don't have to fight so hard. You can have joy. You can delight in the small things. You can change the way you fight your battle, especially when it's a long one. Until then, I'll fight at his side. We'll do it his way.

CHAPTER TWENTY-NINE

SEPTEMBER 8, 1901

The plants and grasses around the lighthouse yellow in September's changed air. The shrubs begin to take on golden edges. We've settled into a routine of avoidance, barely overlapping in the morning light and the evening dim. We leave cordial yet inconsistent notes for each other about the rotten floorboard on the porch or the busted latch on the mule's paddock.

The sourness of our discontent lingers in the house, like something rotten left on a windowsill, growing stronger with every gust of fresh air. There is no levity between us. Just awkward pauses as we pass on the stairs and frustrated mumbles as we pick over each other's messes.

Mannix comes every week. At least there's no hint of the old tension between us. He seems to have forgiven me for my past transgressions. He brings letters from Emmett and Bea. She's introduced him to her parents, officially, and Emmett has made a good enough impression that Leta doesn't fret about them being alone together in the newspaper office. He's done a good job of paying the bills, by Hazel's report, and she's dropped a few hints that she might like to move north, to Philadelphia, for the fashion. Ruthie has started a regular column about suffragist efforts, and I can hear in her letter how much more serious she's grown since we left.

Mannix sits at our table when dawn breaks, as my day begins and Weylan's ends, waiting as I skim my letters because he knows I'll have a million questions. There's nothing urgent this time, though. And that makes it worse, somehow. Like sitting in stagnant air.

At the cupboard, Weylan grinds coffee beans.

"Is there any news about Stoke?" It's my routine question. The expectation of actual news grows with each of Mannix's visits. Eventually something has to happen. But the disappointment continues to grow.

"No news." He strokes an eyebrow. "Not yet. I know you're eager to escape from seclusion out here, but I promise to let you know as soon as there's some legal course that will offer you protection. It will be winter soon. Are you preparing?"

"Chopping wood." Weylan adds hot water to the french press then smashes the plunger.

"Canning too," I say. "Storing as much as I can get my hands on."

Yet another task we divided without talking about it.

Cool air whips in the window, rustling the curtain, and making me shiver. Winter has crossed my mind a lot lately. I had hoped that we wouldn't still be here come time for snow. Lady justice is slow, I know, and she moves at her own pace. Thanks to her blindfold, she can't see a clock any more than she can see bias. I just wish it weren't so glacial. At times I clean the glass in the lighthouse and trim the wicks and wonder if I'll be here forever.

"Good. You'll be well prepared for winter. Then you'll have time on your hands for a project?" The pitch in Mannix's voice is high, excited. I glance at Weylan, and he raises a shoulder. At least he's listening. That's progress.

"I suppose," I say.

"As long as it isn't a joint project," Weylan mumbles.

I roll my eyes, and Mannix smiles, which is only slightly more rare than a tornado or a triple rainbow. "Your Washington lawyer has sent you a task."

CHAPTER THIRTY

JUNE 6, 1902

Mannix won't be here until noon today which is just as well because a storm came through and made a mess of everything. Weylan typically goes back to bed before Mannix arrives, but he must have decided to stay up late after his night tending the lighthouse. He's out there trimming the mule's hoof with a sharp blade, and it sounds like he's slicing carrots on a cutting board. The mule will be pleased. He's needed a hoof trim for days. Every time I try, he quite literally kicks up a fuss. I just don't have the touch Weylan does.

The smell of last night's rain fills my room. From where I change my clothes at the foot of my bed, I have a view across the peninsula and over the bay. Water pools in the low spots in the lawn. I might as well take my time getting ready this morning. Give the earth time to drink it all up.

I don't often see Weylan from this height and distance. He looks different. His shoulders are broader. If we were in town, and I saw him from afar, I might not even recognize him now. I rarely see him at all, actually. We stumble into each other in the hallway, him at the end of his day and me at the start of mine. We move around each other like strangers. A nail and a penny rattling around in the same tin can. Over the last ten months, he's sharpened his mental state against the whetstone of manual labor, and though it's done much for his physique, it's done little for his frame of mind. I miss him. Immensely. And from up here at the window, I can get lost in the momentary dream that all is well between us. That I can walk downstairs, stride across the lawn, and we will be the same people to each other that we once were. I wonder if he ever feels that way about me.

I shake off the thought because it costs too much to entertain it. The hardest part of the last ten months for me hasn't been chopping firewood or slaughtering chickens. It's been letting go. Not being part of his world even though he's right here. The hardest part of every day and falling asleep at night is wondering what's happening in his head. He's a haunted place, and he haunts the places around him.

Brushing my hair in front of the mirror, I stand on my tiptoes to see over my driftwood menagerie. My little coal lion and the duck I carved in Stoke are the engine and caboose to a strange circus train, an assortment of things I've carved over the course of these ten months. They now outnumber all the mermaid's purses I've collected. Fish and ferrets. Mice and moose.

I pause at my door. The people we used to be and all the words we don't say are so loud out there. And on the rare occasions when we're both awake, all the excuses I make not to be near him are so thin.

Weylan's room is at the end of the hall, and his windows are open.

The curtain blows in and the door rattles against the hunk of old metal he uses as a doorstop. At the bottom of the stairs I spin around the newel post, head for the kitchen, and I grab my gathering apron.

The table is still covered with the last pages of the evidence we took from Stoke. My handwritten pages are everywhere. It looks like a mess, but it makes sense to me, and now that I've done all the work the lawyers set me to, all I have to do is put it in the binders that Mannix brought for me and send it back with him today. Finally. But it will only take a moment to pack it all up, so I slip out the door.

The peninsula is more of a bulb of land than a narrow shard, like a thumb jutting out over the water. The drop at the end is sheer, a hundred feet or more. Our two-story farmhouse with its white-painted clapboard sits far back from the edge. It hugs the lighthouse, but they aren't connected, so it's an inconvenience at times to go from one to the other, especially in the winter. For as airy and empty as the house feels, the lighthouse's stone walls, and stuffy watch room and lantern room make me claustrophobic. We're miles and miles from anyone, separated by the wilds, and if I should fall or either of us be injured on those narrow, coiling stairs, help is so far away. With my luck and the state of our relationship, Weylan would leave me there to rot. Fortunately, he's already cleaned the glass this morning, so there's no need for me to go up at all.

I rush through my morning chores. Feed the chickens, gather the eggs, put out fresh water. I need an excuse to keep my distance until the afternoon when Mannix arrives, otherwise, I'll break. I'll snap. I'll push Weylan again and try to make him talk. He'll shut down even more. I regret it every time. Instead, I go in search of wild raspberries in the woods, and that will give me something to do until the ground dries up.

I turn my back on the house and the water, and I slip into the woods in search of solace and berries. I don't have to walk far before I reach the spot where the land dips down and the water rises up, and little coves form. There's a tiny beach of peachy-golden sand that I like to visit, especially after storms, and I fill my apron pockets with raspberries as I go.

Once I reach the little cove, though, the berries are forgotten. The little strip of coast is covered in absolutely shimmering driftwood and pebbles, and I need to see it all. I'm careful not to trip and fall on the slippery logs I must climb over.

There are mermaid's purses and arrow heads of such abundance, stirred up by the storm, and I eat all the raspberries in my pocket to make room for them. I hoard them. I collect smooth pebbles to store in jars on window ledges so I can admire how pretty they are. I pocket mermaid's purses to place on shelves and on the chair rail in my room. But driftwood is a special treasure.

Some of the pieces I find tangled in river grass are practical. One will make the perfect hook for the back of the lighthouse door. There's a longer piece that's flat on one end that would make a perfect shelf, so I tie up my skirt and wade into the water that laps at the shore to snatch it. More precious than that are the animals. I am getting pretty good at seeing them in the driftwood and bringing them to life. And I enjoy the way carving them out of their prisons lets my mind rest.

One whitened, knurled hunk the size of my fist looks like a fish with feathers. Another will become a sweet little beetle with antlers, and another a snake with rows of wings. I sit on the downed log, take my carving knife from my pocket, and pare away at the weathered wood. A fish takes form, then the outline of feathers, and I lose track of time as the sun rises. When my shadow pools beneath me, I brush myself clean of sand.

Mannix should be here soon.

I follow the rim of the peninsula, making the gentle climb, to find Weylan has replaced the missing top rail of the old fence. It looks like it was never broken. But Weylan is nowhere in sight.

With my apron pockets full of driftwood, arrowheads, and shiny pebbles, I leave my driftwood shelf on the porch and go into the kitchen to find Weylan at the table, using a small corner of it to eat a slice of bread. His nose is in a book. Probably trying to finish it so he can give it back to Mannix.

"Sorry I left a mess," I say.

He says nothing, as usual. Like I'm not even here.

My stacks have been disturbed, either by Weylan or wind. I pull them back into order. It's my own fault for leaving them laying around. I've become so lazy and disorganized out here in seclusion.

"Can you move your plate please?" I ask. "It's on the papers. I'll get this out of your way."

He doesn't even blink.

"Please," I say at a volume far too loud for this kitchen.

His jaw clenches as he lifts his plate, and I sweep the pages into a pile—the calendars I made of acts of violence, sicknesses I'm aware of and strikes reported in the newspapers, when bribes were paid, when studies were done, and when letters were written to railroads. Every few weeks, Mannix delivers more evidence for me to sort through, to make connections and tell the lawyers what I know. It's a more time consuming and detailed process than what we did at the newspaper months ago, and I've saved them a lot of time and trouble, apparently. But now I've reached the end of their pile.

I take the pages to the sitting room and spread them on the floor with Mannix's binders. In the kitchen, Weylan turns the page in his book and hums to himself. It's so faint I can barely hear it, but my ears are trained to what he's doing. No matter how long or hard we gnaw at the sinew that holds us together, some little wisp refuses to be severed.

With the last of the papers tidy in their binders, I stack them in the crate and push it by the door. All those months. All that work. I wondered what it all looked like stacked in some Washington, D.C. office with men in suits, glasses poised on the tips of their noses, studying it all. I could picture them arguing with each other, pretending it was a trial, practicing arguments. That's what Mannix said they do. Maybe I should have been a lawyer. I argue with Weylan and myself in my head all the time.

I've been so eager to finish and send the last of it back that it's almost sad to see it go. The fight belongs to everyone now. From here on out, I'll learn about it in bits and pieces. I wonder what Father would say about all this. From his late night speeches at the tavern and standing on the steps of the community building speaking out against Pritchard's cruelty, to this. All the evidence in daughter's hands, on its way to lawyers.

I could sense Mannix before I could hear the horse and carriage come through the parting in the woods. Weylan gets up from the table. He doesn't even look at me as he walks past and slips out the front door.

There's a volley of laughter between Weylan and Mannix, and I step out onto the porch to greet the only visitor we ever have.

"I brought you lemons," Mannix beams. "I know you love them."

He holds one out and I press it to my nose, breathing deep.

"What a marvelous smell," I say. "Like sunshine. I'll make lemonade."

He pats a bag slung over his shoulder. "I have sugar here for you too. Some pins, and other things you asked for. And fabric. You said you wanted to make a coat."

"Oh, thank heavens. The winter mornings last year were unbearable and everything I have is uncomfortable. Come in."

"Heck of a storm last night." Weylan stomps the hay from his boots as he enters the house and shuts the door. "I wasn't sure you'd make it out here. How bad was the ride?"

Mannix sits at the kitchen table. He takes the one chair we have without arms. "Just a few trees down," he says. "Nothing terrible."

I pour water for Mannix and place a bowl of cherries on the table. He clasps his hands in glee. "What a treat. These aren't nearly ripe in town yet."

"Our tree has done well this year. How is Em?" I ask. "Bea? Ruthie and Hazel."

"Fine. All fine." He digs in his bag and passes out letters.

Weylan clears his throat. We don't speak out here very often, and it shows. "How is the newspaper? Have you seen my father?" I can read his father's handwriting upside down. And he has a note from Max.

"Your father is well. Sends his best. The girls seem to be handling the paper just fine. They barely need Emmett's help anymore, but there are vendors who refuse to work with a woman. You know how it is. I think Emmett far prefers working at the newspaper than being at the brickyard. He'll find his place."

Mannix tucks in his chin and pulls the stem from a cherry.

Weylan tugs his ankle onto his knee by hooking his finger in his pant hem, ripping into Max's letter. When our eyes meet, Mannix raises his brows, an imploring look meant to ask how things are here, and all I can do is give a tiny shake of my head as I trace a groove in the table top. It's never any better.

Mannix spits the cherry pit onto a napkin. "Any new hobbies out here this summer?"

"Hobbies?" He doesn't look up. "Like what? Painting? You always ask that."

"Because I'm waiting for the answer to change. Charlie carves all those animals. A man needs something to fight for."

"Fighting for paintings and carvings of mice with flippers?" Weylan sighs and looks to his right, out the window. "Everything is fine."

"It's not fine," Mannix says. "You two are barely speaking to each other."

"I don't know why she's here. I don't need her. I don't need anyone." Weylan's foot hits the floor and glasses rattle in the cupboard. It's his way of saying the conversation is over, that there's no need to speak to each other, but Mannix isn't satisfied. He pushes the bowl of cherries away and rubs his glasses in a circle on his stomach.

"I wish I could separate the two of you. I know it's unpleasant and isolated out here. But all I have is my family's claim to this lighthouse, and with that terrain, you're safe as houses out here."

Mannix winks at me. He probably shares my belief that the Coal and Iron Police are no longer on our tail, that they've let us go because we've been quiet. Leaving Weylan alone out here isn't an option, though.

I follow Weylan's gaze out the window to the land beyond. To the water and the horizon. I wouldn't want to leave this place anyway. It's not perfect, and I'd only intended to be here a short while, but it's quiet and beautiful. Even if Weylan is distant, I know he's safe. Even if he never speaks to me again, he's close. I can sense him in the night. It would be nice to get back to the newspaper someday, but I'm not in any hurry, and I'm not leaving alone.

Mannix slaps the table. "Well, I must get going. I'm turkey hunting." He winks. "If I'm gone too long, people will question my aim."

"Charlie's become very good with a bow and arrow," Weyland says. I had no idea he paid any attention.

"I wish you could stay longer," I say.

"I'll bring a dessert next time."

Mannix collects the crate of binders, and we follow him out to his carriage.

"It's all organized in categories," I say. "Like you asked me to. Have they been happy with my work?"

"Very. You've helped them get into Stoke and collect affidavits to support their case. They think they're closing in on Oran, too."

"Really?" I exclaim. "Why didn't you say sooner?"

He tilts his head. "Because I didn't want to get your hopes up. But now that this is finished, we should start to see some progress soon."

Progress. That means a slow crawl of court filings. And then the injunction Mannix has pushed for. Once a judge is assigned to the case, they'll formally tell the Coal and Iron Police not to contact us or our kin, and then we can go home again. Back into town. Back to the newspaper. The thought of leaving this place coils my stomach into a knot. I don't want to ask Mannix how long he thinks that will take, because I don't want to go.

"Are you relieved this stage is finished?" he asks as he packs it away. "It was a big task. You'd make a good law clerk."

"I'm flattered you think so, but no. You're right, I am relieved. A little hopeful, too. But whatever happens from here, it's out of my hands."

"I thought it would be harder for you to give up your father's fight," he says.

Mannix looks a little proud of me. At least I think that's what that lopsided grin means. But Weylan folds his arms and plants his stance wide, bowing his head. He does that when he abandons a conversation.

"I'm ready to live my life." It's strange to say it out loud, to hear it carried on the wind. It won't be the life I thought it would be or the one I hoped for, but it's the one I have, and I'm ready to live it. The only problem is that I love this place, and I want to finally build a life with Weylan. I want to build it here. But one glance at Weylan reinforces my suspicion that he doesn't care whether the case goes forward or what his future looks like.

"What do you want to do when this is over?" I ask him.

He rocks. Toe, heel. Toe heel.

Just as I'm about to give up and thank Mannix for everything, Weylan says, "You can leave, if you want."

"I don't want to go."

"I'm terrible company, and it's not your fault. I have no desire to go back to any of that. I'm happy out here."

Part of me wants to say that he's clearly not, because he's always miserable. There's no life in him. There's no spark. But I don't want to set him off again, so I say, "Well, I'm happy here too," and I leave it at that. "We've been lucky to have this place, and I'll stay as long as Mannix will let me."

Because I'm not giving up on Weylan.

He may not realize it, but he's lucky. He's not a price tag. Men like Father and Emmett were assigned a value at birth. An amount of money they needed to generate for the coal boss, and an amount he is willing to pay for their keep. That's all they mean to the world. Money. When they die, there's only enough space in their obituary to name the place they worked for. The only column on the census that says anything about them is the one that identifies who profits off their life. Cabinetmaker. Cobbler. Miner. The boys born in Stoke had no choice what to put in that column. They would always be miners. It's work to be proud of, but it never gives you a choice or pays what you're worth. Weylan gets to be his own man, though, and I will not let him lose himself to hopelessness.

"Oh! I almost forgot." Mannix jumps and reaches into the carriage and passes me a bag. "Vegetables for you. From Leta. Some beans, fruit. Some honey."

"Thank you!" I say. "You should take some eggs. We have far more than we know what to do with."

Without a word, Weylan launches to the chicken coop. He's suddenly light on his feet, as if he's eager to enjoy the distance. As soon as he opens the gate, Lady Peckington Von Bolter shoots out like a frantic, feathered cannonball and rockets toward the cliff, squawking and kicking up her little legs.

"She always does that," I say.

"I'll get her in a minute." Weylan dives and shoves his hand in the coop, rustling around for eggs. He collects a handful.

We make our goodbyes which are always bitter to me. Mannix never stays long enough, and strange feelings of loneliness always stir and swirl in his wake. We wave goodbye as his carriage disappears through the trees, then Weylan launches toward the seam where the land meets the sky, bent over, hands down, chasing Lady Peckington. I retire to the kitchen, to clean up the last of the cherries and to start some lemonade. I open the window to dump the cherry pits out into the lawn, and something is different.

It takes me a moment to figure out what's changed. Down by the cliff's edge, a shrub is gone.

The line of trees is the same. It ends at that heap of leafy mess I can't identify. Turns red in the fall. But the shrub near the middle of the point is gone. The storm must have loosened things and caused another little landslide. It happens. But the sense of dread that rises in my throat and makes my hands sweat is not normal at all.

I step out the door.

"Weylan?" I call out, hand over my eyes to shield from the sun.

There's no answer. No Lady Peckington either. I call again. I run past the chick coop, past the stable, past the patch of the corn that's barely knee high.

I run. My skirt tangles between my legs, and I run.

The drop from the peninsula is at least a hundred feet of sheer straight-down terror. I skitter to the edge, to the tip of the earth, with the whole world pushing at my back.

"Weylan!"

"Here." His voice calls up to me, full of grit and strain.

To my left, he clings to a rock embedded in the cliff's edge. I fall to my stomach.

"Help me," he gasps. "Don't let me die. Don't let me fall."

I reach and wiggle my fingers, stretching my arm as far as it will go. Sweat streams down my back. The sun sears my neck.

"I can't reach."

"Mannix?" he asks.

He's gone. I shake my head and wriggle myself as far out as I can, fear of heights be damned. I'm not long enough. I reach and stretch and turn to the side to make my arm as long as it can be.

"A rope," I say. "The mule."

"Not strong enough," Weylan says.

He's right. The mule had been sick and couldn't even pull the mowing machine yesterday.

I stretch and stretch. "I'm sorry I ruin everything," I say.

The earth crumbles more around me, and Weylan turns his head, squeezing his eyes shut. He's going to fall, and he'll never survive the drop. Sweat glistens on his hand. He'll soon lose his grip.

"I let you down," he says. "If I'd stopped Carlin…"

"No, it's my fault. If I'd fought for my own life instead of against everything else, you'd be home. We'd be happy." In a cottage instead of out here. I'm so stupid and stubborn. I put my life on hold to fight Pritchard. Because my parents weren't alive to see me live. Because I had to finish the mission they started.

"I'm sorry I was afraid to live," I say.

I hadn't wanted to admit that my family was dead and never coming back. And I refuse to believe this is the end for Weylan. I'd been so afraid to accept that I was on my own for the rest of my life that I couldn't see I wasn't lonely. I had a life and a future all along. And now…

I wiggle my fingers and lean. Another millimeter. Clumps of soil and grass fall away.

"Leave me," he says. "Let me go. I'm ready." His eyes soften as the strain of clinging to the rocks, to this life, falls away, and I know he's telling me the truth. He's ready to let go. But I'm not.

"Are you insane? No. I'm not going to let you die like this."

"I deserve it."

"No. You do not."

Soil falls from beneath me, pebbling on his hands. His whole body trembles.

"Get back," he says.

"No." I'm afraid to lean any more, that I might cause a landslide, and we'll both be at risk, but I can't worry about that because it's the only chance I have to save him. I start to cry, tears pricking my eyes, and the vision of him swims. I stretch. My side burns. Just a millimeter more. I cannot let him fall.

If I can only pull him up and over the edge, I will give him anything he wants. I'll go back to town. I'll move back to Stoke or go to Philadelphia with Hazel. He'll never have to see me again, if that's what he really wants.

Cool air brushes across the peninsula, blowing my hair into my face and my eyes, but I see so much clearer now. Something within me chips off and crumbles away.

"Charlotte." His voice is almost a whisper. "Charlie."

I blink away tears and find him calm. There's the most peaceful look in his eyes.

"It's okay," he says. "Let go. I have a plan."

There's sun on my back, but my spine goes ice cold.

"What will you do?" I ask.

His eyes glisten, rimming in red. "I'm sorry for not saying every day that I love you. I do. With so much of me that there's nothing left to pretend with. If I were stronger, I could have been better. But I'm a monster, and I deserve this. I love you. I don't want you to watch."

"No," I bark. "You listen to me. You are not giving up. Not today."

"I'm going to let go now." His fingers tremble. They're white. He can't hold on much longer. "I need to know you'll keep living. Promise you'll step back and go to the house. Don't watch. Don't look."

"No."

I don't know where I get the sudden surge, but my hand lands on his fingertips, and I inch them down to his wrist, and he clenches mine. A block of earth falls away from under my armpit, and I reach his other wrist. With both hands I yank and pull. My stomach burns and my shoulders feel like they're being severed by razor blades, and I yell. And I pull.

His feet scramble.

Dear God, you can take anything you want but you can't have Weylan. You have taken the last thing you'll get from me, and I can't live without Weylan.

That damn chicken pops up to my right and looks over the edge.

"You wait right there. I will wring your neck," I scream.

Weylan's eyes are squeezed shut, his left foot digs and kicks and finds a little purchase. He straightens his leg, slowly, and he's just a few inches closer.

There's no more waiting. It's now or never. There's no time to bargain with the universe or pray. There's no chance to try harder tomorrow. He can't give up. It's now or never. Either my arms dislocate and he falls, or I can do this.

I can do this.

I pull and heave. His right hand reaches the edge. Then his left.

He fists the grass, but his feet dangle. He kicks at the soil and curses, and earth falls away, bouncing until it splashes, silent, to the water below.

He cries out as he reaches the land. Shoulders first. Hips. Then knees.

We crawl a good ten feet from the edge and roll onto our backs, panting. I would grip my shoulder but both of them hurt, and so do my elbows and wrists.

"I think I cracked a rib," I say between coughs that are more like whimpers. "No, I know I did."

He rolls onto his back. Sweat streams down his temples and into his hair. His face is red as a summer sunburn, and tears glisten in his eyes. Real tears.

He'll be alright. He's here, and that's all I care about.

His fingers inch along the ground until they find mine. His hand is trembling, but his grip is strong.

"I told you to let me go," he says.

"I told you a long time ago. Never."

CHAPTER THIRTY-ONE

MAY 13, 1912

Ice-cold creek water laps at my rolled-up pant legs. I curl my toes over the curve of a weathered stone and wait for the dog to bring the stick back. Minnows scurried past me.

"You're going to catch your death out there." Weylan stands on the bank, hands on his hips, squinting in the angle of the late afternoon sun. He raises his hand and shields his eyes.

Rocky is a mutt. He showed up on our doorstep one day, howling during a summer storm. Weylan brought him in, cleaned him up and set him in front of the fireplace as best as you can a dog with his own mind. Rocky never left. Five years on, and he still doesn't understand the concept of fetch, but if you stand still long enough, he'll come back around — with or without the stick.

Rocky drops it at Weylan's side and shakes water from his fur.

"Thanks, Rocks." Weylan holds out his arms and assesses his mud-splattered shirt.

"He loves you," I say. "Also, if you stood in the creek, you'd already be wet and you wouldn't care."

He grins and shrugs. "It's almost five," he says. "That man will be here soon. I wonder what he wants."

"Maybe they finally came to an agreement about Stoke."

Weylan throws the stick, and Rocky bounds across the creek after it. Another fifty feet away, Finn pulls in a net and untangles fish into a bucket. He straightens as much as he can and puts a hand on his lower back, arching until he's stretching in the sun. He waves, and I wave back.

I shield my eyes and glance up the creek to where our two daughters skip stones on the water. Frankie's blonde hair doesn't shine in the sun quite as much as it used to. She's nine now, and the older she gets, the more chestnut and amber it becomes. She got Weylan's nose, too, for that matter. But Beatrice is only five, and I hope she stays blonde. At least one of our girls has to take after me.

Frankie snaps her wrist and a stone skims the water's surface, hopping along until it splashes.

"Be careful," Weylan calls out to her. "Finn is fishing up there. Don't hit him."

Frankie turns and says she isn't even close, but she's closer than she thinks. She has a heck of an arm for her age.

The grumble of an automobile on the path precedes its arrival through the trees. It kicks up dust on the drive that cuts between our little brick house and the garden, where the corn is almost shoulder high, tomatoes climb their cages, and cucumbers crawl across the ground. Chickens scatter and squawk as the automobile rounds the corner.

I turn to our daughter. "Beatrice, get your sister and run up the hill to get Em and Auntie Bea. Tell them the man's here. And then go up to Uncle Max's. We'll meet you there for dinner in a bit."

The girls scramble across the creek on high, flat rocks and race up the hill to the house where Emmett and Bea raise two sons and a daughter of their own.

The man tips his hat as he lowers to the ground and tugs a brown leather case from the back of the automobile. We settle in rocking chairs on the porch while the car pings and bangs in the driveway, cooling down from its long journey. Harold's visits have decreased in number over the years, and shortened in duration. There truly isn't much to say about the slow erosion of the coal town and even less to say about the fate of its possessors. I simply don't want to hear about anything other than the demise of that coal operation and the success of people who moved on to better things, so Harold's visits dissolved into letters and news clippings about court cases, appeals, and the occasional apology that the wheels of justice roll so slowly.

"I apologize for the short notice." Harold sets his briefcase at his feet. "And for being early."

"Think nothing of it," I say. "I suspect you're tired of keeping us updated. It was nice of you to come all this way."

"A letter wouldn't do this time," he says as Emmett and Bea make their way across the creek and pull chairs closer. "I hope you will all be pleased with the news."

"They settled?" Weylan leans back and laces his fingers, splaying his hands across his stomach.

Harold nods. "The company has been dissolved."

"They need to do better than that," Emmett snips. Bea places a hand on his knee.

"What about the town?" I ask.

"It has been divided among the claimants. You and Emmett will share twenty-three point three five acres between you."

He reaches down and opens his case, drawing out a map page about a foot square in size. Dark lines trace the roads with rectangular parcels fanning out, each of them numbered. Harold points to one outlined in yellow. The little square drawn within our parcel marks the home we grew up in. It's been empty for years, but it still stands. "It will be up to the two of you how you use it."

"What if I don't want my share?" I ask.

Emmett and I have had nearly a decade to hash it out, talking it over with Weylan and Bea, guessing what might become of justice and how we'd accept it. All of us have cycled between anger and acceptance a thousand times, but the longer the whole thing dragged on, the less I cared about it. Living has filled in the empty places. "I have a life here. We built this house. It's the only home our girls have ever known. I have no intention of ever going to Stoke again. We've spoken to Sophie and she's settled in Mauch Chunk. She doesn't want anything to do with it either."

"That makes three of us," says Emmett. "I won't ever go back to that place."

Harold extracts some papers from his case and hands twin stacks to Emmett and me. "You're not the only ones to say so. Many families have chosen to sell their properties. There's a man willing to buy the land at its current, undeveloped value. He wants to turn it into housing. The group of current residents who wish to stay are meeting to determine whether they'll form a new town or become part of New Kingsley. If you choose to live there, I'd encourage you to participate in those discussions. If not, the man has sent along this offer."

The papers are covered in legal phrases about the size of the lot and descriptions of the woods, the creek that runs through it, the house and its pig pen. I remember Emmett clinging to the fence as we waited for the man from the state to arrive, dabbing his pink gums on his sleeve.

On the last page, there's an offer number.

"Six thousand dollars? That's a mountain of money. This can't be right." I hand the papers to Weylan.

"There's a lot of potential in that land," Harold says.

"Of course there is," Emmett agrees.

"I have to talk it over with Weylan," I say.

"What's to talk about? Three thousand dollars each sets the girls for life." Weylan hands me the papers back. "They can build their homes and never have to worry about a thing. It's your decision, but unless there's something you haven't already said, you made up your mind a long time ago."

I glance at Emmett. His mind is made up, too. He likes running the brickyard, which has slowly become a lumber yard too. He even has his eye on a shop downtown where he wants to open a hardware store. Bea's family is here; our friends are here, except for Hazel who sweeps into town from Philadelphia with presents from the city that make the girls swoon. Frankie and Beatrice love living down the hill from Cousins Matthew and Vernon and little Sophie. It took Max forever, but he finally married Ruthie, and in a few short weeks, they'll welcome their first child. I don't want to miss those moments. I'm where I'm supposed to be.

And that money could do a lot for our girls. Weylan does well with the paper. He's built a home for us, and we want for nothing. I don't make a big income from my job as mayor, but it helps us put away a little savings. With the money from the land in Stoke, the girls could even go to college if they want to.

"This is it, Charlie." Emmett rolls the papers into a scroll and taps his knee. "It can be over. All we have to do is sign."

"Feels good, doesn't it?" Weylan asks, one eyebrow arched. "After all these years."

Harold holds out a pen. He rambles on about deeds and bank accounts and when we'll receive the checks.

All these years, it's never been about money or the land or seeing the end of the drawn-out battle. There can't ever be vindication for the things we lost. We've already taken all the rough pieces and the jagged shards and rounded them off by building joy.

As for the battle for justice, I retreated from the trenches and left the front lines long ago. This is nothing more than the end of a war. A treaty for peace that's been hard won. It's one less thing to think about while my focus is on this town I call home, on paving roads and keeping the waters clean.

I hand the pen to Emmett. He signs with no more emotion than I did. He passes the papers down to me, and clasps Bea's hand while I sign my own name below his.

It feels good to hand the signed contracts to Harold.

"If you'd like to go back and see the old house one more time, I can arrange that," Harold says. "I know that place meant a lot to you."

I have fond memories of the old house, of the way it grieved and wore its scars, of the path etched into its floors by my parents and my childhood. But it isn't my home anymore.

"I can't speak for Emmett," I say. "But I don't need to go backwards. I have everything I need."

ACKNOWLEDGMENTS

First, I would like to acknowledge Shelly Campbell, Al Hess, and Cassie Greutman. I sometimes say that writing a book is like waging a psychological civil war, and it's fun to laugh about the ups and downs with soldiers at your side who truly get it.

Charlotte and Weylan were such a joy to write, and it was fun to walk through these settings again. The coal patch of Stoke is far more bustling than Eckley Miners' Village is today, and I loved adding life and color—along with a dash of corruption—to a place of such rich history. Wrapping dystopian, slightly speculative fiction around a skeleton of real history is always a treat. Charlotte and Weylan's story is one of resiliency and hope, of curating a life during chaos and carving tangible joy out of an invisible war. It reflects a stubbornness of human spirit that I hope is universal to readers for all good reasons and no bad ones.

Extra special thanks to Jennifer Babineau, whose skill made this shine. To Shelly Campbell, who took my vague idea for a cover and turned it into stunning art. And to Donna Sullivan, whose kindness is a light.

I am eternally grateful for the spirit and kindness of my local writing group for the friendship and encouragement. Especially Allison Lattanze and Amber L. Werner. I've had so much fun building a community of writing warriors with you. I know I'm forgetting others with whom I tossed around early ideas for the book, but I'm no less grateful. Charlotte and Weylan owe much of the love they built from the ashes to you.

And above all, thank you to Matthew.

ABOUT THE AUTHOR

A Maryland native and Pennsylvanian at heart, Jennifer M. Lane holds a bachelor's degree in philosophy from Barton College and a master's in liberal arts with a focus on museum studies from the University of Delaware, where she wrote her thesis on the material culture of roadside memorials. She resides with her partner Matt and a tuxedo cat named Penny.

Receive free prequel stories, news about upcoming releases and more by signing up for the author newsletter at jennifermlanewrites.com

OTHER WORKS BY THE AUTHOR INCLUDE

Of Metal and Earth,
Stick Figures from Rockport,
*the six-book series **The Collected Stories of Ramsbolt,***
*and the Poison River Duology: **Downriver** and **Upstream.***